SHROUDED SOUL

HIDDEN: BOOK 3

CLARE DAVIDSON

Published by Smudged Ink Press
Copyright © 2014 Clare Davidson
ISBN: 978-0-9926113-3-0

First Paperback Edition: August 2014

For Eleanor, my beautiful daughter with huge dreams.

Acknowledgements

Edited by Rebecca A Weston
Proofread by Megan Payne
Cover illustration by Bramasta Aji

Special thanks to Rebecca Tsaros Dickson, Renee Dillon and Graham Austin-King.

Thank you to everyone who supported me while I was writing 'Shrouded Soul', especially Tom, Eleanor, Mum, Dad, Kim and Ellen.

CHAPTER ONE

I frame AJ's face in my phone's camera and use my thumb to take the shot. He laughs and turns away as the electronic shutter clicks, leaving me with an image of his profile. His cheeky lopsided smile is hidden from view.

"Spoilsport," I say. "I'll hold your hat for ransom until you let me take a proper photo."

I tap the black fedora, which is currently sitting on my head, and ready the phone for another shot.

This time he holds still, allowing me to capture his smile and the cute dimple that forms between the corner of his mouth and his cheek—two of the many reasons I fell for him. I put my phone away and twist around so I can flop against his chest. A blanket of musty copper leaves rustles beneath us. Twisting, bare branches stretch into the pale grey sky above our heads. I snuggle against him, glad when he wraps his arms around me as it helps to stave off the chill.

"Did you ask your mum about Christmas?" I say.

It's hard to believe it's only a couple of weeks away. I'm not ready to spend a second Christmas without my sister, Charley. I hope having AJ there will help to ease the pain.

My hope dissipates into a frown as his chest rises but doesn't fall.

"You haven't, have you?"

"There hasn't been a good time," he says.

I twist out of his arms and onto my knees. "It's only an invite to Christmas dinner," I say. "Why would she be offended by that?"

His jaw stiffens into a rigid line. "Mum's really tense, Kim. I don't think she can believe it's okay for us to stay. I'll ask her when she's calmed down a bit."

I arch an eyebrow. "Just make sure you ask her before Christmas Day." I prod him in the chest, prompting him to smile again.

I love his smile. I grin at him, feeling my eyes widening like a doe's as I lean in for a kiss, keeping my lips light against his. A giggle tickles the back of my throat, bursting out in a puff of air over his face. I begin to tickle him, playfully fluttering my fingertips across his throat and underneath the collar of his coat, then slipping my hand inside the slit between his coat buttons so I can tickle his armpits. Laughing, he returns the favour. Although his hands remain outside my coat, he applies enough pressure to make me squirm and giggle. We tumble into the leaves in an explosion of laughter, AJ's chest almost resting against mine. His hat rolls off my head and tumbles onto the ground, rustling the old leaves.

My laughter is cut short when AJ kisses me firmly. I smile into it, allowing my eyes to drift shut. I brush my fingertips across his shoulders and twine them together at the back of his neck, feeling the tightly woven texture of his coat. My thumbs stroke the tips of his coarse hair, and I apply a little pressure through my palms, encouraging his body to sink closer so there's no longer a gap between our chests.

AJ freezes and presses his palms into the leaves on either side of my head. Our stares lock, his chestnut eyes dancing with worry. He lifts his body so we're no longer touching and scrambles away, sitting with his back pressed rigidly against the tree.

"What?" I say, trying hard not to scowl.

He shakes his head. "We shouldn't get carried away."

I let the scowl crumple my forehead. "We were having fun." And now we're not. "What's the matter, AJ?" I try to hold his hand, but he snatches it away. I sigh. "This isn't about me and what happened with Gage anymore, is it?" My tone is flat.

At first I thought AJ was being careful not to push me into anything I wasn't ready to do. Gage had used magic to seduce me. He'd been the first boy I'd kissed and been even remotely intimate with, but the entire encounter had been a lie. It hurt and almost broke me emotionally. Being with AJ has helped me heal, and yet he still pulls away.

There are so many things he won't talk about—things that drive a wedge between us. I've tried hard to wait for him to tell me, but I'm pretty sure he never will. He's been keeping secrets his entire life. It's a habit for him.

I fold my arms, as much to warm my hands as to prevent myself from reaching out to him again and risk being rejected. I wish I understood why he keeps pushing me away at the first hint of things progressing beyond a kiss and a hug.

"AJ, you know how much I care about you, don't you?"

I'm afraid he doesn't. I know the depth of his feelings for me. He almost died saving my life. I don't think I'll ever be able to repay him. I blow out a miniature sigh when he nods.

"So why won't you talk to me? What are you afraid of?"

I already know what I think is his deepest secret: His father was a Baneem, part of a magical race of people who hate humans. Gage is also a Baneem.

AJ tips his head back against the tree's rough bark. "It's not just Mum who's afraid this is all too good to be true."

"So that's why you've been pulling away from me? Because you're still in flight mode?"

His brow twitches into an apologetic frown. "I wish I felt differently. I wish I could stop being scared, but the truth is I can't."

"But Matthew gave his word he would leave you alone. Matthew doesn't lie."

Matthew is Shamari. Or, as I prefer to call him, a not-angel. It's their job to stop the Baneem from hurting humans.

"I know that." AJ sighs and rakes his fingertips across his forehead. "It's not just the Shamari I have to worry about. There's a Baneem who knows about me. Or at least knows Matthew didn't drag me into purgatory when he should have."

I press my lips together. AJ was unconscious for a lot of our encounter with Taylor. I've never told him Taylor knows Matthew couldn't tell he was of Baneem descent. I didn't think it would matter. I still don't. Anything I tell him is just going to raise his anxiety levels further. Instead, I try to soothe him.

"Taylor is in purgatory," I say. "He'll be there for a long time."

"But he will get out, and in the meantime, prisoners talk."

I stand, angry my legs are wobbling, angry we're arguing about ifs, buts, and maybes.

"Are you breaking up with me?" I say, dragging leaves and twigs out my hair. "Are you going to leave?"

He hurries to his feet so we're level again. The low sun casts eerie shadows across his face, making his honey skin appear several shades darker.

"No," he says, but there's no conviction in his voice. "I don't want to." He kicks out, sending up a shower of leaves that drift down to the ground slowly. "I want to stay here. I want to be with you." He puts his hands on my arms. "I love you."

I blink at his words, tilting my head back a little so I can focus on his face. On his eyes. I barely have time to register what he's said, let alone reply, because he ploughs straight on.

"But even if I was absolutely sure I'd be safe here, it's not the only reason I should walk away from you."

I shake my head, not understanding.

"I shouldn't be with anyone."

He releases me and wheels away, resting his head and hands against the tree trunk. He hunches his shoulders up to his ears and takes several deep breaths.

"Why not?"

It's all I can think to say. I'm not sure if I'm feeling angry, confused, or sympathetic. From the way my stomach churns and flutters, it's probably all three and a few more unidentifiable emotions on top.

"Because of what I am," he says in a quiet whisper.

I put my hand on his back, between his shoulder blades. I move my hand in slow, firm circles.

"It doesn't matter," I say. "I thought you knew that."

"Yes, it does," he breathes. "It might not now. But in a few years' time, you're going to want to start a family and that can never happen with me."

I slip around him and lean against the tree. I have to bend my knees to stand in the limited space carved out by the angle of his body. I lift my face, so he's forced to look at me or turn away again.

"Are you scared of hurting me or of getting hurt?" I say.

"Both?" He straightens up but doesn't tear his gaze from mine. "Sooner or later, we'll have to end things. The longer we're together, the harder it will be for us both. Maybe we should back off and go back to being friends."

I narrow my eyes, pushing myself upright. Those aren't his words. I might have only known him for three months, but this isn't coming from him. It's coming from his mum. I bite the inside of my cheek to stop myself from badmouthing her.

I force a smile to my lips. "Didn't we cover this when we first got together? All I care about is how I feel about you right now. I'm not ready to get married. I'm definitely not thinking about having kids."

"But at some point, you will."

"Yes, I will. In maybe five or ten years. Not now. But if you want to throw away what we have because of a problem that's a long way off, then you're an idiot." I cross my arms. "And if you can't let yourself relax with me when I know what you are, how are you ever going to have a relationship with anyone?"

All he does is stare at me, his chin dimpling under the pressure of a sad frown. Slowly, my arms drift apart until they're hanging loosely by my sides. I feel like I'm standing in a vacuum. All the pressure has been sucked out of my lungs and dragged into the air around me, suffocating me.

He won't be with anyone else. That's the point. He said it, and I wasn't listening.

"You can't spend your life alone," I say, my voice rising into a semi-cry.

I stand and cup his face in my hands, running my thumbs over his soft cheeks. I pull his head down until our foreheads touch and I can feel his breath on my face.

"I get you don't want to hurt me," I say. "I get everything feels uncertain. But you need to stop worrying about what might happen a few years down the line."

"And stop jumping at shadows?"

"That, too."

I raise my mouth to his. I half-expect him to pull away again, but he doesn't. He presses into the kiss, applying soft pressure that sends little pulses of excitement and desire shooting up and down my spine.

As soon as our lips part, I say, "You need to relax, enjoy what we have, and stop pushing me away."

"I'll try." He leans in for another kiss but pauses when his phone bleeps.

"Ignore it?"

He shakes his head. "It'll be Mum. No one else has my number except you and Sophie."

I suppress a groan as AJ pulls out his phone. Sometimes, Phailin acts more like a prison warden than a mother. Deep crease lines slice across his forehead as he reads the text.

"What's wrong?" My heartbeat increases at the thought she's giving him cut-and-run instructions, making me tremble.

"She wants me to meet her at school."

"Now?" School ended almost an hour ago. "Why?"

"Mr. Whittaker wants to see us both."

"Did she say why?"

"No. But I can guess."

I raise my eyebrows in a questioning expression.

"We might not be sharing classes anymore," he says. He kisses me on the forehead. "I'll fill you in later, okay?"

I don't want him to walk away without explaining his cryptic comment, but now isn't the time to push him.

Instead I say, "Promise?"

He smiles as he stoops down to retrieve his hat. "I promise."

CHAPTER TWO

I'd rather be with Kim than facing Mum and Mr. Whittaker. Mum's waiting for me at the school gates. I don't get a chance to question why she's wearing jeans instead of the smart black skirt suit she normally wears to work. She grabs my arm and frog-marches me up the drive toward the main entrance.

"Don't say a word," she says sharply. "I'll do the talking."

I don't argue. All Mum and I seem to have done lately is argue about the same things: whether or not we should leave and whether or not I should be with Kim. Besides, I'm pretty sure we both know what's coming. We've been here long enough for our lies to start catching up with us.

We're shown straight into Mr. Whittaker's office. It's the first time I've been in here. When I started at the school in September, he met Mum and me in reception for a quick chat before escorting me to my form room. I sweep my gaze over the shelves of ceramics made by students past and present. The bright colours and imperfect designs cheer up the drab office.

Mr. Whittaker makes a token gesture of shaking Mum's hand before motioning for us to sit down. I slip my hat off and let it drop onto the carpet with a quiet puff. Mr. Whittaker's face is scrunched into a suspicious frown as he regards me and Mum. He rests his palm on a buff file.

"When a new student starts at the school, it's standard procedure for us to request information from their previous school," he says, not bothering with any niceties. "Aran's information came through today, and it was quite disappointing."

My heart should be racing as I wait for him to continue, but it isn't. I feel oddly empty. I've been waiting for everything to start collapsing around me, even though I hoped it wouldn't.

He opens the folder and lifts up a printed sheet of paper. "You were only there for two weeks, and you left before taking any exams."

"There must be some mistake," Mum says, smiling warmly. "Maybe I wrote the wrong school down by mistake. Aran has good exam results."

I glare at the desk. For once I wish Mum would stop lying and say something resembling the truth. We've been caught out. Surely she has to know it?

Mr. Whittaker straightens his back. "I assumed you had made a mistake as well, so I asked my secretary to make some enquiries with the exam boards and with the other schools you listed on his entrance form. Aran hasn't taken any exams and has very little formal education to speak of." He snaps the folder shut.

I sink down in the chair a little, hunching my shoulders. There's no lie Mum can tell to make this better.

"Obviously, we require a certain standard of grades before students can be allowed into the sixth form," Mr. Whittaker says.

His voice is beginning to grate on my nerves. He sounds smug, as though he's won the grand prize in a raffle.

He switches his attention to me. "What I don't understand is how you've been able to maintain a high grade average this term. You've been spending a lot of time with Kimberley Welles. She's a smart girl. Has she been helping you?"

Mum inhales sharply. "Are you accusing my son of cheating?"

"After discovering you've lied about his education and exam results, cheating isn't a huge leap to make."

I want their angry conversation to wash over me and dissolve into a muffled echo I can't make out.

"That's ridiculous," Mum says. "My son is a bright boy."

"Who hasn't even had a basic education."

I curl my hands around the arms of the chair. I'm not supposed to say anything. Mum doesn't want me to defend myself. As always, she wants to handle the situation.

"He doesn't have complete school records, granted," Mum says. "We moved around a lot. You can't penalise him for that."

"I cannot allow a student into the sixth form without their GCSEs." Mr. Whittaker taps his fingertips against the desk. "I'm sorry. I'm going to have to ask Aran to leave the sixth form."

Mum's smile morphs into a snarl. "You can't do that." Her expression isn't backed up by her tone of voice, which lacks strength and conviction.

"As the headmaster of this school, I can."

"I'll complain to the board of governors."

Mr. Whittaker shrugs. "They will agree with my decision."

Mum sighs. "Fine. Thank you for your time, Mr. Whittaker."

Isn't she going to put up more of a fight? I'm not sure why I'm surprised. She wants to leave, and me being thrown out of school will only make her argument stronger and mine weaker. Unless I stand up for myself and find a way to change Mr. Whittaker's mind.

Mum stands and walks to the door but pauses when she realises I'm not following her. "Come on, Aran. Mr. Whittaker has made his decision."

"I learnt at home," I say.

"Aran." Mum's sharp voice lashes out at me in a warning I don't heed.

"I downloaded the curriculum from the Internet and bought second-hand textbooks and study guides. I work hard, Mr. Whittaker. If I don't get some qualifications, I won't be able to do anything with my life. I'm sorry we…I lied." The leather chair creaks as I lean forward. "Will you at least let me take my G.C.S.E.s this year? If I do well, I could restart the sixth form next year." I need to believe we'll still be here.

Mr. Whittaker leans back and thatches his fingers beneath his chin. "I suppose we could consider that an option. You could join the re-sit groups for English and maths, but you'd need to sit in on some year eleven lessons for the other subjects. You'll have to take at least five, and there would be a lot of work to catch up on. All the year ten coursework, for a start."

"I can catch up," I say quickly. I start thinking through a study plan, working out which teachers I need to talk to. I'd take the sciences, of course. I'm best at those.

"How much work?" Mum asks. "Don't you think it's too much to ask of anyone to do five two-year courses in less than a year? There's, what, a term and a half before the exams? Less before the coursework deadlines."

I resist the urge to look around at her. I know why she's being so negative, why she's finding it so hard to relax here, because I feel the same way. But surely she doesn't want to sabotage my future?

Mr. Whittaker knocks his fingertips against his lips. "Yes," he says after a long pause. "It is a lot of work. Perhaps too much."

No. I won't let Mum talk him out of this. "At least let me try. Please?" My voice is over-eager, but I don't care. I need to make them both understand how much I want to pass my exams.

Mr. Whittaker clears his throat. "Miss Jao, would it be possible for me to speak to Aran alone?"

"I don't think that's necessary," Mum says.

"Please." He isn't asking. It's a polite statement, but spoken in a tone that would make most of his pupils quake.

Mum isn't that easy to intimidate. "Anything you have to say to Aran can be said in front of me."

I twist around and lean on the back of the chair so I can stare at her with wide, imploring eyes. "Mum, it's fine. I'll see you outside in a few minutes. Okay?"

She squeezes her eyebrows together. "Fine." She holds still for a couple of seconds. Her expression is blank, but her eyes whisper a warning to me. Then she rolls her shoulders back, holding her head high, and stalks out of the office.

I take a deep breath before turning to face Mr. Whittaker.

He reaches for a sheet of printer paper and a pen and starts to scribble something on it. From my upside-down viewpoint, it looks like a maths equation.

"Is everything all right at home, Aran?"

I smile and nod. "It's fine."

"It must be hard, moving around so much."

"Yeah, it is."

I watch him closely to try and work out what he suspects, so I can make sure I don't give any wrong answers. The last thing we need is Mr. Whittaker poking his nose into our lives.

"Is there any reason you move so much?"

"Mum gets bored at work easily," I say. I've said that lie so many times it sounds more natural than the truth.

He turns the piece of paper round and pushes it and the pen to me. It's a complex equation. A-level stuff.

"So each time she wants a new job, you move to a new location?" A note of disbelief hangs in his voice.

I shrug. "Pretty much." I start work on the equation. It gives me a good excuse not to look at him anymore.

"Even though that's meant your education has suffered?"

I wait until I've solved the first part of the equation before answering him. "She home-schooled me a lot of the time, and then I taught myself."

"Is your mother likely to get bored again?"

I imagine him curling his fingers into quote marks. In reality, his hands remain flat on the desk.

"She's trying really hard to settle down this time. She knows how much it means to me to pass my exams."

"It's a shame she didn't feel that way last year."

I can't say anything to that, so I concentrate on the last part of the equation instead. It's obvious my lies are more transparent than I want them to be. It made more sense when I was younger.

"Often, when families move around a lot, it's because they have something to hide."

I pause halfway through crossing out a carried number. "We've got nothing to hide." At least not along the lines he's thinking.

"Do you get on well with your mum?"

"Yes." I finish the equation and pass it back to him.

He looks at it, pulls out a calculator, and works out each part individually. His eyebrows rise when he discovers I've got it right.

"I'm not a cheat," I say. "And I do get on with Mum. She'd never do anything to hurt me."

Mr. Whittaker purses his lips, staring at me. I can't help but squirm. I cross my legs and uncross them again, rest my elbow on the arm of the chair, and place my fingertips beneath my lower lip, before folding my hands in my lap.

"If there is anything you're concerned about—"

"There isn't." I wince, conscious my answer came too quickly and earnestly. I tilt my face toward the ceiling, desperate to come up with words he'll believe, something much closer to the truth. Breathing deeply, I tip my head forward and stare at the desk.

"We move around so much because of my dad." I pause, waiting for Mr. Whittaker to say something, but he doesn't. I can't bring myself to look up at him. "He...umm... He..." I clear my throat, unsure why it's so hard to spit the words out. Maybe I'm scared Mr. Whittaker will think I'm still lying—or worse, speak to Mum.

"He hurt Mum a lot. Physically, I mean. She left him when I was a baby, but he's not the type of man to let go so easily." I force myself to lift my head and look at Mr. Whittaker. His cheeks are puffed out a little, his steady gaze holds mine. "We've been running away from him for years. It's why we move around so much. But we haven't heard anything from him in a while now. So hopefully we've lost him for good."

If only the last part could be true. More than anything I want to stop running. I wipe my clammy hands on my jeans. For some reason, I thought telling a mundane version of the truth would make me feel better, but it hasn't. It's left my gut twisting and churning.

Mr. Whittaker leans back in his chair. "Thank you, Aran."

I blink.

"It must have been hard for you to tell me about your father." He sighs and offers me a small smile. "I'll have my PA organise a new timetable for you first thing tomorrow. Come to the office straight after registration. All right?"

I can't stifle the gasp that leaps out of my throat. "Thank you, sir."

He nods. "You're obviously a bright boy, Aran. It would be a shame to waste your potential."

I stand, almost tripping over the chair in my rush to leave the office, grab my hat, and tell Mum the good news. I bite my lower lip, pausing with my hand on the door handle. Mum won't think it's good news at all.

*

Mum won't ever argue with me on public transport, but her silence isn't a reprieve from the tension mounting between us. By the time we arrive back at the flat, I'm braced for an onslaught of shouting and tears. The muscles in my shoulders and back ache from being held so tensely.

I follow Mum into our tiny sitting room, waiting. She sinks onto the sofa and drops her arms to her thighs so her hands hang limply between her knees. She stares at me and says nothing. I wait in the doorway, shifting my weight from foot to foot. When she still says nothing, I take my hat and coat off, intending on retreating to my room, except I can't make myself take the handful of steps to get there.

"Mr. Whittaker said he would get me a new timetable tomorrow, so I'll be able to get started on catching up straight away."

I watch Mum's face carefully, looking for any hint of what she might be feeling. Her lips are pressed together tightly, leeching them of colour.

"We can't stay, Aran." Her nostrils flare as she speaks.

Here it comes. I take a deep breath and step into the room properly, tossing my hat and coat over the fold-up table. I sit in the armchair.

"School's sorted out, and we don't have to worry about the

Shamari while we're here. You've got a good job—"

"No, I don't."

"What?"

She wrings her hands. "They fired me. None of my references checked out, and they got sick of trying disconnected numbers."

I flop back against the sagging cushion, letting my hands curl limply in my lap. "I thought they liked you."

"It doesn't matter. They think I'm a liar. I even heard two of the girls gossiping that I was probably in trouble with the police." She leans to the side, so she can put her hand on my knee.

It should feel like a comforting gesture, but all I want to do is jerk away. Somehow I force myself to resist, remaining steady under her touch.

"If I don't have a job, we can't afford the rent. Or the bills. Or food." She says each statement slowly, pausing between them to ensure they sink in. "The past is catching up with us, Aran, and the only way to escape it is to start afresh somewhere. Just the two of us."

I pull away and lean my elbows on my knees, wiping my hands over my face. "Did they fire you today?"

Her breath hitches in her throat. "No. Last week."

When was she going to tell me? I should have known. I should have seen the signs. I tip my head back onto the top of the sofa cushion. I've been so caught up in what I should and shouldn't tell Kim and how close I should let myself get to her, I'd stopped noticing Mum. I practically sleepwalk through our daily arguments. I became numb to them because I didn't want to face the reality of my fears.

"I tried to find another job but couldn't."

Did she? I'm not sure I believe her. If she'd ever had any intention of finding a new job, she would have told me as soon as she lost her old one.

"Go and pack. We'll go to the train station and pick a direction. North. South. East. Wherever you fancy."

"I want to stay here."

"No. You want to stay with that girl." Impatience has crept into her tone.

"She has a name, Mum."

"Kim," Mum says through gritted teeth. "You can't make a girl your reason for staying. You don't have a future. You can't be with her."

I press the heel of my hand hard against my forehead. The pressure grounds me, allowing me to take a few deep breaths to calm myself before I speak.

"I love her."

Mum laughs in my face. It's not a jovial sound or an explosion of surprise. It's haughty and patronising. "You're a child. What do you know about love?"

"I'm almost seventeen."

"Exactly. Aran, I'm fed up of having this conversation with you. When will you see sense? You can't be with her."

I'm sick of it, too. All of it. Sick of moving every few weeks. Sick of never being allowed to have friends without Mum warning me off. Sick of being constantly alone and afraid.

I stand and pace while I try to gather my thoughts into a coherent argument. The trouble is I never win. Mum's logic-and-lioness act always whittles me down. I've never had much of a reason to fight against her before, but now I have Kim and the weight of Matthew's promise of protection from the Shamari.

"I can get a part-time job while you look for something. It won't bring in much money, but it might be enough to tide us over."

Mum laughs again, a horrible snorting laugh that makes me feel like I've said the most stupid thing in the world.

"You're going to take five exam courses in less than a year and hold down a part-time job? When are you going to sleep? What would you even do?"

I shake my head. "I don't know. Wash dishes in a restaurant or something."

"Or something? You really don't have a clue, do you?"

Her cruel words cut into me, but I refuse to show how much they hurt. I fold my arms and jut my chin into the air. The effect is lost when she gets to her feet and stands practically nose-to-nose with me.

"Do you really think some crappy minimum wage job would even come close to paying the rent on this place?"

"It would be a start," I say through clenched teeth. I won't let myself lose my temper, because the second I do, she'll win.

"You'd really run yourself into the ground for a girl?"

I shake my head. "No, Mum. I'd do it for us. We've got a chance to stop running and build a life here. I don't understand why you're afraid of that."

She gapes at me. "I'm afraid of losing you." Tears glisten in her eyes. "I've sacrificed my entire life to keep you safe."

Every time she says those words, I can't help but wonder if she's trying to make me feel guilty. I probably should. If it wasn't for me, she would have had a life, she would have been happy.

"If we stay here, you won't need to sacrifice anything else. Go and speak to your boss. Explain why you don't have references. Tell him we've been running away from Dad, but he isn't a problem anymore. He'll understand."

"No, he won't."

"Mr. Whittaker did."

Her mouth drops open, and her skin pales. I bite my knuckle. What a stupid thing to say.

"What did you tell him?"

My voice sticks in my throat, so all I can let out is a series of squeaks while I try build up the courage to speak.

"What did you tell him?" She steps even closer to me, forcing me to shrink away. I know she'd never hurt me, but she can be fiercely intimidating when she wants to be.

"I told him Dad hit you, so you ran away from him."

She turns away, shaking her head as she clamps her hands against her hips. "You idiot. Do you think he'll leave it at that? He'll want to know your father's name. He'll talk to social services and probably the police, too. He'll stick his nose even further into our business." She takes a couple of deep breaths before stepping back toward me and placing her hands on my cheeks. "You foolish boy," she whispers. "You've just made everything worse. Pack your bags."

I don't know what else I can say. I don't think I made things worse. Mr. Whittaker didn't push me to tell him anything more. He didn't ask me anything about Dad. I made things better and gave myself a chance at a future. How can Mum say any different? I'm losing control and edging closer to shouting at her by the second. Her close proximity to me isn't helping. I take a step back, bashing my leg against the low computer table. The plastic base of the monitor whines as it wobbles.

"Why won't you try and talk to your boss?"

"It's safer to run, Aran. Especially now you've told your headmaster a fraction of the truth."

Something inside me snaps in two. "You don't want to stop running, do you?"

"It's not that simple." She tries to touch my face, but I flinch away.

"Yes, it is." I clench my hands into fists. "We've got a chance to have a normal life here."

She presses her trembling hand to her lips and breathes slowly. "Grow up, Aran."

I'd rather she yelled at me, so I could put her words down to the heat of the moment. But her insult shivers through me and makes me feel like crap.

"Maybe you should go without me."

Tears slip from her eyes down her cheeks. "You don't mean that."

No, I don't, but I'm not going to admit it out loud yet. What I need—what we both need—is some space to breathe and calm down.

"I'm going out," I say, putting a firm snap into my voice, which I hope will prevent her from trying to stop me. I need time to pretend my life could be normal, if only for a couple of hours.

She waits until I'm in the hallway before calling after me. "Going where? To her?"

I pause for a second, hunching my shoulders and clenching my teeth against her words. Why does she hate Kim so much?

"I'll be back in a bit," I say, refusing to be drawn into yet another argument.

I'm almost out the front door before she tries again.

"Aran—"

Ignoring her voice, I slam the door behind me.

CHAPTER THREE

The heavy black ball drops away from AJ's fingers and rumbles down the slick surface of the bowling lane, wobbling before thudding into the gutter. By luck, it wings one of the pins, which teeters from side to side before knocking into its neighbour. They both topple to the floor as the ball thunks against the back of the lane, triggering the pinsetting machine, which rattles down to collect the eight pins still standing. The outcome was almost as bad as his first roll.

"Better luck next time." Sophie grins, patting his shoulder as she passes him and carefully selects a dark purple ball.

I grip the edge of the cream plastic bench as AJ comes to sit beside me. It's the first time we've had a moment alone since he arranged this odd evening out.

"Is this your idea of telling me what happened with Mr. Whittaker?" I say.

He leans against the back of the bench, gaze fixed firmly on Sophie as she readies herself to take her first roll of the opening frame. "I thought it would be nice for the three of us to hang out together, that's all."

I narrow my eyes. "So you went to Sophie's to arrange it?"

"Her house is closer to my place than yours."

"You could have called me." I would have suggested that we went for a walk, just the two of us, so we could talk about what happened.

"I left my phone at home."

I tilt my shoulders back, away from him. "Along with your coat and hat?"

He winces and then starts to clap. Sophie whoops and punches the air. It takes me a second to realise she's scored a strike, ending her turn.

"You're up next, Kim," she says, grinning.

I don't really want to bowl. I want to talk to AJ. Sighing, I start to stand, but pause when AJ's fingers curl between mine.

"Let's have some fun. We can talk later, okay?" His eyebrows lift, illuminating the spiraling golden flecks in his chestnut eyes. His expression planes the sharp edges off my mood. I smile as I disentangle my fingers from his and go to select a ball.

I test the weight of a few before finally choosing a bright red one. I haven't been bowling since my birthday. My kid brother, Chris, took delight in beating me and Dad. Although, if AJ's first turn is anything to go by, my only real competition is Sophie. I ready the ball, run forward a couple of steps, stoop, swing, and release. The ball spins down the right-hand side of the lane, gradually curving toward the center. A moment before it reaches the pins, it slips off course into the left-hand side of the lane. It slams into one of the side pins, knocking it into the air and against the surrounding pins. Only four are left standing.

I wait for the ball to rumble through the ball return beneath my feet, so I can use it again. I glance back at AJ and Sophie. They're smiling and chatting. AJ looks more relaxed with her than he did with me, but she's probably not hassling him. I blow out a breath and take my second roll. I watch the ball spin down the lane on a direct path for the center of the four pins I left standing. It veers off, plummeting into the gutter without striking a single pin.

I shrug my shoulders and return to the bench, brushing my fingertips against AJ's arm as we cross paths.

"Question," Sophie says when I sit down. "How does AJ know where I live?"

I make the mistake of missing a breath before replying. "Haven't we all had a study session at your house?" I fight to make my voice sound genuinely confused.

"No," she says firmly. "AJ's never been to my house. You haven't even been over since Gran and Aunt Liz got better." She folds her arms. "Not once."

I focus on the bright scoring monitor, suspended above our heads. I can't tell her I don't want to come around anymore because of her dad. I'm not sure what to say. Why did AJ have to go around to her place? He's supposed to be better at managing lies than I am. He's been doing it for a lot longer.

"Things seem a little tense between you two," Sophie says.

I'm glad she's the one changing the subject. She turns onto her knees and takes a sip from a tall cup of Coke on the table behind us, grabs a handful of French fries, and sits back down.

"Is everything okay?"

"Everything's fine." I pinch a French fry and munch on it to avoid further questions.

Sophie tilts her head to the side as AJ fluffs his second shot. "Either he's rubbish at bowling or he's got other things on his mind. He didn't knock a single pin down that time." She pats my knee. "Looks like I only need to worry about beating you."

She brushes her salty fingers on her jeans as she trades places with AJ again.

"Why did you leave your coat at home?" I ask AJ. It's too cold to be wandering around in only a T-shirt and thin jumper.

He hunches his shoulders. "Mum and I had an argument after the meeting at school." He glances at me from the corners of his eyes. "I'd rather not talk about it right now."

Of course not. He wants to run away from the problem instead. The possibilities of what they might have argued about run through my head. I keep coming back to the same thought: They fought about leaving. My heartbeat increases to a frenzied flutter, which leaves me breathless.

AJ kisses me without warning, calming my heart into a slow and steady rhythm. "Relax," he whispers, barely parting his lips from mine. "I'm not going anywhere." He cups my cheek in his hand and kisses me slowly and deeply.

When we finally pull apart, Sophie is standing over us with her arms folded.

"I got a spare." Her mouth curls up into a smirk. "I guess I'm less distracted than you two."

My cheeks blaze with heat, forcing me to dip my face toward the floor. I brush a strand of auburn hair behind my ear before blowing out a sharp breath.

Unsurprisingly, my next frame is terrible. Not as bad as AJ's, but my total of three doesn't help to close the growing gap between Sophie's and my scores.

Sophie wins. I'd feel better about winning second place if AJ hadn't been so obviously preoccupied throughout the entire game. He smiled at all the right times and kept up cheerful chatter with Sophie, but there was a tension in his gaze that betrayed his concern.

"Another game?" he asks, once Sophie has finished her victory dance. He lifts his eyebrows into a hopeful expression.

Sophie shakes her head. "Not for me."

"But you won," AJ says. "I thought you'd enjoy beating us again."

She blows on her fingertips and rubs them against her plum-coloured T-shirt. "I can't help being brilliant. Seriously, though, we've all got school tomorrow, and I have a ton of homework. We're working with clay in art, so I have to finish my sketches." Her eyes twinkle. "Besides, I think you two could do with some alone time."

"Sophie." I say her name in a high-pitched growl while hiding my face behind my hands.

"What? Am I wrong?"

I exchange a glance with AJ. We need to talk, but I also want to hold him and kiss him. Not that we've got anywhere where we can be alone in the way Sophie is intimating. I'm pretty sure Phailin hates me, and my mum watches us as closely as a prison warden. Dad is a little more accommodating by leaving the room, although he does insist on the door staying open. I know what my parents think might happen, even though I've tried to assure them I'm not ready to jump into bed with AJ.

"Do you want us to see you home?" I ask.

She checks the contents of her purse. "No, I'll grab a taxi. It's too cold and dark to take the bus."

After Sophie has rung for a taxi, the three of us exchange our shoes and wander outside to wait. Sophie was right—it's too dark and too cold. At least it's dry. I pull my gloves on and clap my hands together, shifting my weight from foot to foot in a bid to stay warm. AJ stuffs his hands in his pockets and hunches his shoulders up to his ears. His jaw wobbles as his teeth chatter together. He must be freezing without his coat.

I'm relieved when the taxi arrives and Sophie jumps in. We wave her off before AJ turns toward the bus stop. I grab his arm and shake my head.

"Fancy a walk first?" I grimace at my own suggestion. "Or maybe we can find somewhere warmer to talk."

"A walk's fine." His breath crystallises into a miniature cloud as he speaks.

Hand in hand, we wander across the road toward the promenade. The moonlight illuminates the white crests of small waves as they break on the manmade beach. I can feel the chill of AJ's skin through my woollen glove, so I rub my thumb quickly over the back of his hand in a failed attempt at warming him up.

"What happened at school?"

"Mr. Whittaker discovered Mum and I had lied about my G.C.S.E.s."

I look up at him sharply. "Lied? How?"

He bows his head. "I never passed them, Kim. We were too busy running for me to stay in one place long enough to do coursework or take exams."

I blow air into my cheeks and hold my breath. I'm not surprised, but it hurts that it's taken him this long to tell me.

AJ waves his free hand dismissively through the air. "It's fine. I convinced Mr. Whittaker to let me take them this year. If I pass, I can restart the sixth form next year."

"If you're still here," I say dully.

He squeezes my hand. "I will be."

"Is that what you and your mum argued about?"

He nods. I stop abruptly, sucking my lower lip in as I try to work out what to say next. He pulls his hand away from mine and tucks his hands under his armpits, clamping his arms against his chest.

"Why is your mum so desperate to leave?"

He shifts his weight from foot to foot. "She's not."

I arch an eyebrow. I'm not sure if it's his abrupt tone or the way he evades my gaze as he speaks that tells me he's lying. Probably both.

"Can we please not talk about it?" He curls his mouth into a lopsided smile. "I arranged to go out bowling with you and Sophie so I could forget about my argument with Mum for a couple of hours. I know that probably makes me a jerk, but right now I'd like to feel like a normal teenager, not a frightened half-magical freak. Okay?"

I breathe in the cold air and release it again, forcing the action to soothe away the tension in my shoulders. I unzip my coat, pry his arms away from his chest, and coax his hands inside, around my back. I press my chest against his, resting my chin on his shoulder. I can feel his chattering jaw vibrating against my head.

"A normal but cold teenager?" I say.

He coughs out a laugh. "Yeah, it was pretty dumb of me to storm out on Mum without my coat."

"Shhh, we're not talking about your argument any more, remember?"

He grins at me, his eyes twinkling brightly in the moonlight. Behind me, the waves whisper rhythmically against the beach. This place, this instant, couldn't be more perfect. I lift my lips to his and sink into a kiss. I rest one hand in the dip between his shoulder blades and curl the other around the nape of his neck.

I want nothing more than to be able to completely lose myself in the moment. I want us both to be able to fool ourselves into thinking we don't have a care in the world except the cold. But it isn't true. Sadness and fear cling to AJ even now, robbing his embrace of true strength. I break our kiss and bury my face against his collarbone, wishing we could find a way to make him safe from the Baneem and the Shamari. Forever.

CHAPTER FOUR

After walking Kim home, I end up on the towpath. It's pitch dark apart from the reflection of the stars and moon on the still surface of the canal. I put my hands in my pockets, as though the denim will protect them from the cold. My breath hangs like a pale ghost on the air in front of me. It serves me right for walking out on Mum, which was a childish thing to do.

Tiny loose stones click beneath my trainers. There's a splash as I kick one into the water, and pause, watching as the surface is disturbed by circles increasing outward, shattering the re-flected pinpricks of light.

A crunch to my right drags my attention away from the water. A man is wandering along the path, whistling. I'm not sure why my pulse quickens. There are a dozen reasons why someone would be walking here in the dark. It's not very late—he's probably on his way home. I stand still, watching the man from the corners of my eyes as he wanders past me.

I almost laugh at my own paranoia. I've spent so long being afraid I've forgotten how to relax. I can't even loosen up around Kim.

The surface of the water has settled again. I turn and con-tinue ambling down the towpath. With every step, I try to convince myself to go home and apologise to Mum. But if I do, I'll lose. She'll have us packed and on a train by morning. I don't want to leave, but Mum doesn't want to stay and she never backs down.

I head up a set of stone steps that lead to a road. It takes a few seconds for my eyes to adjust to the artificial amber of the streetlights. I head toward the city center. A steady stream of traffic travels in the opposite direction. Pedestrians huddled in coats, scarves, and gloves hurry past me, their arms laden down with shopping bags bearing a variety of Christmas logos. They look happy. I sigh. It's time to go home and make my peace with Mum. At least I've had time to clear my head and calm down. Maybe this time we can talk without us both getting angry.

I wander down the alleyway between the main road and the flats. As usual, the streetlight at the far end is broken, casting me in darkness.

Footsteps pound behind me, and I glance over my shoulder. A man is standing at the end of the alley, arms folded. I turn back just as a second man steps into my path.

My heart pounds. Two men. I can barge past one and outrun the other. I shift my weight onto the balls of my feet, preparing to run.

"Hello, Aran."

Hearing my own name makes me falter, especially because I don't recognise the voice. The man in front of me, the one who spoke, strides toward me.

"I just want to talk, Aran."

I squint, trying to see his face in the darkness, but there's no expanse of water to reflect the stars high above my head. Instead, the tall concrete walls on either side of us absorb the light.

"Who are you?"

He stops half a dozen paces away from me. Through the shadows, I can see his mouth curl into an approximation of a warm smile.

"Your father."

My chest feels paralysed, trapping air inside my lungs, forbidding me from breathing.

"Can we talk?"

I force my frozen body into life again so I can gulp in a cold breath of air. "If you want to talk, why have you brought along a pet thug?" I jerk my thumb over my shoulder in the direction of the burly man.

My father—Saul—inclines his head to the side. "Forgive me. I wasn't sure how you'd react to seeing me." His gaze flicks up and down, probably taking in my tense stance and the way I'm still tipped forward onto the balls of my feet, ready to run.

"How did you think I'd react?"

He shrugs. "Badly? I'm sure your mother hasn't told you anything good about me." He presses his lips together, smothering a sigh. "I would have liked to meet you before now." His words are sincere, but the timbre of his voice isn't.

"We've got nothing to talk about." I glance at the thug behind me. He hasn't come any closer, but I'm less confident now about barrelling past Saul. He's considerably taller and broader than I am.

"I was afraid you would feel that way," Saul says. "Will you at least hear me out? You might have nothing to say to me, but I have a lot to tell you."

I hesitate. I'm pretty sure telling him to stuff his words is the wrong thing to do. If all he really wanted was to talk, he would have come alone and he wouldn't have cornered me in a dark alley. But I don't want to talk to him or be anywhere near him. I shudder, wondering how long he's been watching and waiting for the perfect moment to approach me.

"Fine, talk." I drop off the balls of my feet in pretence at relaxing.

He steps forward. I'd back off, except I don't want to get closer to the thug, so I put my hands up, palms facing Saul.

"I said talk. You don't need to come any closer."

He raises his eyebrows in what should be a regretful expression but doesn't quite manage it. "I was afraid your mother would have made you hate me. It was naive of me to think anything different. You must believe me, Aran, I wanted to be a father to you."

I don't believe anything he says, but I bite my tongue and keep my acidic thoughts to myself.

"I've been looking for you since she stole you from me. I wanted us all to be a family again."

I feel the tang of blood as I bite my tongue a little too hard, quickly followed by a prickling sensation as my magic regenerates the small amount of damage I've caused.

"And the truth is I need your help. Your people need your help," Saul says.

I clench my teeth together to prevent myself from laughing in his face.

"I'm sure you're aware of the conflict between us and the Shamari? Your mother did tell you, didn't she?"

I nod sharply.

"We want to end the war and live peaceful lives. Will you help us?"

I tense my cheeks until they're pinching against my eyes. "What would you want me to do?"

"Come to Uralahnd with me, and I'll explain everything." He extends his hand toward me.

"Tell me now."

"There are things I need to show you. Things you won't believe unless you see them with your own eyes. Please, Aran. Come to Uralahnd with me. If after you know the truth you still don't want to help, I'll bring you home. I promise."

If I had only heard the words, I might believe him, but there's something low and dangerous in his voice, an implied threat that sends fear tingling up and down my spine. I've played along for long enough, now I need to get away from him.

I take a step back, but the other man thuds toward me. I swallow, duck my head, and run toward Saul, but I swerve to the side at the last moment. For a second, I think I've made it, but then something hard smacks against my shin. I fall, slamming onto my hands and knees. Fingertips curl through my hair and jerk my head backward, forcing me to stare at Saul's upside-down face. Through the shadows gathering around his features, I can make out a pair of hard chestnut eyes.

"I tried to be reasonable," he snarls. "I tried to give you a choice."

"Some choice."

I grab at his hand and writhe in his grip, kicking and shouting as he drags me to my feet and slams my back against the wall. I gasp as a sharp pain drives into my gut. I can just make out the hilt of a knife, protruding from my stomach. I drop my hands and make a grab for the hilt, but Saul seizes my arms and pins them against the wall.

"Relax, Aran. We both know you won't die. Your magic won't let you."

As if on cue, dizziness hits me, making the dark alley spin. My fingers and toes buzz with pins and needles that creep through every part of my body. My legs sag, but his grip forbids me from crashing to the ground. I hate the sensation of healing. The nerves in my gut become raw as my body fights to heal the stab wound, but the knife is still there. Fresh pain collects in my stomach, driving tears to my eyes. I try to cry out, but the exhaustion caused by the healing renders me dumb and helpless. Darkness gathers at the edge of my vision, but I fight it. I can't let myself pass out.

He releases my arms but is there to catch me as I collapse forward.

"I'm sorry it has to be like this." His voice is low and soothing, like he's trying to calm a frightened child.

I doubt he's sorry at all.

I want to struggle, but I can only let out the softest whimper as Saul and his thug drape my arms over their shoulders. The tug on the knife wound causes my body to shudder. My magic, trying once again to heal the injury, saps the last shreds of my strength. I try to fight the numbing darkness, but it consumes me and drags me under. In my mind I cry out for Mum, but in reality I make no sound at all as I plummet into unconsciousness.

CHAPTER FIVE

AJ isn't in form. I keep glancing at the door to the room, my forehead developing a growing series of creases as the fifteen minutes drag by.

"Maybe he slept in," Sophie says as the bell goes. "It happens."

I nod and put a fake smile on my face. AJ doesn't sleep in. Did he go home last night to find Phailin had packed his bags? They could be several hundred miles away by now or on a plane heading who knows where. I stuff my planner away with enough force to wrench my rucksack out of my hand. The weight of chemistry textbooks makes it crash to the floor with a loud thud. The students freeze on their way out, staring at me. I hunch my shoulders against the handful of snickers, which are cut short by Sophie's fierce glare.

"Off you go," our form tutor says, hurrying everyone on their way.

I grab my bag and pull it onto one shoulder. AJ wouldn't have let Phailin take him away without calling me.

"I bet he's in school, talking to another teacher," Sophie says, looping her arm through mine.

She leads me out of the classroom toward English. Another teacher. Yes, that has to be it. Maybe Mr. Whittaker needed to talk to him again about taking his G.C.S.E.s. AJ did say that a new timetable would be ready for him today. The creases on my forehead slowly work themselves out. By the time I'm sitting down in English, I feel lighter and satisfied about my explanation for AJ's absence.

We're part way through a discussion on "The Yellow Wallpaper" when a phone starts to vibrate. My phone. Muffled by my bag and its contents, it's hard to pinpoint where the drilling sound is coming from. I know because I can feel it vibrating against my foot. Our teacher looks up from her book and scans the class, her eyebrows pinching down.

"Whoever's it is, turn it off or hand it over. Just because you're in the sixth form doesn't mean the school rules don't apply to you."

Heat rises up my neck into my face, creating a beacon of guilt. Keeping my head low, I pull the phone out of my bag and check who was trying to call me. The frown returns to my face as I see AJ's name plastered across the screen.

"Kim?" My teacher is standing by my desk, with her hand held out. "Turn it off or hand it over."

I don't want to do either. I want to call AJ back and find out what's going on. If he's calling me in the middle of lesson, he can't be in school and it must be important. But my teacher isn't going to let me skip part of a lesson to talk to my boyfriend, and I can't afford to have her confiscate my phone. I switch it off and slip it back into my bag.

"Thank you. Now, as I was saying, I want you to think about how the description of the wallpaper changes throughout the story. Why do you think it changes and what do you think it's supposed to represent?"

The rest of the class turn to one another and begin to discuss the questions.

Sophie nudges my arm. "Fun questions for first lesson, huh?" Her voice drips with sarcasm. "So what do you think?"

I shrug. I can't concentrate on the symbolism of wallpaper in a short story when I don't know where AJ is or what's going on with him. I slide down in my chair so I can sneak my hand into my bag.

"What's wrong?" Sophie asks, lowering her voice to a hoarse whisper. "Was it AJ calling?"

I shake my head as I grab my phone with my fingertips and slide it up into the sleeve of my jumper. As I sit back up again,

I notice Sophie is staring at me with one eyebrow raised. She banishes her expression and taps her fingertip against her copy of the story.

"We're meant to be discussing this. Are you going to focus or are you going to tell me what's wrong?"

I put my hand up, attracting the attention of our teacher.

"Kim—" Sophie hisses, cutting herself off as we're interrupted.

"Yes, Kim?"

"I don't feel well. Please could I go to the toilet?"

Sophie clamps her lips together. I wait until our teacher nods before bolting out of the room.

I don't go to the toilet. I make my way to the memorial garden. No one questions why I'm out of class, probably because they assume I'm on a free period. I shiver as I step outside the school building, wishing I'd been able to work in an excuse to bring my coat with me. I slip through the gate into the walled garden. My ankle boots crunch against the gravel path as I make my way to the bench dedicated to Charley. I sink down on it, wrap one arm around myself to try to keep warm, and call AJ.

The phone is answered within a couple of rings. "Kim?"

I gape at the voice on the other end of the line. "Phailin?"

"Where's Aran?" Her voice is high-pitched, her words fast and clipped. She hisses in a sharp breath. "Please tell me he stayed at yours last night. Tell me he's in school with you."

I find myself shaking my head before checking myself. I snap my mouth shut, swallow, and take a breath before replying. "We hung out together last night, but he went home." My hand is shaking. My nerves jangle, and my mind races with questions I want to ask her. But most of all I want to know where AJ is.

"They've got him, haven't they?" she says.

I twist the hem of my jumper through my fingers. I want her to be wrong, but I can't come to any other conclusion that makes sense. He told me they'd argued. He'd refused to talk about it. He'd seemed happier when he left me than when we first met at the bowling alley. He'd smiled and kissed me. I touch my fingertips to my lips, feeling the echo of his mouth against mine.

"I told him we should go," Phailin says. "I told him it wasn't safe to stay. But he wouldn't listen to me."

And I don't want to listen to her desperate babbling, but I can't bring myself to hang up. What if she's right? What if the Baneem do have him?

"If they've got him, it's your fault," she says. "He wanted to stay because of you."

I press my hand to my mouth and choke back a sob. I kept things from him. I didn't tell him how much Taylor knew about him.

"Where is he?" Phailin says, her voice sharp.

I don't answer. I can't speak. Phailin hangs up, leaving my listening to a solid beep. The phone slips from my hand and thuds onto the floor. The gravel crunches behind me. I jump, swivelling round on the bench as Sophie approaches me. She's carrying my things as well as hers.

"What's wrong?"

I flap my mouth open and closed a couple of times. "AJ's sick."

She scoops down to retrieve my phone. "He seemed fine last night." There's a sharp edge to her casual tone.

She hands me the phone, but holds onto it for an extra couple of seconds as I accept it.

"You'd tell me if something was wrong, wouldn't you?"

I nod. "Of course."

She releases the phone. "Because I'd never hide anything from you, Kim."

Her words multiply the guilt I'm feeling one hundred fold. I tug the corners of my mouth into a smile. "Ditto."

She purses her lips, and the muscles beneath her eyes flex. "So what's up with AJ? Man flu?"

An odd strangled noise slips from my mouth as I think of a response. "He doesn't know yet. He's going to the doctor later today." It's the best lie I can come up with on the spot.

She rolls her shoulders back. "I hope it's nothing serious." The school bell rings in the distance. "Well, time for art. What have you got?"

"A free period." What's one more lie to add to the multitude I've already told her?

She arches an eyebrow. "Really? Well, have fun." She drops my coat and bag down on the bench, spins round on her heel, pauses, and glances over her shoulder. "If you speak to AJ again, tell him to get well soon."

I nod. "Sure."

As soon as she's gone, I pull my coat on, grab my bag, and head out of the garden. I don't go back into the school. Instead I head to the bus stop. I have to talk to Phailin.

*

I'm still running through what I'm going to say to Phailin when I see her in the alley. She's crouched halfway down, running her fingertips over something dark on the ground. I edge closer, watching as she raises her hand and inspects her fingertips. From over her shoulder, I can see flakes of deep red on her honey skin. Dry blood. My chest tightens, forcing me to breathe shallowly.

"It might not be AJ's," I say, but the way my voice quivers shows I don't believe it.

I can't look away from the blood. It isn't big—just a small neat stain on the concrete. Not enough for the wound that caused it to be life-threatening. Especially not for AJ. His body would have started to regenerate the damage. If it's his blood. I wish I could believe it isn't.

She stands and turns half a step round, flicking her gaze up and down as she brushes a strand of long dark hair behind her ear.

"Why aren't you at school?" Her voice is flat and hollow. Her eyes are sunken into dark rings. I doubt she slept at all last night. "Last time you skipped school, you almost got Aran killed."

I clench my jaw but don't rise to her sharp words. AJ chose to go with me that day. Neither of us expected to be abducted at gunpoint and delivered to Taylor. We didn't know Sophie's father would be desperate enough to use the gun. AJ chose to heal me when I got shot.

"I thought looking for AJ was more important," I say. How else did she expect me to react when she called me at school in the middle of a lesson? "Have you called the police?" I'm not sure why I'm bothering to ask. I already know what the answer will be.

She shakes her head.

"Have you called the hospitals?"

"What's the point?" she says.

"It might not have been the Baneem. He could have been mugged. He didn't have his coat with him." Yet again I don't believe it. He did have his wallet. Surely there would have been ID in there?

She folds her arms. "You're right. It might not have been the Baneem. It could have been the Shamari."

"It won't have been Matthew."

I'm absolutely certain of it. Matthew promised he wouldn't take AJ away and he never lies. I lost faith in him once before when I didn't tell him about AJ. I won't doubt him again. I owe him more than that. I owe him my life.

I tighten my grip on my bag's shoulder strap. I want to hold out hope we'll find him if we look. What if he slipped and fell somewhere? Deep down, I know it isn't true. I know the dried blood on the ground by Phailin's feet isn't a coincidence. I know she's right. The Baneem have AJ.

"Yesterday, we argued about whether or not we should leave," Phailin says. Her lips pull tightly across her teeth. "It looks like I was right. It's your fault he stopped listening to me. It's your fault he wouldn't leave. It's your fault they have him." She jabs her finger at my chest, punctuating each statement.

I knock her hand away and rub my breastbone. The pain from the pressure of her finger makes my chest contract tighter, but I try not to show her how guilty I feel. I square my shoulders and roll them back, so I'm standing tall.

"Why would they want him?" I say.

It's something AJ never really explained. He thought they would hate him because he was half-human but had innate magic. I'm not sure he really knew the reason he'd spent his whole life running. It felt like he accepted they did want him but never questioned it. Why would he? He trusted his mum.

Phailin rests one hand on her hip and the other across her stomach. I'd love to know what she's thinking about with those steely eyes. A cold breeze trails through the alley, disturbing her dark hair. Her shoulders are tense, her expression as fierce as a lioness. But behind that mask is a quivering vulnerability. It's the vulnerability of a mother who has lost her only child.

"This isn't a good place to talk. Let's go inside."

She pivots round and strides toward the block of flats without waiting for an answer. I follow because it's the only thing I can do.

*

Phailin pours herself a tumbler of whisky before joining me in the sitting room. The ice clinks against the glass as she sits in the armchair. I run my fingertips over the arm of the sofa, remembering sitting here with AJ. Holding him. Kissing him. I shut my eyes and take a deep breath before opening them again.

"Why do the Baneem want AJ?"

If I can understand why, maybe it will help me find him. I've stopped them twice before. I can and will do it again.

"I don't know." She takes a sip of the amber liquid and presses her lips together, savouring the taste.

I've only had a drink once, right after Charley died. Vodka. It tasted vile and made me lose control. I'm not sure it's a good idea for Phailin to be drinking before mid-morning, but I'm not the one whose son is missing. I didn't dedicate almost seventeen years to keeping him safe.

I twist my fingers together. "If you don't know, how can you be sure the Baneem want him?"

"I just am." She takes another drink, a gulp this time.

"You haven't spent all this time running for no reason. How do you know?"

She cradles the tumbler in her hands, her expression distant. But whereas the muscles around her mouth slacken off, a vertical line runs down her forehead to the bridge of her nose.

"I was your age when I met Aran's father," she says. "Young and stupid enough to fall for him because he was charming and handsome. Saul." As she says his name, I hear something beneath the venom in her voice. A tender shiver?

"You were in love with him?"

She shakes her head. "I thought I was, but it wasn't real. Our relationship was a sham."

I nod, remembering what AJ said about his father. He lied to her, manipulated her, and ruined her life. Was it a similar arrangement to the one made with Sophie's family? The regular opening of a portal allowing access to and from Uralahnd in return for something magical? In their case, enhanced intelligence. My two encounters with Baneem have taught me two things: They always want something, and they are vindictive.

"What did Saul want?"

"Before I got pregnant, he made me believe he loved me and in return I opened gateways for him whenever he asked me to. Once I fell pregnant, the only thing he wanted was Aran."

"But why?"

She downs the rest of the whisky and puts the tumbler on the burgundy carpet. Sighing, she tilts her head back and clasps her hands between her knees.

"He didn't tell me why. He never openly told me he wanted Aran. Do you think I'd have stayed with him for as long as I did if I'd known he wanted to take my child from me? I'm not stupid."

I slide from the sofa onto my knees and shuffle over to her. "What happened?"

"What's the point?"

I shrug. "It might give us a clue?"

She hitches her upper lip into a snarl. "Do you think I haven't gone over what happened between Saul and me over and over? I've had sixteen years to think about it and try to work out what he wanted." She wipes her hands over her face. "All I know about the Baneem is what Saul told me." She narrows her eyes. "I'm sure all you know is what Matthew has told you."

Her words make a painful lump lodge in my throat. I swallow it away. "What did Saul tell you?"

"He told me the Baneem were a superior race, banished by God because he was afraid of their power."

"And the Shamari? What did Saul tell you about them?"

"That they were the angels and demons from the bible. God's warriors, sent to destroy the Baneem and keep humans ignorant."

I'd rather believe Matthew's version of the truth. "Do you still believe him?"

She tilts her head to the side. "It doesn't matter what I believe. The fact is the Baneem want to steal Aran from me and the Shamari would kill him if they caught him."

"Saul told you the Shamari kill Baneem?"

She nods. I open my mouth, about to correct her, but snap it shut instead.

"You think I'm stupid," she snaps. "You think I'm naive."

I shake my head. "No, of course not." If I'd been targeted by Gage, like Charley and Tia had, I would have believed anything he'd said, too.

"He was all I had." She wrings her hands as her voice rises in desperation. "My parents were dead. I was seventeen years old and had no family, nowhere to live, and no job. He picked me up. He showed me magic and angels were real. I had no reason to doubt him."

She picks up her glass and presses it to her lips. Only a single drop remains, which she allows to slip into her mouth before placing the tumbler on the carpet again.

"Can Saul heal, too?"

"No. He leaches life energy." She holds my gaze steadily as she speaks.

My brow crumples into a frown. "That doesn't make sense."

"Why not?"

"I'm pretty sure the Baneem inherit their magic." It's not what Matthew believes. He told me each Baneem had magic as individual as human fingerprints. "The Baneem AJ and I stopped wasn't old enough to have struck a bargain with

Sophie's grandfather," I say, barrelling on before Phailin can derail my theory. "But he was maintaining the magic, so he must have had the same ability as one of his parents."

She purses her lips.

"But if AJ can heal and Saul can hurt people…it's like Saul's magic was inverted in AJ. Why?"

She shrugs. "Why doesn't his ability to regenerate release a beacon for the Shamari to track?"

"And the Shamari can't tell he's half-Baneem," I say, nodding in agreement. "He's an enigma. But I still don't get why you think Saul wants AJ."

"Because he's such a mystery? Because he's half-human? I don't know." She inhales deeply. "Saul changed when he discovered I was pregnant. At first he got angry and accused me of cheating on him." A bitter smile crosses her lips. "That's how I discovered what his magic was. He used it on me in a fit of anger, trying to make me admit to an affair."

"He didn't believe the baby could be his," I say. "He didn't think humans and Baneem could have children together."

She nods. "I thought he was going to kill me, but he didn't."

Or couldn't because of AJ's ability to heal. I keep the thought to myself.

"When he calmed down, he begged for my forgiveness. He told me it had never happened before, so he didn't think it was possible. And then he was so, so happy and I forgave him. He almost killed me and my unborn child, but I forgave him." She grips the armchair cushion tightly, revealing the whites of her knuckles. "I should have run away. I shouldn't have stayed." She reaches for the tumbler. "I need another drink."

She starts to stand, but I put my hand over hers and apply pressure to encourage her to sit back down.

"I need you to tell me what happened next," I say.

"And I need a drink."

I don't release the pressure on her hand. "Once I've gone, you can drink yourself into a stupor," I say. "But right now I need to know everything that happened with Saul." My eyes widen as a thought occurs to me. "And I need to know what Saul's magic smells like."

I'll never forget the metallic stench of Gage's magic, a smell I mistook for blood. Taylor had magic that reeked of rotting garbage. AJ's smells of damp moss. I half-smile at the memory of his comforting, earthy scent.

Phailin sinks down again and drops the tumbler. It thuds onto the carpet, the glass too thick to break.

"Burning rubber," she says. "That's the closest thing I could equate it to anyway."

My nose wrinkles as I imagine the smell. I've smelt rubber tyres on a swelteringly hot day. It's the kind of scent that coils up your nose and feels like it's coating your insides with bitterness.

"Saul had me open gateways for him regularly," she says. "He'd go back to Uralahnd, and then twenty-four hours later, I'd open another gateway so he could come back." She stares at her hands. "So when he asked me to open a gateway when Aran was a few days old, I didn't think anything of it."

"What happened?"

"The night before he wanted the gateway opening, I woke up to the sound of voices—Saul's and one I didn't recognise. I crept out of the bedroom so I could hear what they were saying. Saul was saying he was going to take Aran through the gateway with him." Her chin quivers, and she clenches her teeth. "His exact words were: 'I'm going to take my child and ditch that stupid human whore.'" Her eyes glisten with tears. She wipes clear snot from her nose, sniffling.

"What did you do?"

"I went back to bed. I let him sleep next to me and kiss me. And in the morning, I told him I was taking Aran out for a walk."

"And you ran?" I say.

"I've been running ever since." She stares at me. "Saul wants Aran. I don't know why, but he does. And because we stopped running, he probably has my son."

"I'll find AJ," I say.

"How? You're a child."

I stand. "A child who has faced the Baneem twice before and won. I'll find AJ, I promise."

CHAPTER SIX

The house is empty when I get home. Mum's at work and Chris is at school, where I should be. I check my phone. Unsurprisingly, I've got half a dozen texts from Sophie: *Where are you? Are you okay? Did you skip school to see AJ? Text me. What's going on? Seriously, Kim, TEXT ME.*

I send her a quick reply—Not feeling well—and discard my phone on the hall table.

If I'm going to find AJ, I'll need help. Even though Sophie's family made a deal with a Baneem, she knows nothing about magic. I want to keep it that way. I can't shatter my best friend's view of the world or of her family. I don't know how she'd react if she ever found out her dad almost killed me. The only person I can ask for help is Matthew. If he'll listen.

I go upstairs to my room and open my desk drawer. At the bottom, there's a large sheet of sugar paper, folded in half. I take the paper and a charcoal pencil out and lay them on my bed. I unfold the paper, revealing a large white feather with pale grey mottling.

When we were trying to stop Taylor, Matthew trusted me with two of his feathers so I could contact him if I needed to. I puff my cheeks out. What right do I have to ask Matthew for help? He trusted me with a part of his soul, but I didn't trust him. I tried to emotionally blackmail him. I don't think I can ever repair the damage I caused our friendship.

My cheeks deflate as I release my breath. I don't have a

choice. I pick up the charcoal and draw the symbol for "speak" on the feather: two arcs joined at the edges, like a child's interpretation of an eye without the iris and pupil. The symbol burns blue the moment I finish drawing it. The flames devour the feather, moving quickly across the surface. I don't have much time. I squeeze my eyes shut and form a plea to Matthew in my mind: I need your help. Please. AJ is missing.

When I open my eyes, the feather is gone, as though it and the flames never existed. I rock onto my heels and pray that Matthew answers.

*

I glance down every side street and alley I pass, searching and hoping, but there's no sign of AJ. The wind has picked up, cutting through my coat and whipping strands of auburn hair around my face and into my mouth. I shove my gloved hands in my pockets and bury my chin in the top of my coat to try to stave off the cold as I trudge along the sea front. My feet ache from the miles I've walked.

The brown sea is choppy and heavy clouds have descended to cloak the hills on the other side of the bay. Charley and I used to walk along here regularly after school. I still have the photo of us both, with our backs to the sea, as the wallpaper on my phone. I wish she was here to help me.

I hunch my shoulders and scan every inch of the beach. There's no sign, but I still look. I have to feel like I'm doing something positive, even though I'm really waiting for Matthew to show up.

I stop when my phone rings. Mum. Sighing, I sit down on a bench and answer the call.

"Hi, Mum."

"Where are you? Dinner's on the table."

I almost smile at her brisk attitude. "I went for a walk with Sophie. Sorry I'm late."

"I'll put yours in the oven, shall I?"

"Thanks, Mum."

I expect her to say goodbye and hang up, but she doesn't.

"Kim, are you all right?"

There must be something in my voice, which is making her worry.

"I'm fine." I can hear the note of drained weariness now, too. "I'll be home soon, I promise."

"All right," she says, before hanging up.

I put my phone away, but I can't motivate myself to stand and move. The dark clouds have rolled in so they're almost above my head. To my left, the sinking sun blazes streaks of red and orange across the horizon, turning the crisp white walls of a hotel into a squatting silhouette. Darkness gathers. The temperature begins to drop.

"Hello, Kim."

I bite my lower lip, not daring to look round. "Matthew?"

He steps over the bench and sits down, resting his arms loosely on his thighs. He joins me in staring out across the bay. There are so many things I want to say to him: I'm sorry. I missed you. I thought you wouldn't come. I press my lips together instead. I can't express doubt in him again, especially not as he's come so quickly.

"Is there any sign of AJ?"

I shake my head. In Matthew's presence, I can't hold my tears back any longer. I turn and press my face against his chest, clutching his dark T-shirt in my fists as I let sobs shake my body. He puts a hand on my back. The still pressure helps to ground me. Gradually, my sobs morph into hiccups. I pull away, wiping the tears and snot from my face with a scrap of tissue I discover in my coat pocket.

"I'm sorry."

His eyebrows lift. "For crying? I'd expected it under the circumstances."

I shake my head. "For everything. For lying to you. For emotionally blackmailing you." I twist the soggy tissue round my fingers. "For not believing in you."

His cheek muscles flex. "It's all right."

"No, it's not. How can it be? You trusted me with your feathers, and I betrayed you."

He puts his hands on my shoulders and utters a calming noise, which begins somewhere deep in his throat. "It's not important right now."

I stare at him. "How can you be so calm and forgiving?"

What if he isn't? What if he's just pretending it's okay? I press my hands against my face, hiccupping into them, and what I'm really trying to do is get my breathing under control so I can stop crying. I hate crying.

"Do you have any idea what's happened to AJ?"

I shake my head and then nod. "His mum is convinced it's the Baneem. I've been trying to hope it isn't." My voice echoes against my palms. I part my fingers, so I can peer through them. "The Baneem know you can't see him."

Matthew scowls. "Taylor knows, but he's in purgatory."

"Prisoners talk," I say, using AJ's words. God. It was only yesterday he said them to me and I dismissed them.

Matthew's hand rests on my shoulder. "I'll look for him."

I take three deep breaths before standing. My legs are shaking as I turn to face him.

"I'm going with you."

"I can cover more ground faster without you."

I clench my teeth and speak through them. "I'm going with you."

His mouth twitches. Was he going to object or smile? He does neither. "All right."

I gape at him for a second before sending a quick text to Mum. As I do, Matthew's wings sprout from his back. The mottled waterfall of feathers and light never ceases to leave me breathless and wide-eyed. The tattered remnants of his T-shirt cling to his chest and shoulders.

"You don't half go through T-shirts," I say in a half-hearted attempted at humour.

He shrugs. "Not really. It's part of my manifestation."

I arch an eyebrow. Why does he create such an elaborate illusion of reality when no one but me can see him? I don't ask and he doesn't offer an explanation. Instead, he holds his arms out, inviting me into them. I allow him to rest one arm under my thighs and the other around my shoulders. I lean against his chest as he begins to ascend.

"Thank you," I say.

He nods. I whisper a prayer to whoever's listening because deep down I know even Matthew will struggle to find AJ.

CHAPTER SEVEN

I'm not ready to wake into a nightmare of captivity, but I can't fight my mind's slow journey to consciousness. It feels like I'm on a boat, rising and falling with powerful waves. The light comes and goes with the rise and fall. I've woken up from enough healing-induced stupors to know I'm not moving at all and that the light is static. I'm not in pain anymore, and the sharp pins and needles have gone, leaving me with a heavy fuzziness I imagine must be similar to a bad hangover. It's hard to force my eyes open, and every time I do, exhaustion drives them closed again. My mouth is dry, my tongue heavy, and my gut is twisting in on itself.

My heavy head rolls back and smacks against a solid brick wall. I shrug my shoulders, encouraging my head to loll forward so my chin strikes my chest. In the few seconds I'm able to keep my eyes open, I become aware I'm not alone.

Saul's thug is standing by a door, tree-trunk arms folded across his broad chest. A table stands off to one side with a jug and a glass on it, illuminated by a single bare light bulb. I try to speak, but I can't control the dehydrated muscles in my mouth, so all I can manage is a grunt.

My eyelids flop shut again. For the first time I'm aware of something cold and heavy around my wrists. I try to move them, but the metal bracelets cut against my skin. A chain clanks against something metal and hollow.

I force my head up and my eyes open so I can properly take

in my surroundings. My stiff shoulder is pushed up against a solid, old-fashioned radiator, which I'm handcuffed to. I'm propped against a painted brick wall with my legs splayed out in front of me. My bloodstained T-shirt has a jagged hole where the knife was thrust into me. My jeans are stiff and chafing. I stink of blood, stale sweat, and piss. I grimace, embarrassed despite having been stabbed, abducted, and unconscious.

My head drops back down to my chest, and my eyes drift shut again. Without food and drink, it's going to take me a long time to recover from the energy my body consumed to heal me.

I don't move when the floorboards creak beneath the thug's feet. The air around my face is disturbed. The smooth edge of a glass is pressed against my chapped lips, and a dribble of warm water slips into my mouth. I swallow, tentatively at first and then more greedily as he increases the flow of the water. It becomes too much for my swollen throat to cope with, making me cough and splutter. My chin and T-shirt become drenched in water. He pauses, letting me recover before allowing me to take more cautious sips.

Once my thirst is sated, I turn my head away, refusing any more. The dusty floorboards complain as he walks away. There's a dull thud as he places the glass down, followed by a squeak.

The water has given me enough energy to open my eyes and keep my head steady. The thug has returned to his post at the door. There are no windows, and by the way two of the walls slope, I guess we're in an attic room. My chest lurches as I realise we're probably still on Earth. If they haven't taken me to Uralahnd yet, I've still got a chance to escape.

I fix my stare on the thug. "What's your name?"

The corners of his mouth twitch, but he doesn't reply to my question.

I shuffle up the wall a little, so I'm more upright. "Mine's Aran."

His gaze flicks to me as he shrugs his shoulders back. He already knew my name.

"My friends call me AJ."

His eyes narrow, and he tugs his heavy black eyebrows down over them. "Save it, kid. No one's listening."

"What's Saul going to do to me?"

He shrugs, which is at least proof he is listening to me. I tell myself it's a good sign, that there's still hope.

"Why does he want me?"

"Ask him." The thug turns his face so he's glaring at the corner of the attic, rather than at me.

I rattle my handcuffs against the radiator to force his attention. "He's not here, is he? He's left you to babysit." I'm not sure allowing anger to flood into my voice is a good plan, but trying to make him see me as a person wasn't working. "He did tell you why he wants me, didn't he?"

The thug clears his throat, which is as close to a "yes" as I need.

I lean forward as far as the handcuffs will let me. "Help me," I whisper. "Please let me go."

His jaw sets into a rigid line, looking everywhere but at me.

"He's already stabbed me. What else is he going to do?"

"You need to be quiet." His voice is low and tense.

"Please—"

"I said shut up," he says, his voice rising to a roar that fills the small attic.

I curl against the radiator, flinching away from the anger burning in his wide eyes and snarling face. I was a fool to think he might help me. Heavy footsteps pound up the stairs. My body quivers, but I'm not sure if it's from anticipation or fear. A second set joins in, a lighter footfall clacking a few steps behind.

The door flies open, bashing into the wall with a loud bang. My heart jumps in my chest. The thug retreats into a corner of the room. Saul stands in the doorway, shoulders hunched, teeth clenched. A small blonde woman peers round him, resting her hands on his bare torso.

"Who the hell is that?" she says.

"I told you not to come up."

Panic fills her eyes. "Seriously? You're keeping some kid up here? What's going on?"

"He abducted me." I try to shout the words, but they come out as a hoarse whisper. I do my best to clear my throat and try again. "He abducted me." My voice is a little clearer this time, even though it's flooded with panic and fear.

Saul strides over to me and backhands me across the face, whipping my head to the side. Warm blood trickles from my nose, and my cheek flushes with warmth. He grabs my T-shirt and tugs me up so I'm half-hanging from his grip. I swear he'd haul me to my feet if the handcuffs would let him. He slams my back against the wall.

"You need to shut up," he says. Flecks of spittle fly from his lips and splatter over my face. Still holding me, he glances over his shoulder at the thug. "You were meant to keep him quiet."

The thug inclines his head slightly.

"Didn't your mother teach you obedience?" Saul says. He slams the heel of one of his hands against my forehead, crashing my skull into the wall again.

My eyelids flicker open and closed as dizziness hits me. Pins and needles crawl across my face like an army of ants as my magic begins to heal the damage he's caused.

"Don't mention her," I say. He doesn't have any right to speak about the woman he used.

He lets me go. I slide down the wall and thud against the floor, allowing myself to sag against the radiator, too exhausted by the regeneration to try to fight back. I could kick him, but what good would it do? He'd repay me with even more violence.

I stare at the woman, knowing she's my shot at freedom, but like the thug, she staunchly avoids my gaze. Saul saunters back to her and wraps his arms around her waist.

"The kid's one of mine," he says in a husky tone. "A traitor. I'm taking him home to face trial."

He grabs the back of her head and pulls her into a kiss before she can say anything. I wish I could shut my ears to the sickening slurping sounds their conjoined mouths make.

After a few seconds, he pulls away. "Can you see why I need the gateway opening soon?"

"He's lying." But as I say the words, my magic betrays me. Already the blood has stopped flowing from my nose and the heat in my cheek is dissipating. It won't take long before the force of Saul's attack will be nothing more than a memory.

She rests her chin on his shoulder. "Healing magic," she says. "Cool."

"You'll open the gateway?" Saul says.

"You know I will, babe," she says. "After you've paid me."

His hands slide under her lilac blouse, and he begins to walk her out the room.

"What do you want with me?" I yell before they cross the threshold.

Saul pauses, but doesn't turn to face me. "I already told you."

"You told me nothing."

He shrugs. "You didn't want to listen."

Tears sting my eyes. "Well I do now."

He untangles himself from the woman, strides over, and crouches down in front of me. A smile teases at the corners of his lips.

"We've been searching for a way to destroy the Shamari and it looks like you're the key to doing that." His smile spreads as I continue to stare at him blankly. "The Shamari can't see what you are."

It feels like someone is reaching down my throat and into my chest to pull my lungs out. I wretch, but there's nothing except stomach acid to bring up. It burns my throat and mouth as I choke it out, spewing the yellow-tinged liquid onto my clothes. When I stop, I breathe slowly through my nose, which makes me feel sick again as I inhale my own stench.

Miserably, I tilt my head back against the wall. "I won't help you."

He chuckles. "You won't have a choice, Aran. I don't need your permission or your help." He stands and joins the woman in the doorway, looping his arm around her waist. "Give us a few minutes and then bring him down. It's time we left."

I close my eyes, flinching as the door slams shut behind them. Unconsciousness beckons me, and part of me wants to drift into it. At least asleep I'll be oblivious to my situation, but I also won't be able to help myself.

"Let me go," I whisper. Surely it's worth another shot? "We can fake a struggle. All you have to do is undo the handcuffs, nothing more. Please?"

The thug rubs the bridge of his nose with his thumb and forefinger. His gaze softens from anger to regret. "I can't."

He strides over, jaw set and muscles tensed, as though he's hardening himself to any further pleas I might throw at him. He pulls a small silver key out of his pocket and slots it into the handcuffs.

"Do yourself a favour, AJ, whatever Saul wants you to do, do it."

I grit my teeth. "I won't help him."

He sighs. "Things will go badly for you if you don't. Your magic makes you much easier to break than most." The left handcuff clicks open. He yanks it off my wrist and frees the chain of the radiator. "And he will break you." He closes the handcuff around my chaffed wrist again.

I want to swear that Saul won't break me, that I'm stronger than they all think. But I can still feel the echo of the blows he rained upon me, and I'm still fighting to resist the suffocating lullaby of my magic.

"Please let me go."

He must have a shred of regret about what he's doing. I saw it in his eyes, and he said my name. Not Aran, but AJ.

"Please?"

My words are futile. His fear of Saul is greater than any compassion he might feel for me. I have to find another way of escaping.

The thug grabs me by the collar of my T-shirt and half-pushes, half-drags me toward the door. It takes a few steps for my legs to work properly and actually walk. I try to resist, but he's too strong and I'm far too weak. My writhing actions are as futile as a fish flopping about on land. My breathing becomes harsh, rasping in my chest, tightening my windpipe until each quick gasp becomes a stabbing pain. I don't want to go to Uralahnd. I don't want to be at Saul's mercy.

Do the gateways send up a magical flair? I've no idea. I never thought to ask Mum. I frown. They probably don't, otherwise the Shamari would sit around waiting for gateways to open up and send the Baneem straight back. That would be the end of the war. But why don't they? They must still be magical. I don't have time to care, let alone figure it out. I need to find a way to trick Saul or the thug frog-marching me into using their magic.

My stomach sinks as I realise they won't. They didn't use magic to catch me, so why would they use it now? I'll have to use mine, but my own regenerative ability doesn't send up a flare. I'll have to heal someone else. I know Kim still has one of Matthew's feathers. She might have called him for help. I clench my fists. I have to stake my life on the hope she called him and he came.

We're out the door and on the steep staircase. The thug is pushing me ahead of him, his firm grip stopping me from falling down the stairs. I'll only have one chance. With an apologetic grimace he can't see, I step to the side and twist round. His grip on my collar strangles me. Unable to breathe, I smash my fists into his groin. He lets me go and doubles over, grunting and cursing. I bring my fists down again, this time on the back of his neck. He topples, grabbing at me as he crashes down the stairs, pulling me with him. The wooden steps are unforgiving as we slam into them.

I land on top of his twisted body. My chest and back ache, my eye is swollen shut, and my cheek feels like it's been smacked by a meat cleaver. I can't move my jaw. In a few seconds, my magic will start to regenerate, healing the damage, and I won't be able to resist being dragged into unconsciousness. I press my palms against the thug's chest. Thank God he's still breathing.

I trigger my magic on him before it has a chance to start working on me. He groans as I pull his injuries onto myself.

His wrist cracks back into a normal position while the transferred damage drives a stake in my mind. His ribs mesh together, but blood floods from my nose. The bruises on his face
vanish to nothingness, as my lips crack and bleed. His ankle
rights itself, and something deep inside me breaks.

He opens his eyes and stares at me. For a second, I don't
understand his expression. His mouth is twisted in anger, yet
the softness around his eyes suggest he's grateful. His eyes
widen, as though a light bulb has just gone off in his mind.

"You shouldn't have done that," he hisses.

I'm aware of someone else behind me, but I don't have time
to react before something heavy and cold smashes into my head.
I collapse to the floor. From the corner of my vision, I see Saul
towering above me. Something shiny flashes in his hand, driving
toward my skull. But before I feel the pressure of the blow, my
magic smothers me in its power, drowning my consciousness.

CHAPTER EIGHT

I'm not sure how long Matthew and I have been searching for AJ, but it's dark and I'm finding it hard to stay awake. This high up it should be cold, but Matthew's strong presence warms me. We've circled the city several times. The first time we flew low so we could peer through every window. Most people had drawn their curtains on the wintry night, and it was strange, looking in on people who were oblivious to our presence. I'll never get used to being invisible when I'm in Matthew's arms. I'd hate to live like that every day. I'm not sure how he doesn't go insane through loneliness.

Now we're flying higher, twenty or so feet above the buildings. I should be afraid as we pass over streetlights that resemble strings of Christmas tree lights. If I fell, I'd die. But I know Matthew won't let me go. There are fewer cars on the road now, alerting me to how late it's getting. I sent Mum a lie in a text message, pretending I'd gone to Sophie's. I hate that dishonesty is becoming second nature because I've been doing it for so long.

Matthew stops. The strong beat of his wings make our bodies rise and fall a fraction as he turns his head sharply to the left.

"What is it?" I use his neck to pull myself more upright in his arms.

"Magic," he says. "AJ's magic." He moves forward at speed, changing course.

My heart flutters against my ribs. "Are you sure?"

He nods.

"How?"

AJ has only used his magic when Matthew's been around once, when he healed me. It felt like an entire lifetime passed as he took the force of the bullet wound into himself, but in reality, it was seconds.

"The magic of every Baneem feels different," Matthew says. "AJ's is the cleanest I've ever felt." He clenches his teeth in annoyance.

"What?" I say, although I can already guess what his answer will be.

"It's gone."

I shuffle again, twisting round so I can peer in the direction we're flying. I wish I could sense magic from a distance as well. Even though he can no longer feel it, Matthew doesn't stop. He flies faster. The wind whips against my face and through my hair. For the first time, I feel the chill of the night. It makes my teeth chatter and stiffens my fingers. I cling more tightly to Matthew and press my forehead against his chest, whispering a prayer to whoever will listen to let us find AJ. If his magic was visible to Matthew, he had to be healing someone else. But who?

Matthew stops as if a hook has grabbed him and yanked him to a halt. The quick change in motion steals my breath, leaving me gasping. His upper lip curls.

"Matthew?"

"More magic," he says. "It feels like it's coming from the same place, but it's oily."

He darts forward again.

"What does AJ's magic feel like?" I say, unable to stand the silence. If we talk, maybe the distance between us and AJ will fall away faster.

Matthew shrugs.

"You said it felt clean."

"Cleaner," he says sharply. "Not clean."

I press my chapped lips together, feeling like a child who's been scolded. "When you protect me, it smells like cut grass,"

I say, even though I'm sure he knows already. "When AJ healed me, it smelt earthy like moss. It was comforting."

His only reaction is a brief glance at me before setting his jaw into a determined line. He beats his wings faster. I don't ask him why I perceive his abilities in the same way as magic. I know how angry he gets at the insinuation that the Shamari use magic at all. But I do wish he would talk to me because the seconds are stretching out. I need to crowd out the voice of doubt in my mind that whispers we won't find AJ. I grit my teeth. We have to find him.

I inhale sharply as Matthew's body angles down. He tightens his grip, holding me against his chest. Over his shoulder, I can see his wings are stretched back as we plummet toward the ground. The wind whistles past us but doesn't disturb his massive mottled feathers.

At the last second, he pulls his shoulders back. His feet hit gravel with a crunch, and he sets me down gently.

"You should wait here."

"No way," I say with a firm shake of my head.

I wait for him to argue, but he doesn't. He leads me over the gravel, his wings slowly vanishing into nothingness. Darkness lies around us, broken only by the pale moon, hanging far above our heads. A battered mini sits in front of a large detached house.

The house is dark and, as we get closer, it becomes obvious the windows have been blacked out. The paint is chipped on one pane of glass, allowing a thin trickle of light to escape and spill down the red brick wall onto an empty flowerbed.

Four stone steps lead to the front door. Matthew clears them in one stride, leaving me to jog up behind him. He puts his palm against the door and pushes. The wooden frame splinters and the door swings inward. The house is silent. Cold. We step into a massive hallway, illuminated by the light flooding out of an open door to our left. I curl my trembling hands into loose fists, resisting the urge to call AJ's name.

Matthew heads toward the open door. His feet don't make a sound over the bare floorboards. Mine do. I cringe every time the wood creaks beneath my boots. With each step, I expect a Baneem to rush out of the room toward us. I expect to smell magic the instant before it strikes us.

Nothing happens.

Matthew reaches the room first. His bare shoulder muscles twitch into tense knots. He drops his head forward a little. "I'm sorry."

"Sorry? For what?"

I have to push past him to get into the room. My eyes widen. There's a single naked light, which reveals a charcoal pattern on the far wall. It looks like it might have been circular, with a series of glyphs and lines inside, but it's smudged beyond recognition. The wall and floor are charred. A body lays in the center of the room—a petite blonde woman. Her eyes are open. Her expression is fixed in twisted shock. The fading scent of burning rubber lingers in the room, the only confirmation I need that Phailin is right: Saul has AJ.

I fight to suck in air as my windpipe constricts. I press my hand against my chest, turn and run, making my way through every dark room in the house. Most are empty. My eyes strain to penetrate the darkness. What little furniture there is appears as dark grey static. Two rooms contain nothing but a bed. A staircase leads to the attic, where there's a table, jug, and cup.

It's not until I'm back downstairs in the hallway that I realise Matthew didn't follow me. He didn't need to search the house. He knew it was empty.

"It's a gateway," he says, nodding toward the charcoal mess on the wall. "Or it was. We were too late. I'm sorry."

I stare at the woman on the floor.

"She's human," Matthew confirms. "They will have needed her to open the gateway."

I swallow. "How did she die?"

He crouches down beside her and holds his hand a breath

away from her chest. "Magic. The same oily magic I felt when we were on our way here."

"Why?"

His brow collapses into a frown.

"If she opened the gateway, she must have been on their side. Why would they kill her?"

"AJ used his magic," Matthew reminds me. "Probably for the sole purpose of me sensing it. It was a good bet that a Shamari would be on the way."

"But you can't go to Uralahnd." My voice holds no emotion. My body is numb. I'm standing, but I might as well be floating. It's like I'm detached from my body and if I let myself back inside, I'll crumble.

"No," Matthew says. "But you can."

I gape at him.

"You think Taylor has been talking while in purgatory. He probably mentioned you as well, Kim." His eyebrows rise a fraction. "Gage might have done, too."

I swallow. "I can go to Uralahnd?"

I hadn't thought about the possibility of going there until this second. Now it's all I want to do, which is crazy because I know nothing about it. Matthew has told me precious little. All I really know is that it's where the Creator dumped the Baneem when He banished them from Earth. A shudder slithers across my shoulders. If it was supposed to be their punishment, it can't be a nice place. I don't care. Rescuing AJ is the only thing that matters.

I lift my chin. "I'll find someone who can open a gateway. Maybe AJ's mum remembers how to."

Matthew shakes his head. "You can't go there—not alone. They'd kill you."

I scrunch my mouth into a tight circle. After everything we've been through, I hoped Matthew would have more faith in me. The tension in my lips starts to dissipate as I see fear in the dark depths of his eyes. He's only openly shown fear once before— when he asked me not to go after Tia. Then it was fleeting. Now his fear grips me, shaking my resolve. I know he's right. My head tells me it would be madness to chase after AJ. I'd be on my own, against God knows how many Baneem. I wouldn't be able to find him before they found and killed me.

Would I be willing to risk my life for a boy I've known for three months? It's crazy. I know a large part of my intense feelings for him are the result of teenage hormones. We've joked about it often enough when we've pulled away from each other, on the verge of intimacy that neither of us has admitted we're ready for.

The answer coils in the pit of my stomach and grips me with fear. Yes. Yes, I would risk everything for him because he did it for me. Because it's my fault the Baneem caught up with him at all. I kept the truth from him. I gave him false hope he could have a normal life. It's my fault he's in Uralahnd.

And yet I'm terrified of going. I'm relieved there's no one to open a gateway for me right now.

"They didn't need to kill her," I say, blinking back tears. "AJ's gone, hasn't he? Whatever they want him for, they're never going to let him go, are they?"

"I don't know, Kim."

Yes, he does, and I know it, too. The realisation is all it takes. I snap back into my body. My knees give way and I crash to the floor. I slump over, pressing my eyes against my clenched fists. Tears flow freely. Sobs make me cough. My chest heaves. My throat aches.

"Kim." Matthew's hand rests on my back, firm and comforting.

I snap my head up, narrowing my eyes. "Don't give me sympathy."

His head jerks back a little.

"This is my fault."

"No, it's not."

"Yes, it is." I jerk away from him, stand and pace. "Of course it is. AJ stayed because of me. Taylor found out what he was because of me. I asked you to give him a free pass. If I hadn't… if you hadn't…he would have kept on running. He would have been safe." I sweep my arm to the side hard, jarring my shoulder.

Matthew grabs me and pulls me to a halt. "No, Kim, he wouldn't. They would have caught up to him sooner or later. The Baneem are fanatics. They don't give up."

"Phailin kept him safe for sixteen years by running, which is exactly what I stopped him doing."

I don't want to hear his logical arguments. I don't want him to come up with a way to absolve me of my guilt. It's my fault. I need to direct my anger somewhere. Because if I don't feel angry, all I'm going to feel is grief. I don't want to feel the hopeless sense of loss that engulfs and devours me. I can't feel it again. I can't.

I press my hands against my face, unable to do anything but cry.

"Kim."

"I don't need your sympathy." I slam my fists against his chest in time with each word I spit out. "AJ is gone and it's my fault."

My arms drop to my sides. I stand there, sobbing and coughing so violently I know I'm going to make myself sick. All the energy has drained from my body. I want to collapse into Matthew's arms. I crave comfort I know he can't give me. But I don't move. I don't let myself fall. I repeat the same words over and over in a frenzied whisper: "It's my fault."

Matthew's left hand curls tightly around my shoulder, holding me fast. I try to step back, but I can't break free of his grip. He presses his right thumb against my forehead.

"I'm sorry." He runs his thumb down toward the top of my nose and then hooks it back up. "Sleep."

I don't fight the word. I can't. He catches me as I fall. As my heavy eyes drift shut, I'm struck by a distant memory, one locked away in the depths of my consciousness. Matthew has done this to me before. And last time, I slept for two days.

CHAPTER NINE

I wake gasping for breath, my eyes squeezed shut. I was dreaming about Mum. She was reaching out to me, calling my name: Aran. Strange that even in my dreams she won't call me AJ. I breathe in and out slowly until the adrenalin-fuelled panic begins to subside. I open my eyes, trying to work out where I am and if I'm alone. I'm lying on a thin mattress, which does little to protect my back from the hard surface beneath it. My stomach is so empty, I've gone past hunger into a numb hollowness. An odd buzzing sensation zips around my skull, making my teeth feel like they're about to explode. All I can hear is my breathing.

I open my eyes. The ceiling is black and textured. An orange glow leaps and flickers. I push myself up on my elbows, glancing around until I catch sight of a lantern hanging from the wall. My view of it is obscured by black bars. The bunk is bolted to a wall, which is made of the same material as the ceiling. The only other thing in the cell is a wooden bucket. With a grimace, I realise it's probably intended to be a toilet. I'm surrounded by stone on three sides and bars on the other. Beyond the cell, there's a short corridor leading to a set of tall double doors made from dark wood. A pile of folded clothes has been set on the bottom of the bunk, waiting for me.

I yank my T-shirt over my head and wipe it over my skin in a poor attempt at ridding myself of sweat, grime and blood. I check I'm still alone before unbuckling my belt and tugging my jeans off. I practically have to peel them away from my raw skin. I pull on the shapeless brown clothes. They're made from itchy wool, but at least they're clean. I still stink, but something tells me I'm not going to be offered a shower or a bath anytime soon. I kick my clothes into a corner and then sit down on the bunk, pulling my knees up to my chest and leaning against the wall. The rough surface is cold against my back and the buzzing in my head intensifies until I'm forced to drop my forehead onto my knees. I grind my aching teeth together and press my palms against my skull.

"It's the obsidian."

I snap my head up, but the pain stops me from opening my eyes wider than a squint. A woman is standing outside my cell with her arms folded and her weight shifted onto her right hip. She's tall and has a generous figure, especially her bust. Her dark hair is cut into a blunt bob, just above her shoulders.

"It's stopping you from using your magic," she says. "I'm sure you can understand why that would be important here."

Here. Uralahnd.

"Who are you?"

Her eyes gleam as she slips her hand through the bars, an invitation for me to get up and shake it. When I don't move, she tuts and shakes her head.

"No manners," she says. "My name is Adele. Your father has asked me to find out why your soul is invisible to the Shamari."

Given that the entire room appears to be lined with obsidian, my guess is she can't do that here.

I dig my fingertips into the thin mattress. "Why? I won't help you."

She lifts her chin a little. "Your father knows that. Perhaps if you had been brought up here, as he intended, you would be more amenable to our cause."

My sharp intake of breath hisses in my throat. The thing is, she's right. If Saul had brought me here as a child, I'd behave like they do.

"Your cause? You mean hurting humans for kicks? Or… what was it Saul said?" I make a show of clicking my fingers. "Finding a way to end the war with the Shamari?"

"For kicks?" she says, narrowing her eyes. "Is that what you believe?" She curls her hands around the bars. "Let me guess: The Baneem came first. We failed in the eyes of the Creator and were kicked off the Earth. When He installed humans in our place, we were angry and jealous and we've been trying to make them fall ever since. It's the Shamari's job to stop us from doing that, to protect the humans." She smiles. "How warm am I?"

I rake my teeth over my lower lip. Mum never told me anything about the origins of the Baneem or the Shamari. I don't think she knew. But Adele doesn't need to know I'm clueless.

"Lies," she hisses.

"Why don't you tell me the truth?"

"Have you read the Bible, Aran?"

I shake my head. Mum wasn't religious and even if she had been, she would probably have been Buddhist like her parents. It's the only thing I know about them. She never even told me their names.

"Humans came first," Adele says. "We were created to be the proverbial serpent. It was our job to tempt them."

I breathe sharply through my nose. "Why would the Creator want to do that?"

She shrugs. "Funnily enough, no one has ever had the chance to ask Him," she says. "The thing is, we did too good a job. So He created the Shamari to be a positive influence in their lives. In human terms, they were angels, except we managed to portray them as demons, so they stopped being able to show their faces." She smiles smugly. "It makes their job quite a bit harder. The thing is, some of us are bored of our role in His experiment. He wants us to tempt humans but uses the Shamari to punish us for doing it, by catching us and throwing us into purgatory. Then they release us and expect us to do it all again. It's time for it to stop."

"I don't believe you," I say. "It doesn't make any sense."

"And the version of events you believe does?" she says. "Think about it, Aran. Humans don't need our help to destroy one another. Right now, how many wars are humans embroiled in? How many people are dying because of the weapons they created?"

I flinch back, as though the extra millimetres between us will stop her words from making sense.

"We tempt humans to use magic," she says. "Not to create weapons of mass destruction. That's all on them."

I stare at the ground, which is obsidian like the walls and ceiling. "If you don't like your role, why don't you stop doing it?"

She pushes away from the bars. "Because we want more, Aran. We deserve more. We've done the Creator's bidding for three millennia without questioning Him. We've done our job and taken the punishment without complaint."

"So stop." I don't attempt to hide the anger that makes my voice louder. "You have a home here. Just live your lives and leave the humans to live theirs."

She laughs, a soft condescending sound that makes my skin crawl. "Live here? No, we want to retire to the Earth. But the Shamari will never allow it. They'll never believe we simply want to leave peacefully. They are standing in our way and you are the key to getting rid of them."

I rub my knuckles against my jaw to drive out the buzzing pain so I can think more clearly. Whether what she's saying is true or not doesn't matter, the fact is she believes it and so does my father. I'm not sure if it even matters whether Adele's version of events is right or not. I can't let them use me to hurt the Shamari or humans.

"I won't help you," I say.

"Aran, why do you still think you have a choice?"

I know I don't, but if all I can do is put on an act of defiance, then I will. I cross my arms and stare at her with all the determination I can summon.

"I won't let you use me to hurt anyone."

"You can keep telling yourself that," she says. "I might even let you believe it for a little while." She takes a couple of ambling steps toward the door before stopping and looking back over her shoulder. "Loneliness is a brilliant weapon against defiance. So are hunger and thirst. Remember that."

She closes the hatch on the lantern, cutting off its supply of air, and chuckles to herself as she carries on walking. She and Saul are clearly not in a rush to examine me. I clench my fists. If they think I'm going to give up just because they leave me alone in a cell, they're idiots.

I hug my knees as the starved light flickers and dies, leaving me in suffocating darkness. They don't care if I stop fighting. They've already told me I can't prevent them finding out what they want to know. Being left alone with this constant buzzing in my head is part of their game. They're playing with me and there's nothing I can do about it.

CHAPTER TEN

I expect to wake up in a hospital bed surrounded by beeping machines and flowers. It's what happened the last time Matthew made me sleep. Although my memories of finding Charley are still hazy, I'm beginning to gain more clarity. My first burst of recall came under hypnosis, shortly after Charley's death. I remembered Matthew's voice telling me to forget. The second burst was when I found Kevin with his wrists slashed and I remembered Charley laid out on her bed, her blue eyes staring at the ceiling.

Now I remember Matthew commanding me to sleep. Sleep and forget.

Did AJ believe Matthew and I would reach him before he was taken to Uralahnd? He must have clung on to that hope, even when they were dragging him through the portal. We failed him.

I roll over and bury my face in the pillow, inhaling the familiar floral scent of Mum's favourite fabric conditioner. Downstairs, the vacuum cleaner makes a triumphant sucking noise. I'm at home. I lift my head. There's a mug of hot chocolate and some toast on my bedside table. I tap the toast, but it's cold and the hot chocolate has a rigid film on top. How long has breakfast been sitting there?

I sit up and shove the quilt aside. Heat rushes to my cheeks as I realise I'm in pyjamas. Who changed my clothes—Mum or Matthew? I'm not sure which scenario is worse. I don't care that Matthew has no physical urges, he's still a guy. And I'm the girl who tried to kiss him, because I thought I was falling in love with him. Matthew getting me out of my clothes and into pyjamas is wrong on so many levels.

I grab my phone and run my thumb over the screen. It's just gone ten on Sunday morning. Damn. I've lost more than a day.

Mum is putting the vacuum away as I wander downstairs. She smiles at me and ushers me into the kitchen.

"I didn't hear you come in last night. Did you and Sophie get a lot of work done?"

I stare at her blankly for a second too long. She twitches her eyebrows together into a knotted frown.

I make a show of yawning and rubbing my eyes. "Sorry, I'm not awake yet. We got lots done, thank you."

"You look tired." She stares into her half-drunk mug of coffee. "I'm still worried you're taking too much on. You're seventeen. You shouldn't have to spend your entire Friday night and Saturday doing homework."

Not this again. For a moment I can't think of anything to say. It's not school work that's making my insides twist into tight knots.

"You were so busy, Sophie's father had to call me to let me know where you were. Couldn't you send me a text?"

I curl my hands in my lap. I can't tell her I couldn't text because I was unconscious. Thanks to Matthew. Why did he have to get Sophie's dad involved? Couldn't he have used my phone to send a text to Mum? I roll my eyes up to stare at the ceiling. I don't suppose not-angels have mobile phones in heaven.

I'm relieved when Chris opens the kitchen door and peers in, bopping his head in time to whatever music he's listening to on his MP3 player.

"I'm off out." He starts to leave.

"Wait," Mum says. "Where are you going?"

"To David's."

"When will you be back?"

Normally I'd shake my head at the familiar list of questions.

Instead, I stare at the breakfast bar, tuning out their voices as I try to piece together what happened after Matthew made me sleep. If he didn't bring me straight home, where did he take me? Does Sophie know I allegedly spent over a day at her house? There's one thing I'm sure of: I need to speak to Matthew, assuming he's still around. He might not be. AJ's gone and so are the Baneem who took him. I press my hand to my mouth and breathe in deeply to stop myself from crying.

I barely hold it together when Mum squeezes my shoulder.

"Why don't you go back to bed?" she says. "And no studying today. You're pushing yourself too hard."

I nod and flee the room, heading up the stairs as Chris makes a swift exit out the front door.

Once in my room, I nudge my curtain back. My body sags into a sigh as I see Matthew standing on the other side of the street. He gives me a nod and a slight smile. Despite the distance between us, the power of his smile is enough to make me feel a little stronger. A little less hopeless.

I take a hot shower instead of going back to bed. I need to speak to Phailin.

*

"You didn't have to knock me out," I say, as Matthew falls into pace alongside me.

He hangs his head. "You were hysterical, Kim. You needed to rest."

I grit my teeth in an attempt to be annoyed with him. I understand why he made me sleep, which makes anger hard to summon.

"You got Sophie's dad involved," I say. "You shouldn't have done that."

"Would you rather I'd revealed myself to your mother?"

I bite my lower lip. "Of course not."

I stop at the bus stop, pat my gloved hands together, and tilt my head in a questioning manner. You didn't take me straight home."

"I took you somewhere safe until I sensed you'd drifted into a more natural sleep. Then I took you home." He scuffs his foot against the floor in a very human gesture of embarrassment. "I used your key to get you into the house once your mum and brother were asleep."

My face burns with heat. "So it was you who changed my clothes?"

He avoids my gaze. So, so wrong. I press my hands against my cheeks in an attempt to rub the red glow out of them. Fear ignites within me, bubbling from my gut up into my throat in a squeak. I've lost a day. Who knows what Saul has done to AJ while I've been asleep.

"Why are you still here, Matthew?" I trace the toe of my boot round in a circle. "I mean, I'm glad you are. I just don't get it."

"We're friends," he says slowly. "And you're hurting. I wanted to make sure you were all right."

I shake my head. "I'm not all right. I've already lost my sister because of the Baneem. I've lost AJ, too, and according to you, there's nothing I can do about it. Now I've got to go and tell Phailin her son is gone." I breathe in and out through my nose to calm myself. "How do you expect me to be okay?"

"I don't," he says. "Which is why I'm still here."

"But you didn't stay after I stopped Tia, did you?" I drag my fingers through my damp hair. "I needed you then, Matthew. You were the only person I could talk to about what had happened and you left."

Dredging up last year's events brings the anger I was longing to feel with it. Deep down, I know I'm being a bitch. I know Matthew doesn't deserve this, but it's better than hating myself.

"There were other Baneem I had to deal with."

It's not the first time I've been irritated by how calm he can stay while my insides feel like they've been thrown into a blender. "And there aren't now?"

He tilts his face up a fraction. His eyebrows tug down to shade his unnaturally dark eyes. "No." His voice raises a fraction, almost like he's asking a question, except he isn't. "But if you want me to go, I will."

"I don't." I can't make myself speak any louder than a whisper. "I want AJ to be here and safe. But you can't make that happen, can you?"

Matthew shakes his head. "I'm sorry."

I half-heartedly slap him across his arm. "Stop apologising for something that isn't your fault. You tried to help AJ. You did everything you could."

The rumble of an approaching bus makes me push my shoulders back and puff air over my bottom lip.

"I can't put this off. I have to tell Phailin what happened."

"Do you want me to come?"

"No."

It's a lie. I want his support more than anything, but his presence will make things worse. Phailin hates the Shamari as much as the Baneem.

I try to let my mind drift while I'm on the bus, but I can't. I keep running over the events of the last few days, looking for something I could have done differently, something that would have helped to save AJ. I'm not even sure what I'm supposed to feel anymore. Grief? As far as I know he's still alive. How can I grieve for someone who isn't dead? Anger? I can hate myself until the day I die, but it won't change anything. It won't fix this. Nothing will.

I stare at the photo of AJ on my phone, tracing the curve of his lopsided smile and the C-shaped dimple between his mouth and cheek. I remember the press of his lips against mine. The feel of his fingertips brushing over my face. My skin tingles, as if for a second my body believes his touch is real and not a figment of my imagination. I grip the edge of the thin bus seat. I won't accept he's gone. I'm not powerless. I will find a way to bring him back. I don't care if Matthew thinks it's impossible or that going to Uralahnd is too dangerous.

Phailin isn't in when I arrive at the flat. I bang on the door until my fist is sore, just in case. Next I peer through the window. It's hard to focus through the thin sheet of net, but I can tell the furniture and computer are still in place. I lean against the brick wall. The top edge digs into my back, just beneath my ribcage. What was a breeze at street level feels more like the start of a gale on the seventh floor. My thick coat and woollen gloves do very little to stop the chill creeping in. When my body starts to feel numb, I beat my hands together and stamp my feet.

I'm relieved when Phailin appears from the stairwell. She glares at me and, without a word, unlocks her door and goes inside, leaving it open. I guess it's the best invitation I'm going to get. I follow her into the sitting room, where she peels off her coat and gloves. I swallow as I notice AJ's coat and hat lying over the folded table, exactly where they were the last time I was here.

"I was out looking for him." Her voice breaks.

She starts to untie her long boots, the plastic end of each lace clicking as she tugs them through the metal-edged holes. I clear my throat. Phailin pauses and raises her head. Her honey-toned skin has faded to an ugly ashen shade, complimented by dark lines beneath her eyes. I have to tell her about the gateway, but I'm not sure how. Is this how police officers feel when they have to deliver bad news to a family?

"I...we... Matthew and I found where they were holding AJ," I say. God, my voice sounds so rigid and forced.

"Where?"

My chin trembles. If I don't choke out the words now, I'll cry before I get a chance. "They opened a gateway before we got there. He's gone." My voice breaks into a sobbing cough. I brush the fresh tears away from my eyes, put my hands on my stomach and breathe in. "The gateway was too damaged for me to copy the symbols. And they killed the human who opened it for them."

The human. I didn't know her name, but it seems wrong to reduce her to a phrase that makes her sound like a commodity. To the Baneem she was, but she was someone's daughter. Probably someone's sister. Maybe someone's wife or girlfriend. Possibly someone's mother.

"Opening the gateway destroys it." Phailin's voice is even

more mechanical than mine. "The symbols get burned up by the magic." She goes back to tugging at her laces.

I sit beside her, perching on the edge of the sofa. "I'm so sorry."

I expect her to shout at me and tell me it's my fault again, but she doesn't. She doesn't even cry. She pulls her left boot off and flings it aside before starting on the laces of the other one.

I want to be able to calm her the way AJ soothed me as we waited to hear from Sophie's dad. We sat in this room, on the floor, leaning against the sofa, watching a teen movie. I glanced at my phone every few seconds, desperate to get information about the Baneem who was tormenting Sophie's family. AJ held me, keeping me calm with his supportive quietness.

I know Phailin wouldn't respond to me even if I did try to comfort her.

"Do you remember how to open a gateway?" I say.

She shakes her head. The click-click of the laces is starting to drive me insane.

"AJ told me he'd found a drawing of one in your things. That must have been years after you last opened one for Saul."

"I destroyed it," she says. "It would be madness to go to Uralahnd."

"I know, but I'd do it." I frown. "Wouldn't you?"

A short, sharp laugh escapes her throat. "You're a fool, Kim. Would you really throw your life away over a boy you've only known for three months?" The anger I've been waiting for finally creeps into her voice, her flared nostrils and the hard light in her eyes.

"I love him." Regret smothers my heart, as I wish I'd said those words to AJ.

Phailin snorts. "He said the same thing about you."

I let my tears escape and run down my cheeks freely. Phailin tuts and shakes her head before edging closer and wrapping her arms around me. She pulls me into a stiff embrace. I'm not sure why I let her, except for the hope she'll listen to me and help me if she feels we're bonding in some way.

I sob against her shoulder until I feel washed-out and sick. When I pull away, I notice her eyes are damp, but her cheeks are dry. How she can keep herself together?

She releases me and eases her right boot off. She doesn't throw it away. Instead, she runs her thumbs over the soft leather. My chin trembles. AJ used to do the same thing with the brim of his hat when he was nervous or thinking.

Phailin lets out a heavy sigh, which makes her shoulders droop and her head sag. "I always knew I'd lose him. Sooner or later, I had to, didn't I?"

"He's not dead."

"It doesn't matter. Saul has him now and he won't let him go."

I shake my head. The AJ I know won't settle for being a prisoner for the rest of his life. The AJ I know will fight back. I turn and put my hand over Phailin's. "Try to remember how to open a gateway. How many times did you do it for Saul?"

"I can't remember." She snatches her hand away and paces to the window, where she stands and glares at me.

"We'll find someone who can," I say. "We'll bring him back."

"We?"

My jaw becomes slack for a second before I shake myself. "Yes. You and me. Matthew can't go to Uralahnd, but we can. If we work together—"

I stop talking when she stalks toward me and drags me to my feet. She grips my hand, digging her nails into my flesh.

"How did your sister's death affect your family?"

My hand shakes in her grasp, but I don't pull it away. "It devastated them. Mum's paranoid about everything and is protective of me and Chris. Dad tries to put on a brave face, but I know he still cries when he's on his own. Chris spends most of his spare time playing video games. He jokes around and stuff, but I know how scared he is of doing or saying the wrong thing." I haven't summarised the mess my family has become to anyone before. Sophie knows, but we don't talk about it anymore.

Phailin nods her head sharply. "So how would they cope if you vanished?"

I stare at the burgundy carpet. "It would destroy them." I brush fresh tears from my eyes.

She releases my hand, leaving red half-moon imprints where her nails were. "Go home, Kim. Go back to your life. Forget about AJ."

"Is that what you're going to do?" I say through gritted teeth. "Are you going to forget about your own son?"

Mum would never do that. She would do anything to protect me and Chris, even if it meant travelling to hell and back.

Phailin slaps me hard across the face. I squeal and clutch my cheek in my hands. "Get out."

I stumble away from her, heading toward the door. I pause when my gaze falls on AJ's fedora. I brush my fingertips against the black felt, desperate to snatch it up.

"You've spent sixteen years protecting AJ. How can you give up the second he's gone?"

She presses her lips into a thin line. "I don't have to explain myself to you."

"No, you don't. But what about when I bring AJ back and he asks you why you sat back and did nothing? Are you going to explain it to him?"

She folds her arms and holds my gaze. Although she's swallowing more than normal, her eyes are drier than a desert. Her silence pours petrol over my anger.

"He needs you. Have you stopped to think what he might be going through? What he might be feeling?" I don't want to think about it, but I know I have to. "He'll be scared. He's probably clinging to the hope we're going to find a way to get to him."

Like he must have prayed Matthew would sense his burst of magic and get to him in time. But we didn't. We failed him.

Phailin's hard expression doesn't quiver. "It's all I've thought about."

I clench my fists. "You're his mother. You have to help me. You have to fight for him."

"I gave up sixteen years of my life." Her voice is low and

sharp with bitterness. "For what? He's been pulling away from me since the day he met you."

I shake my head, unable to believe what I'm hearing. "You're going to give up on AJ because you're jealous of me?"

"If a girl could seduce him so easily, how long do you think he'll fight against his own father?"

"AJ won't help the Baneem."

"Wouldn't he?" She parts her lips, as though she's about to qualify her statement. Although the words don't cross her lips, I understand what she was about to say: He is a Baneem.

Warm tears spill from my eyes and tumble down my lips. Some make it over the curve and into my mouth, like tiny bullets of anger.

"AJ wouldn't side with Saul. He wouldn't." My voice trembles out of me.

I lower my hands, curling them back into fists. I press them against my thighs, digging my knuckles through the thick fabric of my jeans until I feel dull pain against my skin.

"I know you love him," I say.

Her chin trembles, but she remains silent.

I breathe in slowly. "I know you're scared, but you can't give up on him."

She sinks onto the sofa, her gaze never leaving mine.

"I'm sorry if I caused a rift between you and AJ." My voice is hoarse, my throat sore from the hurt, anger, and grief compressing within me. "I know letting go must be hard, but every parent has to go through it. You can't hate AJ for wanting his own life."

"And what would you know about it? Have you ever lost a child? You don't have a clue."

"I lost my sister," I say. "That was bad enough."

She sighs. "I'm sorry. I don't hate AJ, or you."

I press my lips together and push the melting pot of emotions down into the pit of my stomach, where it writhes and congeals.

"Will you help me?" I say.

"I know Saul. If he has AJ, he will have turned him against us both. It's what he does."

She unclips her hair, allowing the dark locks to tumble around her shoulders and down her back. The hair framing her face makes her look younger and more fragile, like the child she was when Saul destroyed her life.

"AJ will do whatever Saul wants him to. By the time we reach him, there will be nothing left to save."

"You're wrong. AJ won't betray us." I grab his hat and clutch it to my chest, rubbing the brim between my fingertips as though it's a comfort blanket. There has to be something she's not telling me, some secret she's buried deeply but is having to face again. "What did Saul make you do?"

She shakes her head and angles her body away from me. Her jaw is clenched, her lips pressed into a thin white line.

"You taught AJ to be strong. Believe in him. Fight for him. Help me."

She pushes her hands across her face and over her hair. "How? I don't remember how to open a gateway. I wish I did."

"When you were with Saul, did you know other humans who helped the Baneem?"

"Yes, but it was a long time ago, Kim. When I ran away from Saul, I cut ties with everyone I'd known. I had to. I couldn't trust any of them."

"But you must remember their names. Couldn't you look them up and try to get in touch?"

She stares at me, tears giving her eyes a wobbly appearance. "Even if I could, why would they help me?"

I catch my lower lip in my teeth, unable to answer her. "I can't think of any other way to find out how to open a gateway, can you?"

She shakes her head. "I'll try. Perhaps I can be as convincing as the Baneem."

I hope she can for AJ's sake.

CHAPTER ELEVEN

I'm still second-guessing myself as I dial Kevin's number and listen to the ringtone. A year ago, he would have answered my call within a couple of rings. Tops. He replied to text messages within seconds. We were friends, until I realised he was involved with Gage. I haven't spoken to him in a year, so I wouldn't be surprised if he didn't answer at all.

"Kim?" Kevin's voice is full of nervous anticipation.

I hesitate, wondering if I should engage him in small talk or just get straight to the point.

"How are you?" he says, beating me to it.

"Okay." It's easy to lie over the phone. He can't see my red eyes and puffy cheeks. "You?"

"I'm good." There's a smile in his voice.

I realise I'm actually glad he's fine. I hope he's happy. He got in over his head with Gage. He tried to put it right and almost lost his life.

He hitches in a breath. "You didn't ring for a chat, did you?"

"No." Guilt gnaws at my gut. "Did you or Tia ever open a gateway for Gage?"

"A gateway?" His voice rises in genuine confusion.

"A door to and from his home." I try to keep my voice calm and measured, but I sound impatient and annoyed.

"No," he says without hesitation. "He taught us about his magic, that's it."

"You're sure?"

"Yes."

I flop back onto my bed. My loose hair fans out around my head. Gage must have had someone to open a gateway for him.

"Could he have taught Tia without you knowing?"

There's a pause. My heartbeat increases to a fast patter.

"No." He sighs. "Kim, Tia didn't keep secrets from me."

Right. He knew she killed Charley and he did nothing about it. Except befriending me. Except lying to me. Except reporting back to Gage. He claimed it was to protect me, but his blabbing tongue nearly got me killed. I shouldn't have called him.

"Even if Tia did know, she's not the same person anymore, Kim. She won't be able to help you."

Her mind broke, something I'm partly responsible for because I took away her ability to create perfect music. Gage twisted her emotionally. I hurt her physically. She's been in a psychiatric unit ever since. But babbling incoherently about magic and angels doesn't mean she's forgotten everything Gage taught her.

"Thanks, Kevin."

"Kim, what's this about?"

Does he really think I'd tell him? Possibly. On the day he left, he still held out hope we could be friends.

"Nothing important."

"Kim—"

I hang up before he has a chance to say anything else. Almost immediately, my phone starts to ring again. I throw it onto my bed as I move to sit cross-legged in my desk chair. I jab my fingertip against the computer's power button. Before it's finished booting up, my phone stops ringing. A second passes and then it rings again. I open up a web browser and type in the name of the psychiatric unit Tia is in. Gage must have taught her how to open a gateway. A text message ping vibrates my phone. A beat later, it rings again. Kevin would ace a course in aggravated persistence.

It doesn't take me long to find a phone number for the unit. I retrieve my phone just as it stops ringing, allowing a text message from Sophie to arrive. I don't open it. I punch in the unit number and press the phone to my ear.

A bored voice answers. "Hello, Millfield House, Robert speaking, how can I help?"

"I want to arrange to visit a patient."

"All visitation requests have to be approved by the doctors. Please call back tomorrow to speak to your family member's doctor."

I almost tell him I'm not family, but I won't get to see her if I do. "I don't know who her doctor is."

There's a pause. "If you don't know the name of the doctor, you probably shouldn't be visiting anyway."

Jerk. It's a good bet that he's guessed I'm not family. "Her name is Tia West. She's a school friend."

I'm stretching the truth by several hundred miles. Tia and I were never friends. But she was Charley's best friend, before Gage tore them apart. She, Charley, and Amy were a trio. Now they're both dead and Tia is locked up.

"Only close family members are allowed to visit. That's parents, siblings, and spouses," he says in the most patronising voice possible.

I roll one shoulder back, then the other, as I shrug away my irritation. "Can I talk to her on the phone?" I wince at how pleading my voice sounds.

"No, sorry. Is there anything else I can help you with?"

"No."

I growl as he hangs up on me. Leaning back in my chair, I tilt my head and elongate my neck, staring at my pristinely white ceiling. There has to be a way to get in there to speak to Tia. Maybe if I hadn't annoyed Kevin, I could have asked him to go for me.

I could speak to her parents. Only, according to Tia, they don't give a crap about her. If they did, there's no way they'd talk to the girl who ruptured their daughter's eardrums. I still feel guilty for doing it, even if it was the only way to stop her creating deadly music and hurting anyone else.

The muscles in my neck are starting to ache. I lean forward, resting my forehead on my desk. I need to speak to someone who knows how to open a gateway in case Phailin can't get anyone from her past to help her. Kevin doesn't know. Tia is out of my reach. I know Sophie's dad and aunt tried to get the same information a couple of months ago, but they failed, too. I snort. It's not as if there's an online forum called Magic Users Anonymous or Victims of the Baneem Unite. It would make my life a lot easier if there was.

I lift my head in response to a soft knock on my door. Mum doesn't wait for me to invite her in before she opens it and peers round.

"I thought you'd be back in bed," she says.

I shrug. "I'm feeling a lot better."

"Do you fancy watching a movie with me? I bought popcorn."

I almost say no, but I'm stopped by the hopeful rise of her eyebrows. We haven't spent much quality time together recently. Before Charley died, the four of us would have movie nights once a week. Maybe a couple of hours of normalcy watching a chick flick will allow me to let go of some of the hurt I'm feeling right now. With any luck, it'll allow ideas to work their way free, so I can figure out who to ask about opening a gateway.

I smile at Mum. "Sure." I wander over, allowing her to hug me and kiss the crown of my head.

"Thanks," she says. She needs this as much as I do.

*

The film has been on for less than ten minutes when the doorbell rings. Mum motions for me to stay on the sofa, where I'm curled up underneath a blue blanket. I hold it up to my face, feeling the fuzzy softness against my cheek, and repeat over and over that I have to hold it together, even if it means struggling through each second. Each minute. Each hour.

"Hello, Sophie," Mum says. I can hear her voice clearly through the open door. "Kim's in the lounge."

"Hi." Sophie pops her head round the door. "Want to head upstairs?" She gives me a tight-lipped smile.

I nod and push the blanket aside.

Mum puts her hand on Sophie's shoulder. "Thanks for studying with Kim yesterday. I hope you encouraged her to take a little timeout."

Sophie's eyes narrow, a look Mum can't see. "It wasn't any trouble at all," she says through a fixed smile.

As she follows me upstairs, I hunch my shoulders, bracing myself for an onslaught of questions. I sit on my bed, crossing my legs. Sophie closes my door with a firm bang and leans against it, arms folded.

"What's up?" I try to keep my voice casual, but tension creeps in. It's also the lamest thing I could have said.

Her eyebrows dip at a sharp angle, meeting in the deep crease above her nose. "You were at my house yesterday?"

I open my mouth and then snap it shut again. I'm not sure what to say.

"If you're going to use me as an alibi, do me a favour and clue me in."

I dip my chin to my chest.

"Or don't. I don't know what's going on with you anymore, Kim. You skipped most of the day on Friday because you 'weren't feeling well.'" She curls her fingers into quote marks as she speaks. "God knows where you were yesterday. You sure as hell weren't at my house. Why are you lying to everyone?" She narrows her eyes.

"I'm not—"

"Cut the crap, Kim. You've been keeping things from me since Charley died, but I let it slide. I figured it was your way of coping and, when you wanted to, you'd open up to me. I guess that makes me an idiot, doesn't it?"

I shake my head, not understanding where the venom in her voice is coming from. I know I've lied to her for over a year, but I was protecting her. I can't let her know magic exists.

"Were you with AJ? Did the pair of you sneak off somewhere?"

I shake my head, unable to say anything to explain what happened. "AJ's sick."

"I covered for you at school."

"Thank you."

"Thank you?" She marches across the room to the bed and stares down at me. "That's all you're going to say? What about an explanation?"

I suck in a breath and hold it, trapping the truth.

"You need to tell me what's going on, Kim. Now."

All I manage to do is stare at her. She wouldn't believe me if I told her the truth. She'd think I was lying and get angrier. I'm making excuses. Why can't I bring myself to confide in her?

"I thought our friendship meant something to you." She turns away and presses her palm to her forehead.

I scramble to my feet and touch her shoulder. "You're my best friend."

She shrugs away from my touch, spinning round to face me. "Best friends don't lie to each other or use each other."

"I'm not using you."

"Yes, you are." The anger in her eyes fades to sadness. "Why won't you tell me what's going on?"

When I don't answer, her mouth quivers and tears spring to her eyes. "Forget it," she says in a rasping tone. She backs away from me. "I wish I knew what was going on with you, Kim. Believe it or not, I want to help."

"I know." But I can't involve her in my nightmare. I can't.

"For the record, I'm pretty sure AJ isn't sick. When you vanished on Friday, I tried to call him, too, but he didn't answer."

I bow my head, tensing my shoulders to stop them shuddering. Sophie hisses and starts to open the door but pauses with her hand on the handle. Through the small crack she's created, I can hear our landline ringing and Mum's voice as she answers.

"Are you in trouble? Is AJ?" She growls when I remain silent. "Something's going on. You know you could have told me anything, Kim. Whatever it is you're involved in, I would've helped."

I clamp my teeth together. She's talking in the past tense, letting me know I'm out of chances. It would be too easy to break down and tell her everything. Her green gaze bores into me earnestly, but I stay silent. I have to. I can't involve her in my nightmare. I can't put her in danger.

The muscles in her cheeks flex as she shakes her head. "Fine. Have it your way. But don't expect me to hang around so you can keep lying to me. I'm done with you. Both of you."

I run down the stairs after her, but she's out the door before I reach the hallway. I'm about to run after her when Mum steps out of the lounge. Her pale face and shaking hands make me stop.

"Mum?"

"That was the police."

Pain stabs at my chest.

"It's Chris." She wrings her hands.

I clutch her shoulders. "Mum, what's happened to Chris?"

Her lips move soundlessly for a second, as though she's trying to comprehend what's happened herself before she tells me.

"Mum." I don't vocalise the questions running through my mind: Is he hurt? Is he dead?

"He's at the police station."

My body sags a little.

The light drains out of her eyes. "Chris was caught shoplifting."

CHAPTER TWELVE

Mum and I are shown into a small room. Chris is sitting, head bowed, glaring at the table. His messy dark hair brushes his brow. His hands are clenched together and, beneath the table, he's jogging his leg up and down at a furious rate. Mum wraps her arms around him, holding him tightly against her chest. He doesn't respond, not even to shrug her away. Mum lets go and puts her palm against his cheek, trying to make him turn to face her. He resists her touch.

"What did you do?" she says. "Chris?"

The door opens and a pair of police officers step into the room—one man, one woman.

"We'd like to question Chris now," the woman says. She puts her hand on my shoulder. "Would you mind waiting outside?"

I don't want to go, but it's obvious I'm not allowed to stay. I slip out the door into an equally bland corridor. The only embellishments are graphic posters warning not to drink and drive. A couple of plastic chairs stand against the wall, so I sit and lean forward onto my knees. I want to call Sophie, but I don't think she'd speak to me unless I promised to tell her everything.

I lean back and tap my feet against the shiny floor. Part of me has always wanted to confide in Sophie. She kept me afloat when Charley died and was the only friend who stood by me when everyone thought I was losing my mind. I don't want to lose her.

"Kim."

I glance up at Dad. His chest rises and falls a little too quickly and sweat dampens his forehead.

"Mum's in with Chris." I jerk my thumb toward the door. "The police are asking him some questions."

Dad slicks his hair back with his hands. "I should have got here sooner." He sits beside me and pats my knee. "I'm sure it's just a misunderstanding. Chris isn't a thief."

I nod. I know my kid brother. He might be an annoying pain in the ass at times, but he's a good kid. He's not a thief and after everything that happened last year, he wouldn't do anything to upset Mum.

I lean against Dad, smiling and ignoring the scent of sweat that his deodorant can't obscure as he wraps his arm around my shoulders.

"It'll be okay, Kimmie," he says.

For a few seconds, I let myself feel like a small child again. Young enough to not hate his nickname for me and believe he can fix everything. I desperately need it to be true.

We both look up as the door opens. The female police officer holds the door for Mum and Chris.

"Let's go," Mum says.

We follow her out of the building and around to the car park.

"I'll follow you home," Dad says.

Mum shakes her head. "I don't think that's a good idea."

Dad takes her arm and pulls her away. Chris slumps against the car, arms crossed.

"Don't cut me out, Cath." Dad tries to keep his voice hushed, but fails. "He's my son, too."

Mum yanks her arm away from him. "Is that why you couldn't have him this weekend?"

"I told you weeks in advance that I had something on. It's the first weekend I haven't been able to take the kids since—" He cuts himself off and shakes his head.

Since their divorce. I fill in the end of his sentence for him.

"Go home," Mum says. "I'll call you later."

I step forward. "I want Dad to be around," I say. "I bet Chris does too, right?"

Chris doesn't acknowledge my words.

Mum throws her hands up. "Fine, whatever. We'll see you at home." She uses the button on her car key to unlock the doors. "Get in."

I do as I'm told, shooting Dad a reassuring smile as I do.

*

Chris runs straight up to his room while Mum shoos Dad into the kitchen and shuts the door behind them. I stand motionless in the hallway, feeling useless. I'm not supposed to listen in, but this is my kid brother they're talking about and I don't know what else to do. I sit on the bottom step, clasping my hands between my knees.

"He didn't say a word," Mum says.

"Chris isn't a thief."

"Well, apparently he is. They caught him on CCTV stealing DVDs." Mum's voice is weary, edged with anger.

There's a long pause. I imagine Dad leaning on the back of a stool while Mum sits and taps her fingertips on the breakfast bar. She'll be waiting for him to say something. He'll be taking it in, not believing it, even though she's just told him there's evidence. I don't believe it either.

Their silences have gotten longer. There was a brief moment, just after Charley died, when I thought they might get back together. Dad wanted them to. Mum didn't. Then the silences started and got longer. They began giving each other pointed looks instead of actually talking. Their relationship is worse now than when they first got divorced. I guess it's because they blame each other for Charley's death.

"What's going to happen?" Dad says.

"It depends on if the store want to press charges or not. The police have suggested Chris writes a very heartfelt letter of apology. It's the first time he's been in trouble, so hopefully the store will accept the letter and that'll be the end of it."

"Fine. I'll go up and chat to him. Get him to write the letter."

There's a slapping sound, probably Mum's palm slamming against the breakfast bar.

"No, you won't. This is your fault."

"My fault?" Dad's voice rises to just below a shout.

"You don't think it's a coincidence that he chooses this weekend to act out, do you? The weekend where you don't take the kids." Mum's voice competes with his, inching slightly louder.

I head up the stairs. I listened to my parents argue enough before they split up. We all did. Charley and I would sit in her room. Sometimes we'd pay attention to their shouting, other times we'd drown it out with music. Chris stayed in his room, too. He never wanted to hang out with his big sisters.

I knock on his door. When he doesn't answer, I let myself in anyway. He's lying on his bed. Black wires trail from his ears to an MP3 player in his hand. I sit on the bed, waiting for him to pay me some attention. When he doesn't, I tug the earbuds out.

He glares at me. "Hey!"

I yank the cord free of the MP3 player and throw the earbuds across the room. They clatter against the door and fall soundlessly to the carpet. He starts to sit up to retrieve them, but I push my hands against his chest, forcing him back down.

"What?"

I fold my arms. "Are you talking now?"

He narrows his eyes.

"What's going on, Chris? Stealing? That's not you."

He clenches his jaw and shifts his gaze out of the window.

"Listen," I say.

Mum and Dad's raised voices drift through the floor. It's exactly like it was two years ago before Dad left. Tears sparkle in Chris's eyes.

"Why did you do it?"

He shrugs and rubs his thumb over the MP3 player. I frown. I haven't seen it before. It's certainly not the crappy old one that Charley and I clubbed together to buy him two Christmases ago. A crippling chill creeps through my body. I swallow to wet my dry mouth. It can't be. Gage is in purgatory. I saw Matthew take him there.

I pry the MP3 player from his fingers. It looks expensive. "Chris, where did you get this from?"

"Dad."

"Really? When?"

I have no recollection of Dad giving him such an expensive present, and we only ever see Dad together. When our parents first split up, Dad went through a patch of getting us presents whenever we saw him. A new game for Chris, books for me, cinema vouchers for Charley. He stopped when Mum accused him of trying to buy our affections. I always thought he was trying to make up for leaving. For not being there for us all the time anymore.

"He posted it. I got it yesterday," Chris says.

I press my hands against my thighs, hoping he won't notice they're trembling. I have to swallow several times before I'm able to find my voice again. I tell myself I'm being paranoid, but why would Dad post us anything when he only lives a few minutes away?

"Did it already have music on it?"

He shrugs. "A few songs. They were pretty good."

"Chris, this is important. Were you listening to any of those songs when you took those DVDs?"

I wait for him to say no and laugh in my face. Instead, he stares at me with slightly wide eyes. It's a look I've seen hundreds of times on thirty different faces. The look that queries whether I've lost my mind or not.

"Were you?"

"Maybe. Probably. I dunno."

"But you were listening to your MP3 player in the record store?"

He nods.

"Why didn't you go to David's house?"

He shrugs. "I meant to. I cut through town and stopped by the record store." He tugs his knees up to his chest and rests his chin on them. "I've really screwed up, haven't I?" He wipes tears from his eyes with his thumb and forefinger and then rests his finger on his lower lip. "I don't know why I did it. I just did."

He presses his face against his knees. His shoulders start to shudder, followed by his chest, but he doesn't make a sound except for the occasional sniffle. I wrap my arms around him and rest my head against his. I can remember the last time he let me hug him. We were waiting for the school bus. He was angry at me because he was scared I was going to "do a Charley." Those were his exact words. I don't want to believe he would purposefully act out by shoplifting.

But the other alternative is both impossible and terrifying. Whether I buy Matthew's belief—that the Baneem's magic is individual—or my own—that their magic is inherited—I'm led back to Gage.

Mum and Dad's arguing has faded, but I haven't heard Dad leave. I expect one of them to come into Chris's room. Probably Mum.

"Chris?"

He lifts his head.

"Mum said you have to write a letter to the store. Want some help? I aced persuasive writing in English."

He uses his sleeve to wipe the snot away. "What mark did you get in grovelling?" He attempts a smile. It's as weak as his attempt at humour.

"Maybe a B." I go to his desk and retrieve a pad of lined paper and a pen. "You write, I'll dictate," I say, handing them to him.

As soon as he's concentrating on the paper, rather than me, I slip the MP3 player into my jeans pocket. There's one way to find out if Chris's out-of-character behaviour is natural or not and to allay my fears. I need to listen to the songs on the MP3 player, no matter how lame my brother's choice of music is.

*

I sit outside on the garden wall, listening to a few seconds of each track on Chris's MP3 player before skipping to the next one. It's probably only a couple of degrees above freezing. My breath forms little white crystallised clouds in the darkness. My scarf covers the lower half of my face and a hat warms my ears, but my nose still stings from the cold. Dad has gone home. The atmosphere inside the house is thick and heavy. I left Mum crying in the kitchen because she pushed me away with sharp words and a glassy stare.

Chris has rubbish taste in music, not that I listen to much since Gage and Tia took Charley from us. Each cheesy pop track is the same for the first few beats and don't really differ when the singing starts. Male voices sing in upbeat harmony, or a squeaky teenage girl chirps into my ears. There's a bit of techno thrown into the mix, distinguishable by the electronic clauses that rise in pitch on each repeat.

The next song is different from anything else on the MP3 player. It's sombre and slow. A familiar, deep male voice sings words that I can't quite grasp, no matter how hard I try to listen. They make my eyes drift shut, leaving me dizzy and disorientated. A strong metallic scent coils up my nostrils and drifts down my throat, invading my body. Gage. His voice. His scent. I want to pull the earbuds out, but my hands don't respond. My body feels heavy and fuzzy. I have an urge to jump down from the wall and walk. I'm not sure where, but I know I need to go.

A strong hand curls around my shoulder, restraining me. The scent of fresh-cut grass explodes around me, driving out the stench of Gage's magic. The earbuds are tugged from my ears. I breathe in, allowing Matthew's scent and the crisp air to drive Gage's pollution out of my body.

"That was reckless," Matthew says.

I switch the MP3 player off. "It was just a hunch. I didn't really want to believe that..." I stare at him open-mouthed. "Gage is in purgatory."

Maybe Kevin lied when he told me he'd destroyed all the recordings he and Tia had made under Gage's instruction. My chest aches as I feel a pang of regret that I needed proof of Chris's innocence.

Matthew turns away and clasps his hands together. "I need to tell you something, Kim."

My heart thuds against my ribs. "What?" I already know his answer, but my numb mind still denies the obvious truth.

"They released Gage. He was sent back to Uralahnd."

"Released him?" And now he's here, screwing with my kid brother. I double over, gasping for breath. "It's his fault Charley and Amy are dead."

"Tia killed them," Matthew says.

"With Gage's magic." I wrap my arms around my stomach. "He tried to kill me, Matthew."

"But he didn't." He shakes his head. "It wasn't my decision. I'm really sorry, but I don't have any say over how long Baneem are kept in purgatory."

"It's barely been a year." I manage to stop my voice rising into a high-pitched yell. I don't need Mum, Chris, or our neighbours to hear me arguing with an invisible not-angel. "How could anyone in their right mind think a year is long enough for what he did?"

Matthew shrugs. "I'm sorry."

His apology slices across my mind, fuelling my anger. It doesn't matter that it isn't his fault. Between AJ's disappearance and Gage's release, I feel like I'm being torn in two and my insides are being shredded by anger and grief. I sink to my knees, too exhausted to cry.

"How long have you known?"

"Kim…"

"How long?" I snap my head up. "Did you find out today? Or did you know when you answered my call?"

His mouth twitches. His silence tells me everything.

"You should have told me."

"I'm sorry."

"Stop apologising." I narrow my eyes. "Did you come because you knew he'd messed with my brother?"

He inclines his head, guilt radiating from the depths of his impossibly dark eyes.

"You sensed Gage's magic." Sarcasm drips from my voice. "But you didn't stop him from making my brother steal."

"It was the same as a year ago. The magic was old and hard for me to track."

"Because it was a recording."

It's why he wasn't able to save Charley's best friend, Amy, when a deadly song prompted her to step in front of a car. I clutch the MP3 player in my hand, wishing I had the strength to crumble it into black powder. Knowing Gage made Chris steal the DVDs doesn't help my brother. I can't explain it to him or anyone else. Everyone will carry on believing he's a thief.

"Why is Gage doing this?"

Matthew doesn't say anything. The truth is I don't need him to. I already know the answer.

"Gage wants revenge. He's going to tear my family apart."

"We'll stop him," Matthew says.

I stare at him with wide eyes. "We?"

"I've given up trying to keep you out of trouble. It's easier if I let you help." His eyes twinkle with a mischievous smile that doesn't reach his lips.

It feels like a weight has been lifted off my chest. Matthew isn't going to fight me or shut me out. He wants my help. I'm torn between hugging him and punching the air in victory. I do neither. I turn the MP3 player over in my hands. It's not a victory. Even if we do stop Gage, it won't help heal the damage he's caused my family.

"Why now?" I say.

Matthew lifts his eyebrows.

"Why has Gage shown up right after AJ's disappearance? It can't be a coincidence."

He shrugs. "He's just been released from purgatory. He's had a year to fester over what happened and how he was caught. I admit the timing is suspicious, but the Baneem aren't organised enough for it to be anything other than a coincidence."

Not organised. According to Matthew, that's the only reason the Shamari are able to stop the Baneem at all—because they don't work together.

"Bad timing?" I say, even though I'm not convinced. "But if I'm trying to stop Gage, who's going to help AJ?"

Matthew shrugs. "For what it's worth, I'm really sorry about AJ."

An apology won't bring AJ back or get rid of Gage. I pick myself up and wrap my arms around my waist.

"We need to prioritise dealing with Gage," Matthew says. "If he wants revenge, the incident with Chris won't be the end. You know that, don't you?"

Of course I know it. Whatever plans Gage has, this is just the beginning.

CHAPTER THIRTEEN

There's no way out of the cell. I've nothing to pick the lock with. There's no window or drain. The bars are solid and don't flex, no matter how much I try to force them apart. Not that I have much strength left in my body. I've been given water at regular intervals. I think it's been regularly, but it's hard to tell when I've nothing to gauge the passing of time by. They gave me food once. A couple of thick slices of bread, which I swallowed down in small chunks, resisting the urge to throw up with every bite. With food and water comes a brief spurt of light, but they never leave the lantern lit once they're gone.

I don't know how long I've been here or how long it's been since Saul and his thug attacked me in the alley. I try not to think about Mum and Kim because wondering what they're doing and how they're coping is more torture than anything Saul could throw at me. It's hard to keep them out of my thoughts. To not dwell on the argument Mum and I had or the hurt in Kim's eyes when I pushed her away. I shouldn't have done that.

The double door whines open on its hinges, allowing bright sunlight to stream into the cell. I raise my hand to shield my eyes as Saul, flanked by two heavy-set men, strides down the corridor toward me. I recognise one of them, but he staunchly avoids my desperate gaze. I bounce to my feet, fold my arms, and regard Saul through narrowed eyes. It's the first time he's bothered to visit me since he dragged me here. I doubt it's a good thing he's come now. I hold my head high and make sure my back is straight. I'm not going to show him their attempts to keep me weak are working.

"Father." The admission of who he is burns my tongue, but maybe if I remind him who I am, he'll think twice before hurting me or forcing me to help him. It works in crime dramas on TV, when victims pretend to play along with their captors. But this isn't TV and Saul isn't a human who's suffered a psychotic break.

His lips, which are pressed into a narrow white slash, twitch at the corners in response. It's a fleeting grimace rather than a smile. I'm not surprised. He pulls a long metal key out of his jacket pocket, opening the lock with a heavy clunk. I consider trying to barrel past him, but it doesn't take me more than a second to realise it's a stupid plan. If Saul didn't stop me, the two guys with him would.

I can't escape, but I won't show Saul any fear either. I stand still, breathing slowly and concentrating on keeping my muscles relaxed. He motions for the men to enter the cell. My cheek muscles twitch as they do, but it's the only trace of emotion I show as they loop their arms through mine. They wrench my elbows back and cross their arms over my spine. If I struggle, I'll dislocate my shoulders.

"What? No niceties?" I say, as they march me out of the cell. I have to twist in their grip so I can keep my gaze fixed on Saul. "The least you could do is say hi."

He lifts his chin. "Hello, Aran." There's no warmth in his voice at all.

I'm not sure why I expected anything other than coldness from him, but his rebuttal hurts. I consider trying to talk to him, but the hard light in his eyes makes the words slip away. Saul isn't a man who's going to listen to my pleas, no matter how impassioned I make them.

I blink my eyes as I'm led out of the door. The unfiltered intensity of the natural light makes them ache. It's suffocatingly hot outside. The humidity is so heavy it feels like I'm breathing soup instead of air. My skin starts to feel damp, but

I'm not sure if it's from the moisture in the air or because I'm sweating. Probably both.

There's a roof above my head, supported by tall columns that create arch-shaped gaps, allowing me a view across a once-lush courtyard. The broadleaf grass is a sickly shade of brown, punctuated by tall palm trees. A dry fountain sits in the center. The floor is made up of giant sandy flagstones with deep fissures running through them, allowing shrivelled-up weeds to gain a foothold.

I glance to my left, at the wall of the building we've just stepped out of. I can make out the uneven shape of bricks beneath a coat of blue paint, which is only a couple of shades darker than the azure sky. Cracks and flakes in the paint mar the beautiful visage of the building. The door and columns have been left bare, revealing sandy bricks that create an illusion of gold trim as the sun beats down on them.

I can't help but stare, open-mouthed. It's like I've been dragged from a modern city and sent back in time to an ancient civilisation.

"What is this place?" I say.

"It was a palace," Saul says. "Now it's where I live."

I'm surprised he bothered to answer my question. "Was?" I'm probably pushing my luck by hoping to get more information out of him.

He sighs as he scans the compound. "We haven't been led in generations."

I'm guessing he wants to change that since he's made this place his home.

"Why not?" I try to keep my voice casual, cutting myself off before I ask what I really want to know: Doesn't someone tell the Baneem which humans to mess with? Does Saul?

"Why do you care?" His voice drops into an annoyed growl.

"I'm trying to understand. That's all."

He turns to face me. "Will understanding make any difference to you? Would you volunteer to help us?"

I try to shrug, but the two thugs are holding my arms too tightly. "It might."

Saul's lips flatten and the muscles beneath his eyes twitch. I can tell he's trying to figure out if I'm lying or not. I hope I'm practised enough at it to fool him. He turns his back on me and carries on walking.

"Let me show you something."

The way the thugs shove me forward, I doubt I have a choice.

When we reach the corner of the building, I'm forced up a flight of stone steps. The building is easily six stories high, only each level is the height of a modern two-storey house. My feet slip and scrape across stone, sending tiny chips of debris clattering down the steps.

"Our people put all their effort into the task the Creator had given us, believing one day we'd be rewarded," Saul says. "There was a foolish myth that those most successful at tempting humans would earn a place on Earth."

"It doesn't make sense." I regret the statement as soon as I've made it.

"Why not?" Saul says.

"Why would you be so eager to trade Uralahnd for Earth?"

He grabs the back of my shirt and wrenches me away from the thugs. I fight to stay on my feet as he propels me toward the edge of the steps. For a second, I'm convinced he's going to hurl me over the edge. We're halfway up—even I wouldn't survive the fall. But he holds me fast at the very edge, with my toes hanging over thin air.

"Look," he says.

The empty palace is surrounded by a tall wall. The land on the other side is barren and dusty. It stretches as far as I can see. Small pockets of green surrounded by half a dozen buildings pockmark the desert.

"All of Uralahnd is like this. Most of it is dead. Earth is our promised land, our reward for doing what the Creator asked us to without questioning."

He pulls me back and throws me onto the steps. The thugs close in on me so I can't escape. Saul shakes his head, forbidding them from hauling me back to my feet.

"Except it's obvious we're never going to receive our reward unless we take it. Working as a disparate race has kept us in this hole for generations. I intend to change that."

"What about the humans?"

He shrugs. "What about them? They were given a beautiful world and what have they done? Fought one another. Created war machines and weapons of mass destruction. They've strangled it with buildings and suffocated it with pollution. They don't deserve it."

I glare at him. "They don't deserve to die either."

He smiles. "Don't they?" He twists his hand in a lifting motion.

The thugs grab my arms and pull me up, forcing my shoulders back again.

"We don't intend to kill them," he says. "We intend to rule them."

My chest clenches painfully, as I notice the gleam in his eyes. "We?" I say, my voice sharp with anger. "I don't see many Baneem rallying to your cause."

Saul's eyes narrow, and the skin around his lips becomes taut. "I didn't think you'd listen to me," he says in a nonplussed tone. He turns and descends the steps.

"There's no one else helping you, is there?" I say. "Did you give up on your home when you set your sights on Earth? Because this compound looks like it was beautiful once. It looks like there was life here until you ruined it."

"You have no idea how this place works," Saul says, without bothering to stop or turn to look at me.

"So tell me."

He rolls his tense shoulders back, signalling the end of the conversation.

I don't bother to try to talk to him again.

They drag me back down to the covered walkway and into a small room with what can only be described as a stone altar in the center. Predictably, the thugs push me toward it. I attempt to slow the inevitable by refusing to walk and allowing my feet to drag along the dusty floor. Hanging in their grip puts more strain through my shoulders, making my muscles and tendons burn. They're too strong for me and before I know it, they're slamming my back down on the altar. They use their hands to pin down my shoulders and wrists. I squirm under the pressure of their grip but can't break free. After a few agonising seconds of trying, I lay still, breathing hard.

Saul leans against the wall, just in my field of vision. His expression is blank, which I guess is an improvement on the victorious smirk I imagined he'd have plastered on his face. I keep my gaze fixed on him, holding the dim hope in my mind that he'll act like a father and stop this. Whatever this is.

As if on cue, Adele enters the room. She lays both her hands on my chest and smiles icily.

"This shouldn't hurt too much."

I scrunch my forehead up. Her words don't fill me with confidence. Bowing her head and shoulders, she closes her eyes. The suffocating scent of rotting fish floods my nostrils. The ammonia tang in the air stings my eyes, making them water so aggressively everything blurs. I gag and swallow in a repetitive cycle that leaves my stomach churning like a whirlpool.

Pain tears through my body. A bright white haze seems to lift out of me, rising a millimetre at a time as Adele slowly raises her hands. I'm gripped by burning agony, as if a dozen knives are tearing their way over my skin, flaying me alive. I grit my teeth to stop myself from screaming. Despite the heavy hands weighing me down, my chest arcs off the altar. The muscles in my neck become as rigid as steel cables as my head tips backward and presses down against the cold stone. Every nerve in my body is ablaze. My breath rushes out of my lungs. The pain consumes me. I scream.

The weight of my body rips away. I'm surrounded by light. Am I dead? Through the bright haze, I can see Adele peering at me. A smile is teasing the corners of her mouth up. She presses her hands down, through the light.

I'm falling back into my body, but it resists me. Adele's hands keep pushing down, forcing me through what feels like a metal sieve. Thousands of crisscrossing threads slice into me. I'm sure

I'm going to fragment and scatter into the ether. I'm surrounded by the suffocating heaviness of my body, which is like an alien cage trapping me. I gasp air in, struggling to drive out the crippling skewers piercing my flesh and deep into my muscles.

"Let him go," Adele says. "He's not going anywhere."

The thugs release me. My skin begins to tingle, a warning sign my magic is about to kick in and heal me. I'm not sure what's wrong with my body, but something inside me feels shattered. I fight against it, gritting my teeth and driving my nails into my palms to try to stay conscious. I have to hear what they're saying.

"Well?" Saul says. "Why can't the Shamari see he's Baneem?"

Slowly, inch by inch, I manage to raise my knee, fighting the lullaby of my healing with every jerky movement.

"It's probably easier to show you," Adele says. "I could do with a flame, though, preferably one that can't be extinguished."

I flop my knee sideways and twist my body after it, rolling onto my side and curling into a foetal position. I'm crying. I press my knuckles against my eyes to try to stem the uncontrollable flow. I don't want to cry in front of any of them, especially not Saul, but the pain consuming my body is unbearable.

Heat flares next to my cheek and I try to shy away from it by collapsing my shoulder and pressing my head against the altar. I lower my fists and peer at the ball of flame dancing in the palm of the thug who helped abduct me. He's a real-life Human Torch. I'm too scared, too weak and too sore to be impressed.

"Imagine the flame is the soul of a Baneem," Adele says. "Or in this case, Aran's soul."

She dangles a piece of white cloth in front of it, but the flame is bright enough to shine through.

"The cloth represents the body of a Baneem," she says. "To the eyes of a Shamari, they can still see the soul, albeit in a muted fashion."

"But in Aran's case?" Saul says.

Adele chuckles. "Let's just say the body of a human is thicker than that of a Baneem."

She grabs my hand and presses it over the fire. Rather than puffing out of existence, like a mundane flame would have done, it continues to burn. The heat prickles and blisters my skin, but it's nothing more than background noise against the agony caused by having my soul ripped out of my body and shoved back in again. I get her point, although it burns my hand, the fire is invisible.

"His body literally shrouds his soul."

I try to wrench my hand away from Adele and the flame, but she's surprisingly strong. Either that or I've been rendered helpless. She smiles and holds my hand in place for a few seconds longer. Twenty-three to be precise. I count each one, fighting her with the fragile shred of energy I have left.

She lifts my hand away from the flame and drops it. My palm is an ugly mess of angry red and glistening moisture.

"A beautiful illustration of my next point," Adele says, dropping the white cloth onto Flame Guy's palm. The fire consumes it. I watch as the cloth blackens, shrivels up and crumbles into ashes. Flame Guy closes his palm, extinguishing the fire. The ashes drift to the floor.

"His soul is too powerful for his body. By rights, he should have burned up before he was even born."

Dizziness makes my eyes roll back and my head flop. The pins and needles consuming my body are no longer content to be held at bay by my stubbornness. Combined with the pain from Adele's experiment, it feels like a swarm of angry hornets is having a party in my body.

"His magic keeps him alive," she says. "It's constantly repairing the damage his soul is causing."

I squeeze my eyes shut, unwilling to look at her smug face. Is she right? I fight against the desire to pass out by digging my nails into the remnants of the burns on my palm. It doesn't feel like I'm healing myself every second of every day, but maybe that's why my magic exhausts me the way it does when I have a visible injury to repair.

"Which is probably why he's one of a kind," she says. "Because the only way the offspring of a Baneem and a human could survive is with the power of healing."

"Can we use what you've learned?" Saul says. "Can you replicate it?"

I have to stay awake, but my eyelids are clamped to my cheeks and the darkness is so inviting. It would ease my pain.

"Sort of, yes."

"Sort of?" Saul sounds impatient. His voice is blunt, his words clipped.

I focus on the pain, welcoming it even though it brings fresh tears to my eyes. It keeps me hovering on the edge of consciousness.

"I could transfer the soul of a Baneem into the body of a human. The body would hide the soul and there would be no active magic for the Shamari to pick up on." Her voice is distorted, like an echo haunting me, sending a shiver snaking down my spine. "But it wouldn't take long for the soul to burn through the body. There would be a very small window of opportunity to act."

"How long?"

She shrugs. "I don't know without further experimentation." She rests her hands on the altar, close to my head. "I suspect the most damage occurs when the soul is first removed and when it is replaced. Would you agree, Aran?"

I don't make any attempt to nod.

"What would happen to the Baneem?" Saul says. He doesn't seem to care that Adele is talking about destroying a human life.

"If their soul was in the human body when it was destroyed, they would die. Of course, Aran's magic might be able to give the body more time." Her fingertips brush against my cheek, making me shudder. "Giving the Baneem a chance of surviving."

And the human. My magic would save the life of the human.

"It won't work," Saul says. "If Aran is healing the human, the Shamari will sense his magic."

"Which is why I need to experiment," Adele says. "If Aran heals the body after the Baneem's soul has been put into it, there might be enough time for the Baneem to complete their task before their soul consumes their host."

"Find out if you're right," Saul says without hesitation.

"Get me a human and I will."

CHAPTER FOURTEEN

Sophie ignores me all day at school. She even finds somewhere else to sit during registration and English. We've never had an argument fester this long. Was it really even an argument? She wanted me to tell her the truth and I didn't. It doesn't matter how many times I tell myself I couldn't because I know it's not true. I could if I wanted to.

Chris heads upstairs as soon as we get home.

"Squirt."

He pauses with his foot on the top step, turns, and scowls at me. "What?"

I don't blame him for being annoyed. It's not just the nickname, he knows Mum has asked me to keep an eye on him. I met him straight after school and escorted him to the bus stop. He even let me sit next to him with only a couple of huffs and puffs.

"How was school?"

He sighs as he sits down on the stairs. "Crap."

I lean against the banister. "Do you want to talk about it?"

"No."

"Tell you what—you can either talk to me or Mum. Which is it going to be?"

His scowl deepens, wrinkling his nose in a comical fashion. "Fine. Half the kids stared at me and the other half handed me shopping lists." He picks at the carpet. "Now I know how you must have felt last year." He dips his face away from me so he's mumbling into his chest. "Sorry."

"It's okay." I know I didn't lose my mind or have a break-down after Charley died. I've stopped caring what anyone else thinks or believes. At least I've tried to.

I put my foot on the bottom step, intending on sitting beside Chris, but he stands and darts to the top of the stairs.

"We did the mushy thing yesterday," he says. "I'm fine, honest, Kim. I've got homework to do."

"Okay."

I don't believe him, but I let him hurry into his room. He closes it a little too hard, making a photo on the wall wobble and bang. It's a picture of Chris, me, and Charley, taken a few weeks before she died. I sniff back tears. I miss her so much, but the pang of anger I felt when I destroyed her prom dress is creeping back into my heart. She shouldn't have gotten involved with Gage. She should have warned us how dangerous he was. I guess that makes me a hypocrite because I know he's back and I haven't said anything to my family. But unlike Charley, I'm not going to shut my eyes to the danger, hoping it goes away.

I slip into the kitchen and open the back door, letting Matthew inside.

"Have you felt Gage's magic at all today?" I keep my voice low so Chris doesn't overhear me.

Matthew shakes his head. "I've been looking, too, but so far nothing."

He'll be hiding and planning his next move. I hate having to wait, wondering what he's going to do to my family next. The problem is I don't just want Gage out of my life. I need to make him help me. The only way he could have got out of Uralahnd to harass my family is if a human opened a gateway for him. I dig my teeth into my bottom lip. I can't let Matthew know what I'm thinking. If he did, he wouldn't let me anywhere near Gage.

I sit down at the breakfast bar and pull out my phone. "Sophie is angry that I used her as an alibi on Saturday."

Grimacing, Matthew leans against the closed back door. "What have you said?"

"Nothing. Now she's not talking to me."

"I'm sorry."

I shrug. An apology won't fix my friendship. I'm not sure Sophie is as predisposed to forgiveness as a not-angel. I need to tell her something, but if I tell her even a small part of the truth, I'm going to have to tell her everything. She won't believe the truth.

"How did you get her dad to help anyway?"

Matthew inclines his head. "Like you, he's more aware. I can reveal myself to him without letting anyone else see me. I stood outside their window. When he saw me, he came out to speak to me and I asked him to call your mother."

I smack my palm against my forehead. "Great. So he probably left the house without an explanation, right?"

His mouth quirks into a grimace.

"No wonder Sophie is suspicious."

"I'm sorry."

I wave his apology away. It was better than him revealing himself to Mum or her panicking that something had happened to me. It isn't the only suspicious thing Sophie's picked up on. She's gradually been seeing through my lies. She's given me several opportunities to start telling her the truth. I don't deserve her friendship.

I push my fingers through my hair. "Lies always catch up to you, don't they?"

Sooner or later, I'm going to have to confide in Matthew about using Gage to get to Uralahnd. I should tell him now, but I'm hoping Phailin will succeed first so I never have to. I pick up my phone and quick-dial Sophie's number.

She doesn't pick up and eventually the call goes through to her chirpy voicemail: Hi, this is Sophie. I'm probably doing something clichéd like washing my hair. Leave a message. I don't. I call her again. And again. And again.

"What?" she says when she finally does answer.

"We need to talk."

"Are you going to tell me what's going on?" Her voice is slightly breathless. Traffic buzzes in the background. She's not at home.

"Where are you?"

"In town. I stopped by the library to pick up a couple of art books." She growls. "Don't change the subject, Kim."

"Come over?"

"We can talk just fine on the phone."

No. We can't. "Please come over."

"Why? So you can ply me with ice cream and we can hug and make up?"

I want it to be that easy, but the acidic tone in her voice makes it clear it won't be. This is an argument we're not going to get over with a few tears. She's not going to let go until she hears the truth. Or something I can make pass as the truth. I press my hand over my eyes. Before Charley died, I would never have concocted lies to tell Sophie or anyone else. What kind of person have I become?

"If you won't come around, how can I tell you what's going on? And don't tell me we can talk over the phone. If you want to know the truth, it has to be face to face."

I can hear her footsteps and the sharp puffs of her breath. I hold my own until my chest hurts so much I'm forced to exhale.

"Or you can come to me. I'll meet you at the coffee shop, okay?"

I'm meant to be watching Chris, but I don't argue. Sophie has thrown me a lifeline and I have to take it.

"Okay, I'll see you soon." I hesitate, unable to say goodbye. "Thank you." I hang up and hop off the tall stool.

I'm not sure if I should feel relieved or worried as I head into the hallway to grab my coat. Matthew follows me like a silent shadow.

I jog up a couple of steps, so I don't have to shout as loud. "Chris, I'm going out."

He sticks his head out of his door, oblivious to Matthew's presence behind me. "You trust me enough to leave me alone?"

"Cut the sarcasm or I'll lock you in your room."

"I can always shimmy down the drainpipe."

"Of course you can if you want to end up in casualty with a broken leg."

He sticks his tongue out at me. "Have fun."

I force a smile as he retreats into his room and slams his door. I don't think "fun" is a good way to describe the conversation I'm about to have with Sophie.

"Are you going to tell her the truth?" Matthew says once we're out of the house.

I shrug. "I've spent the last year trying to protect her from finding out magic exists. I didn't let her dad get punished for shooting me so she wouldn't have her world torn apart like mine was." I clasp my hands together. "But I have to tell her something, Matthew, or I'm going to lose her. I can't lose her."

"It's not an easy choice to make."

I pause at the edge of the pavement, waiting for a break in the traffic before I dart across the road.

"Did you have to tell anyone you loved about magic? When you were alive, I mean."

Matthew sets his jaw into a rigid line. "No."

His abrupt tone makes me stuff my hands in my pockets and hunch my shoulders. I want to know more about his life as a human, but now isn't the time. I'm not sure if I'll ever be able to get him to open up to me. From the little he's already told me, I know he still feels guilty for the events that led up to his execution. People he loved died. For now, that's all I need to know.

"If I do tell her the truth, she'll think I'm nuts." I purse my lips. "Unless I can give her some proof."

"No." His tone isn't as abrupt, but the message is the same.

"I know about you. Her father knows about you." I mumble my plea into my chest, so the cyclist passing us in the park doesn't think I'm talking to myself.

"Her father was magic-aware already."

Now we're alone again, I tilt my head to the side. "I wasn't. Not when I first met you."

What do I count as our first meeting? Charley's funeral? Outside the nightclub? The night Charley died? I tug at my lower lip with my teeth.

"Matthew, there's something I've never understood."

"What?"

"You told me you made me forget seeing you the night Charley died to protect yourself. It didn't make sense then and it doesn't make sense now."

His mouth curls into an amused smile, which makes the pit of my stomach quiver. "I seem to recall you called me a liar."

Heat rises to my cheeks. Whether it's from embarrassment, the effect of his smile, or a combination of both, I'm not sure.

"I was protecting myself," he says. "I should never have let you see me."

"But you did. Why?"

He stares at the floor. "You'd already fallen down the stairs and you obviously weren't thinking straight. I was afraid you would hurt yourself. I needed to calm you down, but to interact with you, I had to let you see me."

I shake my head, still not quite buying his story. "But you let me see you at Charley's funeral, outside the nightclub, and again at school. I get why you saved my life when I almost walked into the road the day Amy died. I get why you let me see you then. But the other three times? I wasn't in any danger."

"I've also told you that once a human sees me, it's harder for me to hide from them. It takes a lot more effort."

"Effort you could have put in if you'd wanted to, right?"

I half-close my eyes. I don't want to remember the details of Charley's funeral, but I make myself anyway. I was standing at the front, reading a poem Mum had chosen and Charley would have hated. "Remember" by Christina Rossetti. I was struggling over the words, unable to choke them out because I was crying too hard. My tears had smudged the ink, making it impossible to read the words, but it didn't matter. I knew every line of it by heart. I tried to compose myself by looking at everyone who had come to say goodbye to Charley. Big mistake. It nearly made me crumble. But then I saw Matthew. He had smiled and I was able to carry on reading.

"You were surprised I could see you," I say, recalling the rise of his eyebrows the moment before he smiled. "Why?"

"I thought making you forget would also stop you being aware. I was wrong." He arches an eyebrow. "I did try to avoid you at the school, remember?"

"Not hard enough."

"You think I should have sprouted wings and flown away?"

I shrug. "It still doesn't explain why you helped me outside the nightclub. I wasn't in danger."

"You were drunk and on your own in the middle of the night. What was I supposed to do?"

"What were you meant to do?" I say, lifting my chin.

A squeak of a failed explanation escapes his lips. He presses them shut and looks away.

"You're not meant to interact with humans, are you?"

I should have realised it before. It should have been blindingly obvious. He paces ahead of me, the muscles in his back taut. Does he have to concentrate on his manifested form to make it appear natural? I file that question away for another time.

He turns around, walking backward with ease. "We used to. It's why you have myths of angels and other similar creatures in human culture. But the Baneem turned humans against us by portraying us as demons, so we had to retreat and become invisible to protect ourselves."

"You broke the rules," I say.

"One rule."

"Two."

He glances at me sharply.

"You should have taken AJ to purgatory, shouldn't you?"

He rubs the back of his neck.

"Matthew, what would happen if another Shamari found out? A true Shamari, I mean. Not one of the Changed."

He narrows his eyes.

"I'm guessing the true Shamari are in charge, right? You're a foot soldier, they command the troops?"

He nods. "Yes. The true Shamari don't come to Earth anymore. It's why the Changed exist and why I was given a chance to redeem myself."

"They use you?"

"It's not like that, Kim. The risks are too great for them. If a Baneem killed one of them, they'd be gone forever. Their soul would be destroyed."

"So would yours."

He shrugs. "But this is my second chance. My second life. It doesn't matter."

"Of course it matters." It's an effort to stop myself shouting at him.

I jab my finger hard against the crossing signal, gritting my teeth and holding my breath as I wait for the lights to change in my favour. I exhale over a count to ten, allowing the tension in my jaw to slip away with each number that runs through my head. "What would happen to you if the true Shamari found out you had broken the rules?"

He doesn't get a chance to answer before the rhythmic crossing warning prompts me to jog across the road. Once on the cycle path, he stops me by holding his arm out in front of me. His dark gaze captures mine, momentarily paralysing my breath until the moment he speaks.

"They wouldn't destroy me if that's what you're thinking. I'd probably be sent to a different area."

I can't tell if he's telling the truth or not. Can he lie? If he is lying, it's because he doesn't want me to worry. The penalty for hurting humans or Baneem is death, why would the penalty for helping a Baneem—even one who is half-human—be any less?

I want to cry. Or scream. Or hold him. I don't understand why he would risk that for me and AJ.

I push his hand away and carry on walking. "Why are you here?" My voice trembles with the effort of holding back the tears burning my eyes. "You shouldn't be here."

"You needed me. So I came."

I shake my head. "You shouldn't have even given me your feathers, should you? I bet that was another rule broken, wasn't it?"

He doesn't answer, which might as well be an admittance of his guilt. I know he won't leave the city, not until he's taken Gage back to purgatory. For all the good it will do if the true Shamari are just going to let him go again.

"I should carry on looking for Gage," he says.

I nod. I don't want him around when I'm talking to Sophie anyway, especially if he's not going to help me make her believe. I still don't know if I should tell her the truth. But if I don't, I'll lose her forever and I'm not sure I want to be as lonely as Matthew is.

"Let me know if you find him," I mumble. I hope he doesn't because, unless Phailin can contact someone who will teach us how to open a gateway, Gage is my only hope of rescuing AJ.

*

I'm almost at the coffee shop when I feel my phone vibrating in my pocket. I tug it out, frowning at Sophie's name splashed across the screen.

"Where are you?" she says.

"Almost there. Did you think I wasn't coming?" I regret my glib words instantly, but I can't take them back.

"What? No. Kim, it's your mum. She's acting…strange."

"Mum?"

She works in the town center, in one of the department stores.

"You need to get here, Kim—now. She's outside the coffee shop…"

Sophie keeps talking, but I stop listening as I spot Mum. She's standing in front of the ATM beside the coffee shop, handing out money. I gasp as she practically shoves a note into a woman's hands. The next person to pass her, a teenage girl, doesn't hesitate to accept the random gift. Sophie is standing with her, tugging at her arm as she continues to talk to me on the phone.

I jog over to them. Sophie hangs up and slips her phone into her pocket.

"She won't listen to me," she says in a harsh whisper.

"Mum?"

Mum smiles at me and presses a note into my hand. I'm not even sure she realises I'm her daughter.

Gage's melodic voice reaches me, his voice intensified by a microphone. It pours over me, but I'm not lulled by it. Nor is anyone around me.

"Stay with Mum," I say to Sophie.

"What? Kim, what's going on?"

She makes a grab for me, but I turn and push through the crowd. The amplifier distorts Gage's voice, making it bounce off the sandstone buildings, only to be absorbed by the bodies of the shoppers. I don't recognise the song, but a name punctuates the chorus: Cath, Mum's name.

I see him standing on a street corner, one hand rests on a microphone and the other taps against the air, as though he's rocking it on a stage. His eyes are half-closed. For a second, I think I can reach him before he spots me. He catches my fierce gaze and winks before turning and running. He doesn't even bother to gather up the plastic bowl overflowing with money at his feet.

I try to run, too, but I'm pushing against a strong current of people, unable to gain any forward motion. As I go past his busking spot, the thick metallic scent of his magic curls into my nostrils. Within seconds, I lose sight of him as he darts down a side street. A growl lodges in my throat, but I hold it there as I force my way toward the last point I saw him. Now free of the crowd, I run down the side street. Stopping, I glance ahead, left, and right. I see the flash of his pale coat as he vanishes down a side street to the left.

"Kim."

I yelp and spin round at the sound of Matthew's voice.

"I felt Gage's magic," he says. "But now it's stopped. Did you see him?"

I gape and then point to the right. "He went that way."

Matthew nods and takes flight in that direction. What am I doing? I don't let myself think about it as I sprint down the side street to the left.

The back entrances of restaurants, pubs, and clubs line the road. There are no cars. No pedestrians. All I can hear is the beat of my trainers against the tarmac and the buzz of traffic from the ring road on the other side of the buildings. I slow my pace. My breathing is heavy as I exhale in sharp puffs. My impulsive plan is crazy. What will I do if I catch up with Gage? I shouldn't have sent Matthew the wrong way. I puff out my cheeks and stop. I have to find Matthew and tell him I made a mistake. I turn, intent on making my way back to him.

Gage is leaning against a massive metal bin, grinning. My breath catches in my throat, and my chest constricts painfully.

"It's been a while." His grin curls into a smirk.

The way his arms are folded makes his muscles bulge. With his dark hair and athletic physique, it's not hard to see why Tia and Charley fell for him. I did. Until I discovered he was psychotic.

"I'm curious as to why you sent your Changed friend away," he says.

He spits "Changed" out like an insult, just like he did a year ago. Do all the Baneem frown upon the Changed so much?

"No time to chat though, is there? Shame," he says.

I'm finally able to make my shaking legs work. I sprint toward him, but he's faster, disappearing round the corner before I'm even close. By the time I reach the next road, he's gone. I lean forward onto my knees. He won't let me get close to him again. I had a chance and I blew it.

I bite my lip to suppress a scream as a strong hand closes around my shoulder. I lurch round, straight into Matthew's piercing gaze.

"What are you doing?"

"I…thought I saw something…" I shake my head. "Did you find Gage?"

"No." There's a cold edge to his voice. His expression is blank and unreadable. "You should go to your mother."

"Is something wrong?"

He lifts his chin. "We'll talk later."

"Matthew—"

He cuts me off with a dark glare that almost drives me to my knees. He turns his face away, strides past me, and takes to the skies with a couple of powerful wingbeats. I cover my face with my hands. He knows.

CHAPTER FIFTEEN

Sophie has taken Mum into the coffee shop. An untouched mug of black coffee sits in front of her.

"Mum?" I pull up a chair and sit down.

Sophie raises her eyebrows at me.

"Thanks," I say.

She shrugs. "It's fine. I hope she's okay." She reaches across Mum and puts her hand on my arm. "What's going on, Kim? Why did you take off like that?"

"Can we talk later?" I can't answer her questions, not here and now when all I want to do is make sure Mum is okay.

Sophie scrapes her chair back and stands. "I understand you're worried about your mum, but you can't keep brushing me off."

"I'm not brushing you off."

"Yes, you are." She grabs her school bag and slings it over her shoulder. "I really do hope your mum is okay."

I let her walk away, out of the shop. Even though my mouth fights to get out the words to stop her, my throat doesn't let them. I turn my attention to Mum. Her hands are trembling and her face is pale. She's clutching her handbag in her lap, as though it's the most precious thing in the whole world.

"I don't know why I did it," she says.

The shop is packed. Christmas music jangles through the speaker system. The warm air is heavy with the scent of coffee and gingerbread. The other customers are chatting and laughing, showing off the presents they've been buying and swapping notes on where to get the best wrapping paper.

"It's okay," I say, rubbing her arm.

Mum's fingers twitch against the brown leather of her bag. "No, it's not." Her voice is an angry hiss. "I gave complete strangers hundreds of pounds, Kim."

"Mum."

She draws in a breath. "I maxed out both my debit cards and my credit card, Kim. That's six hundred pounds. Gone." She shakes her head. "Why would I do that?"

Because Gage made you. I bite my tongue. Even if I did try to explain it to her, she wouldn't believe me. She'd think I was mocking her.

"It is Christmas," I say in as light-hearted a tone as I can manage. "Maybe you were getting into the spirit of the season?"

She stares at me. Her eyes are round and dull, like those of a fish floundering on land. The last time she looked so lost and defeated was just after Charley died.

"Things have been difficult lately," I say in a more serious tone. "But it's only money. Come on, let's go home."

"Only money?" She hugs her bag to her chest. "I want you to call your father and ask him to pick you and Chris up. You need to stay with him for a few days."

"What? Why?"

She turns her face away from me and stares out of the wall-to-ceiling glass window at the throng of people outside. I don't think she really sees them or the winking Christmas lights that adorn all the shop windows.

"I'm going to get myself admitted to the hospital."

It feels like someone has grabbed hold of my heart and is squeezing the life out of it. I press my hand against my chest and fight to breathe calmly.

"You're not sick."

"I've been taking antidepressants since Charley died," she says.

I gape at her. Why didn't I know that? She should have told me.

"A couple of months ago, the doctor prescribed me sleeping tablets as well."

I can't believe what I'm hearing. I knew she changed when Charley died. We all did. She was upset and neurotic about Chris and me. It took her months to go back to work. But I hadn't imagined she was depressed enough to take pills.

"You should have told me," I say.

"It's my job to worry about you, not the other way around." She finally moves one hand away from her bag to pinch the skin at the top of her nose. "I'm going to have myself admitted to the psychiatric ward." Her voice is so calm it sends an icy shiver trailing down my spine. "I need to get myself well, for you and Chris."

"You don't need to go to the hospital," I say through gritted teeth.

She pats my hand. "I do, Kim."

I shake my head. She doesn't. Gage made her withdraw the money and hand it out. She's not losing her mind.

"Please don't do this, Mum." Tears make their way down my cheeks. "Chris and I need you."

She stands, arranging her coat and bag in a neat fashion. "That's why I have to, Kim. I'll be home in a few days. Then everything will be better. I promise." She leans down and kisses me on the top of my head.

I want to grab her and scream at her not to leave us. Even if it is only for a few days, I don't want her to go. Especially not because of a lie. But she wouldn't believe the truth, so I have no choice but to watch her walk out the door and turn up the road, toward the hospital.

What else is Gage going to do to my family?

*

Chris is stuffing his face with a sandwich when I get home.

I sit down at the breakfast bar beside him and drop my head into my hands. My hair tumbles through my fingers. Mum's probably talking to doctors at the hospital right now. Dad is on his way here. I have to explain to Chris what's going on.

Sophie's even angrier with me and Matthew probably is, too. I don't think things could get any worse. I've never felt so alone. Not even when Charley died.

"What's up?" Chris says.

I raise my head and blink at him. I'm not used to him asking about my feelings. He takes another bite of his sandwich, destroying the illusion of concern.

"You're going to cry, aren't you?"

I shake my head, even though it's probably true. "Chris, we have to go stay with Dad for a couple of days."

His brow quivers. "Why?"

"Mum…" I can't find the words. How can I tell my kid brother our mum thinks she's losing her mind?

"It's because of me, isn't it?"

My eyebrows shoot up my forehead. "What? No. Why would you think that?"

He drops the half-eaten sandwich onto his plate, scattering crumbs and creamy globs of mayonnaise.

"Because of what I did yesterday." He lowers his head, probably hoping I can't see how red his eyes have become.

"It's not because of you," I say firmly. I sigh. "I don't want you to worry, but she's had to go to hospital for a few days."

His head jerks up and he stares at me with wide, sparkling eyes. "She's sick?"

"No." I splay my hands on the table. Why is it so hard to find words that aren't as blunt and insensitive as my last statement? "She hasn't been coping with Charley's death as well as she wanted us to think."

"So things happen to get too much the day after I steal some DVDs?" He jumps down, tipping his stool onto the floor with a loud clatter.

I grab his arm as he stalks past me toward the door. "It's not your fault, Chris."

He rips his arm away from me. "I'm going to pack."

I listen to the angry pound of his feet on the stairs and the loud slam of his door. I should pack, too, but all I can do is sit.

I press my palms against my eyes, allowing tears to overwhelm me. My sobs fill the air. My shoulders shake so hard my back muscles start to ache and my throat becomes raw.

There's a slight thud as the toppled stool is set right. I don't look up. I don't need to see Chris's hurt expression again.

"It'll be okay." Dad's voice.

His arms envelope me, drawing me to his chest as though I'm a small child. I cry against his dark shirt, letting him comfort me.

"I spoke to Mum before I came over."

I tilt my head up. My tears blur his face, so I can't make out his expression.

"She's positive."

"She checked herself into a psych ward. How can she be positive?"

He grips my shoulders and pushes me upright before brushing hair and tears away from my face with his large hands.

"The doctors will get her right again."

I shake my head. She doesn't need help from doctors. She needs Gage to be out of our lives forever.

But Gage didn't make her fall apart after Charley died. He didn't make her take pills. Getting rid of him isn't going to be a quick fix for Mum or the rest of my family. It won't erase the past year or the crazy things Gage made Mum and Chris do. I grit my teeth. I wish he were dead.

"Go get some clothes together," Dad says. "Even I know you don't have a great selection of stuff at my place." He winks and grins, which would normally be enough to make me smile or laugh.

Not even Dad can make me feel better this time.

"We'll stop off and grab some takeaway. I don't think either you or Chris would be up for dinner out?"

I shake my head. I don't need anyone to see me right now. I slip off the chair and pad upstairs, heading to the bathroom instead of my bedroom.

I turn on the hot tap and let it run for a few seconds before splashing water onto my puffy face. I stare at my reflection in the mirror, at the droplets of water running down my cheeks, the red and white blotches spattered across my face and the bright red veins marring the whites of my eyes.

It would be easy for people to pity me. Even Dad.

Poor Kim who lost her sister.

Poor Kim who's brother is acting out.

Poor Kim who's Mum is losing the plot.

I turn the tap off and slam my fist onto the edge of the sink. Pain darts through my hand and up my arm. Everything that's happened is Gage's fault.

"Kim? Are you almost ready?" Dad's voice is muffled. He's probably shouting from downstairs.

I dry my face and go to my room. I grab a few changes of clothes, my brush, and hairdryer and stuff them into a rucksack.

Chris is already downstairs, silently cleaning up the mess his sandwich made. He's careful not to make eye contact with Dad and I. Has he been crying, too?

"Let's go," Dad says. "I'm starving. What do you two fancy? Pizza? Chinese?"

I shrug. I'm sick of takeaway. We practically lived on it after Mum and Dad split up. It wasn't until this September that Mum really put any effort into cooking again.

"Indian," Chris says. He grabs his rucksack and heads to the front door.

Dad and I follow him. I let the rage I'm feeling toward Gage continue to build up inside me. What started as a gale of anger is slowly building in intensity into a tornado.

I open the car door and freeze. Matthew is a few feet away, arms folded across his chest. His expression is stern. His dark eyes beckon me to him. It's impossible to resist, even though I don't want to face him right now. I try to get into the car. He shakes his head, paralysing me. He must be angry with me if he's purposefully enthralling me.

I clear my throat. "Dad, I need to go and see Sophie. Can I catch you up later?"

Dad squints at me from the driver's seat. "I can drop you off."

"I'd rather walk."

"Are you sure?"

I nod and fake a small smile.

"Okay," he says. "You can reheat some food when you get in. Don't be too late."

I make the smile a little wider. "I won't."

I wait until Dad's car has turned round the corner, and then I take a deep breath and go back into the house, motioning for Matthew to follow me. Dread makes my insides cold and my empty stomach churn. For the first time since I met him, I wish Matthew would leave me alone.

CHAPTER SIXTEEN

I drop my rucksack in the hallway and head into the living room. Matthew stalks in after me. I sit on the sofa, tucking my feet beneath my bum and straighten my back to brace myself for whatever he's going to say. He leans against the doorframe, arms loosely folded, head tilted to the side.

"I'm not an idiot, Kim." His voice is steady, calm and completely unnerving.

I blink, unsure what he expects me to say to that.

"I could have caught Gage earlier and put a stop to what he's doing to your family. But you sent me the wrong way."

My stomach sinks. "No, I didn't."

He draws his eyebrows down. "Don't lie to me. You wanted to go after Gage on your own. Why?"

I swallow, but the painful lump in my throat doesn't dissipate.

He curls his hands into loose fists. "I trusted you, Kim."

"Are you trying to make me feel guilty?" I grab a cushion and hug it against my stomach, running my fingertips over the tatty tapestry threads. It was made by Charley in textile lessons at school. She hated the sight of it, but Mum insisted it have pride of place on the sofa.

"Do I need to?"

I bow my head, tucking my chin tightly against my chest.

"Why did you lie to me, Kim?"

"Isn't it obvious? The only way Gage can be here is if a human opened a gateway for him."

He smacks his fist against the doorframe, making the room shudder and me jump. "We talked about this."

"No. You talked. And then you used magic to knock me out." I lift my head in time to see his eyes narrow. "Sorry. You used your abilities. Words of power. Whatever. I didn't tell you because I didn't want you to get into trouble. I was protecting you."

He lifts his eyebrows. "Protecting me?"

"You're already pushing it, aren't you?" I toss the cushion aside, stand and stride toward him. "Letting AJ go. Befriending me. I didn't want to add anything else to the list."

I stop a couple of paces away from him, raising my chin so I'm staring him in the eyes. Big mistake. His dark gaze pulls me onto my tiptoes, and I tumble the last two steps forward. He grabs my shoulders and holds me fast. I want to twist away from him, but I'm paralysed, unable to do anything except pant shallow breaths.

"You want to believe that's the reason, don't you?" he says.

"It is."

He shakes his head. "It's because you didn't trust me to help you. Again." He growls the last word through his teeth.

He releases me and turns his face away. My knees sag, but I remain upright.

"I wanted to protect you," I say. "But yes, you're right, I didn't believe you'd help me. Your job is to capture the Baneem and take them to purgatory. When you caught Gage last year, you took him and left me." I slam my fists into his chest. "Gage tried to kill me and you left me." I hit him again, putting all my grief and fury behind the blows. "I needed you and you left me. I couldn't tell anyone what had happened." I clench my fist against my stomach. "I had to keep all the pain inside me. You left me because doing your job was more important than me. So, no, I didn't trust you to help me. You would have caught Gage and gone. Leaving me without any way of helping AJ. Leaving me without anyone to talk to. Again." I clench my teeth. "There's a part of me that will always hate you for that."

As soon as the words leave my lips, something within me unfurls and frees itself from my body, making me feel momentarily light. But then the weight of Matthew's crushed expression presses down upon me. The sad downward turn of his mouth, the deep creases above his eyebrows, and the spiralling darkness in his eyes force me to my knees.

"I wish you'd never walked into my life," I say. "Because everything that's gone wrong since that moment is because you opened my eyes."

Matthew's mouth quivers. For a second, I expect his eyes to brim with tears, but they don't. They can't.

"I should never have allowed you to see me," he says in his irritatingly calm voice. "That was a mistake, one I'm likely to regret for the rest of my existence. And I wish I could have stayed with you that night." He clenches his fists so hard his hands start to shake. "I wish I could have helped ease your pain. But you do not have the right to blame me for everything that's happened to you and the people around you."

I open my mouth to speak, but he cuts me off with a sharp shake of his head.

"I didn't make you look into your sister's death. I didn't make you investigate what was wrong with Sophie's family. I didn't make you lie to her, your family, or AJ."

Guilt stabs at my chest, making it hard to breathe. I want to speak, but I'm rendered dumb by the intensity of his angry stare.

"You don't give anyone a chance to prove themselves to you, Kim. You don't give anyone around you the opportunity to make decisions for themselves. You're not protecting anyone. You're pushing them away."

I wrap my arms around my stomach and tilt my head back so I can look at the tense angles of his face. I'm not sure what's worse, Matthew being angry with me or the fact he's right. I didn't even tell AJ everything.

I should apologise, but I hold the words inside my gut, twisting them and mixing them up into angry exclamations that I don't spit out. I breathe in and out deeply half a dozen times, trying to collect my thoughts. I don't want to argue with Matthew, but I can't tell him I'm sorry for the things I've said and done. He expects me to trust in him completely, but I can't because there's still so much I don't know or understand about him.

"Would you have helped me if I had told you why I wanted to speak to Gage?"

"Does it matter?"

"Of course it does. I need to know if I was right to cut you out."

His lips part and he shakes his head. "It wasn't right. It doesn't matter what I would have done. You should have trusted me."

"If it doesn't matter, tell me. Would you have helped me?"

He lifts his head a little, so shadows gather around his eyes. "No." His blunt reply punches me in the gut, making me gasp. "Gage cannot be trusted," he says.

I want to shut my ears to his reasons. I tell myself they're irrelevant, that nothing he can say will ease his betrayal.

"If he did lead you to someone who could open a gateway, I wouldn't let you go through. I would stop you from going to Uralahnd."

I shake my head and bring my fists down on my thighs hard. "Cut the big brother act. I don't need you to protect me. I don't need you deciding what I can and can't do. Going to Uralahnd is my decision."

"If you go to Uralahnd, you will die."

"That's my choice. It's my life."

Matthew throws his hands up and turns his back on me. "I'm done."

"What? You're losing an argument so you're going to run away? Coward." It's not the first time I've accused him of cowardice.

He shrugs. "Maybe I am. But you're not going to listen to me. You don't want to trust me. You want everything to be on your terms, so I'm done." He tilts his face toward the ceiling. "I can't work with you anymore."

"You're just going to walk out?"

"Yes."

"What about Gage? What about AJ?"

He glances over his shoulder. "I'll find Gage and get him out of your life. As for AJ..." His shoulders droop. "I wish I could help him, but he's beyond our reach. I'm sorry."

I shake my head. "I won't accept that."

"Then we really don't have anything else to talk about. Goodbye, Kim."

I let him walk out. I could call him back with an apology, but I don't.

When the front door clicks shut behind him, I drop to the floor and curl into a foetal position. I don't cry. The vacuum inside my chest has sucked all the tears up, leaving my eyes dry and sore. I feel empty. Drained.

CHAPTER SEVENTEEN

Phailin's worried expression hardens as she opens the door and sees me. She glances past me, her eyes filled with hope for the briefest of moments.

"Have you managed to get hold of anyone?" I say. "From when…" I look away and shuffle my feet.

She shakes her head. "Not yet."

"I tried to track someone down who might know about gateways, but…"

I suck in a breath. I shouldn't have come here. I've got no news and neither does she. If she did, she would have called me. Shoulders slumped, I turn to leave.

"Why don't you come in?"

I blink, hesitating, and raise my face. Phailin's expression has softened a little. Small creases have settled at the corners of her mouth and her eyebrows are raised in an inviting gesture.

"You look upset." She stands aside and holds her flat palm sideways. "Come inside."

I'm not sure why she's suddenly being nice to me, but my only other option is to go to Dad's and pretend everything's okay.

I go inside. Phailin motions for me to go into the sitting room while she heads to the kitchen. I sit on the sofa, threading my fingertips together. I'm glad I've left my coat on because the heating isn't on. Warmth has fled the small flat, leaving it a chilly shell. I look up and smile as Phailin hands me a cup of water. She sits in the armchair, leaning forward onto her knees as she twitches the corner of her mouth into an affected smile.

"What's wrong?"

"I'm missing AJ." I take a sip of the water and then put the glass down on the carpet.

"It's more than that." She purses her lips. "I've spent sixteen years lying to people, Kim."

I shrug my shoulders. "Why do you care?" I don't mean for my voice to be as sharp as it is.

She sighs and leans back, pressing her palms against her flat stomach. "It's a fair question." Her gaze drifts upward to the ceiling. The plaster is cracked and flaking, uncared for like the rest of the flat. "Right now, you're the only connection I have to my son. If…" She parts her lips and runs her tongue over her exposed teeth. "When he comes back, he'd be angry if he found out I turned you away when you were upset."

When. There was no conviction in her voice.

"Besides, I could use the company." She clenches her jaw, making her neck muscles rigid. "All I've done since you left yesterday is listen to out-of-service tones. All I can think about is Aran and what…" She wipes her hand over her mouth and nose. "What the Baneem are doing to him."

My muscles twitch. I want to go to her and hug her, but I know she'd push me away.

"What's wrong?" Her expression turns into a hard glare, daring me to refuse to answer her truthfully.

I draw in a shuddering breath. "The Baneem responsible for my sister's death is back."

She leans forward.

Tears spill from my eyes. "I thought I could get him to tell me who opened a gateway for him."

"You tried to take on a Baneem on your own? That was foolish, Kim."

I narrow my eyes. "I've already have a lecture from Matthew. I don't need one from you as well." I shuffle back on the sofa, hugging my knees to my chest. "I'm sorry. Everything's so messed up. Matthew said I was pushing people away."

"That's what happens when you have to lie to people every day."

A choke splutters out of me. "Are you trying to make me feel better or worse?"

She slips off the armchair and comes to sit beside me. "I'm sorry. It's been a long time since I've had a heart to heart with anyone."

"Even AJ?"

"All we've done recently is argue."

"About me." I feel sick. I want to run out of the door, but the weight of my guilt pins me to the sofa.

Phailin rubs her forehead with her thumb and forefinger. "I don't want to argue with you, Kim. I'm too tired to fight. I just want my son back."

I twiddle my thumbs round one another, unsure what to say. I'd love to give her reassurances that we'll find AJ and that everything will be okay, but I don't believe it. Besides, as she took pains to remind me, I'm just a kid. She should be the one telling me it will all work out.

"You argued with Matthew?"

I nod and drop my head into my hands. "I blamed him for everything that's happened, but it's not his fault. It's mine. I pushed Matthew away. I pushed Sophie away. I'm lying to my family and now Mum thinks depression is driving her mad and my kid brother thinks he's a shoplifter. I…" I bite down hard on my lower lip, forbidding the rest of the words from escaping my mouth: I let AJ believe he was safe, even though I knew he wasn't.

My shoulders and back convulse as tears flood down my cheeks. I start coughing and choking and hiccupping all at the same time, which makes me feel like I'm going to throw up over the dingy burgundy carpet.

Phailin picks up the glass of water and presses it gently against my quivering lips. "Take sips," she says soothingly. "It'll help."

I take the glass from her and take short sips while she uses her palm to firmly rub my lower back.

"Matthew said he'd stop me from going to Uralahnd," I say once I've recovered.

Phailin takes the glass away and puts it back down on the floor. "He cares about you." She puts her arm around my shoulders and pulls me into an embrace. "You shouldn't be angry with him for wanting to keep you safe."

I try to pull away, but her grip is too firm and my actions are too half-hearted. "Are you going to stop me?"

"No. I don't understand why you'd be willing to risk your life for a boy you barely know, but it's not my place to stop you."

I want to tell her that I do know AJ. That I love him. That even though he's only been in my life for three months, it feels like forever. But she'd laugh away my words and remind me my emotions for him only feel deep because of my age. It's only half the reason why I have to save him. I can't tell her how guilty I feel or this brief moment of connection between us will be smashed into tiny pieces of anger.

"If I…we do get Aran back…" She breathes in a deep, shuddering breath. "You must know we'll have to run, Kim. We won't be able to stay. You and Aran will be over."

I stare at the carpet. I've lost count of the number of times AJ and I snuggled up together in this room while his mum was out at work. The times we kissed and held each other, fooling ourselves into believing he could stay and we could be together.

"I know."

"To be honest, I'm glad I'm not searching for him alone," she says. "I'm not strong enough to go to Uralahnd on my own."

"Yes, you are."

She shakes her head. "I'm not strong at all, Kim. Look at me. I'm falling apart." She lets me go and stands. "You should probably go home. Your parents will be worried about you."

I don't move. I don't want to go to Dad's house. He needs to be focused on Mum and Chris, not me.

"Can I stay here? Just for one night?"

She pinches her mouth into a frown. "I don't think that's a good idea, Kim."

"Please?"

A sigh seeps through her barely parted lips. "Fine. But I can only offer you the sofa. We don't exactly have a spare room."

"The sofa's great." I guess she doesn't want me to sleep in AJ's room.

She nods and leaves the room. While she's gone, I pull out my phone and send a text to Dad: *Staying at Sophie's tonight. See you after school tomorrow.* Another lie. If Sophie finds out, it'll give her more ammunition to fuel her anger toward me.

Phailin comes back with a blanket and a pillow. She drops them onto the sofa beside me.

"Thank you," I say.

She shrugs.

"We will find AJ, won't we?"

Her mouth quivers. "I hope so, Kim. I really hope so."

CHAPTER EIGHTEEN

I'm not done fighting.

I throw my weight forward the second Flame Guy and his surly pal lead me out onto the veranda. I ignore the loud pop as my shoulder wrenches free of its socket. The brutes stumble and fall, releasing me in order to save themselves from crashing onto their faces, and I let myself drop into a tumble. Pain makes my teeth chatter as I scramble to my feet and run. I jump over the edge of the veranda into the courtyard. My ankle twists, but doesn't snap. Hobbling, I keep going across the lush green grass, haunted by the sound of Saul's amused laughter.

I've barely reached the babbling fountain when a great weight crashes into my back. I slam forward against the stone, striking my chin. The metallic tang of blood floods my mouth. Water sprays onto my face. I'm pretty sure I only got this far because they let me. Any shred of hope I had that I could get away is sucked into the gathering darkness of my magic as it heals me.

I'm pulled up and turned round to face Saul. He grips my face, digging his fingertips and thumb into my cheeks.

"Don't pass out," he says through gritted teeth.

My body trembles with the onslaught of pins and needles, and my eyes threaten to roll back.

"Fight it," he says. "Learn how to master your magic rather than allowing it to overpower you."

"Why?" I spit out the word, projecting blood onto his cheek.

He flicks it away with his free hand. "I need you to have control of your magic if you're to be of any use to me."

"I won't help you." My voice sounds muffled. The edges of my vision are starting to fade to black.

He digs his fingertips harder into the hollows of my cheeks. "You need to stay awake."

I don't want to, but his grip keeps me teetering on the edge of consciousness. The stench of burning rubber floods my nostrils. I'm unable to breathe. I try to gasp, but all I can do is emit a strangled grunt from my throat.

"Fight it, or I will bring you to the edge of death again and again until you master your magic." Saul releases me.

Air floods back into my lungs.

"Help Aran sort out his arm."

The brutes adjust their grip on me. Flame Guy gives me an apologetic smile as he takes my useless arm and holds it straight. The other wraps his arms around my torso, so I can't move. I bite down hard on my tongue as they pop my shoulder back into place. It doesn't stop a scream erupting from my chest. Saul holds up two fingers and flicks them down. In response, my captors release me. I drop to the floor and crash onto my knees. Saul crouches down beside me.

"Now fight it."

The lull of unconsciousness is so strong as it tries to drag me beneath ice cold waves. My body is heavy, my muscles tired. All I want to do is give in and sleep, but I know he'll punish me. I clench my fists and drive them against the damp grass so I can push my upper body up. I grit my teeth until my jaw and temples ache from the pressure, and I lift my eyebrows, forcing my eyelids to stay open. Nausea sweeps over me, but I manage to swallow it down so I don't lose the pathetic amount of food they've given me.

Every part of my body shakes, making things around me tremble and jump.

"Good boy." A smile touches Saul's lips. "You know, it really is interesting how much of a toll healing takes on you. Maybe it's because your human side makes you weak."

"I'd rather be weak than like you."

He chuckles. "Still putting up a fight. When will you learn you can't win, Aran? It would be easier if you gave in."

I glare at him through narrowed eyes. I won't give in. I channel my hatred toward Saul into keeping myself awake, but it's not enough. I need another diversion. My gaze drops to the grass and my brow crumples.

"The grass was dead before." My voice is distorted by the chattering of my teeth. "How is it possible?"

It's not just the grass that's suddenly healthy—large white flowers have blossomed, framing the veranda.

"Why do you care?" Saul asks.

"If you want me to stay awake, humour me."

Chuckling, Saul bends down and rips a handful of grass tips up. He spreads his fingers wide, allowing the grass to flutter away in the breeze. I frown. There's a breeze. Last time I was out here, the air was stiflingly hot. Now it's almost pleasant. My eyes widen as the grass tips vanish.

"Everything you see is created by my will," Saul says. "I can make my small portion of Uralahnd as beautiful as I want. I can bend it to my will. But when I'm not here, it withers. You were wrong, Aran, when you assumed I'd let it fall to ruin."

I swallow hard, taking in his words. It's hard to make sense of them when I'm still swaying toward unconsciousness. It's the first time I've managed to keep my head above water for any length of time while regenerating, but I need to stay lucid enough to ask my questions.

The effort saps my strength. My arms give way as a wave crashes over me, pulling me down. My cheek strikes the grass. For a second, I'm suspended in darkness. It would be so easy to give in and let it overwhelm me. I dig my fingertips into the dirt and force myself up again, gasping as I break the surface. I'm even more exhausted than I was seconds before.

"Why would you want to leave?" I have to pant the words out.

"Because it's too easy." He grins at me. "Are you done? Adele is waiting for us."

"Too easy?"

"There's no challenge to living. We can have everything we want when we want it. It's hell."

It sounds more like heaven to me.

"But on Earth, we will be treated like gods."

I shudder as I remember our last conversation: He wants to rule humanity and I'm part of his insane plan.

The last shred of pain flits away from my body. Slowly, normal sensation returns to my limbs, starting from my toes and spreading up through my body. I feel no less tired, but unconsciousness is no longer tugging at my heels. I roll onto my back and allow myself to breathe in and out deeply, hardly able to believe I fought the side effects of my magic.

The brutes don't give me more than a couple of seconds to revel in my achievement before they drag me to my feet again.

"You'd better hope you can do that again," Saul says. "Someone's life is depending on it."

*

I have no choice but to let myself get dragged to the room with the altar. This time, there's no scenic route via the massive staircase to view more of Uralahnd. I remember what it looked like outside of the compound: little pockets of life surrounded by desert. If it was as easy to change and mould this place as Saul wanted me to believe, why isn't everywhere teeming with life?

I don't have time to work it out.

When we enter the room, my gaze is immediately drawn to a snivelling huddle in the corner of the room. I can't immediately tell how old the person is or even what gender they are. I can see long blond hair, matted into dreadlocks. They're wearing a waxed jacket, which is so caked in mud it's almost impossible to tell it's supposed to be green. I can just see the soles of odd-sized trainers. This isn't a person anyone is going to miss. Not anymore, anyway.

I'm transferred solely into Flame Guy's grip while the other thug strides to the corner and hauls the figure up. It's a girl, with frightened brown eyes and tear tracks cutting through the dirt smeared all over her face.

"You really want to put my soul in that?"

I turn toward the new voice, even though Flame Guy's strong grip sends a spasm of pain up my arm and into my neck. A young woman stands in the doorway beside Adele. Her dark hair frames a pretty, narrow face, accentuating piercing blue eyes. Her weight is thrown onto one leg and her full lips are pursed in an almost provocative manner. There's a haughty air about her as she places her hands on her hips.

"And I presume he's the one that's going to keep me alive." She flattens her lips into a tight smile. "Shall we get on with it?"

"He will keep you alive, Stella," Saul says. "You have my word."

Adele slips into the room, jerking her arm in a signal to the thug holding the frightened girl. My chest constricts as she's hauled to the altar and thrown onto it. Her sobs become louder, filling the small room as she struggles uselessly against the thug's grip.

"Remember this is an experiment," Adele says. "We need to find out how long a Baneem soul can remain in a human body."

"Your body," Stella says, pointing at the girl.

"Please don't hurt me. Please don't hurt me." The girl repeats it over and over, her wild brown eyes fixing on each of us in turn. When she pins me in her gaze, a painful lump forms in my throat. As much as I don't want to help Saul, I can't let this girl die either.

Adele beckons to Stella. The young woman doesn't hesitate in moving to stand at the end of the altar by the girl's head.

"Don't do this." I know none of them will listen to my plea any more than they're listening to the girl.

I shut my eyes and bow my head, almost gagging as the stench of rotting fish floods the room. I can't close my ears to the girl's screams. They're loud and piercing at first, shrieking into my eardrums with an intensity that makes them feel like they're about to burst. Then they start to fade into gurgling sobs, which are cut off like someone has thrown an off-switch on her lungs. A dull thud comes from the left and in front of me.

I'm wrenched from Flame Guy's grip by the scruff of my neck and pushed forward until I hit the altar.

"Heal them," Saul says.

I open my eyes. Stella's body is on the floor. The girl is still lying on the altar, but she's grinning at me.

"This body is so heavy." It's the girl's voice, but Stella's attitude. She lifts up one shaking hand and then the other. "And it's broken inside. Fix it. And then fix my body. It hurt to get dragged out of there and stuffed in here."

I remember the pain and the amount of damage that was caused to my body. It makes me feel nauseous just thinking about it. I take a breath and lay my hand over the girl's, pulling the damage her body has taken onto my own. It's more than I expected. Gasping, I drop to my knees, clutching the edge of the altar in an effort to stay upright and not plummet into unconsciousness.

"Stay awake," Saul's voice whispers beside my ear. "Like I taught you."

I clench my teeth. He didn't teach me anything. He forced me to learn. There's a difference.

"Heal Stella's body," he says.

I don't move. It's difficult enough to breathe evenly and not pass out. Saul grabs my shirt and drags me the couple of feet to Stella's limp body.

I run my tongue over my cracked lips, tasting blood. "Why isn't she awake?"

"A human soul isn't powerful enough to animate a Baneem body," Adele says. "But the soul will be strong enough to keep Stella's body alive so long as you heal it quickly. She'll sleep until she's switched back."

"If you don't heal the body, they'll both die," Saul says. "Do you want the girl's death on your conscience?"

I don't. I grip Stella's hand. Black spots swim before my vision, and I cry out as pain wracks my insides. My stomach convulses and I choke blood onto the floor between us. Painful tingling consumes my body. Saul's boot connects with my shoulder, but I barely feel it or the flagstones as I topple onto them.

"Recover quickly," Saul says, standing over me.

My eyelids flicker. It's impossible to fight the darkness, so I don't.

*

Cold water trickles over my face, slowly bringing me back from the darkness. I open my eyes a fraction. I'm flat on my back, staring at a yellow ochre ceiling and Saul's face.

"You're needed," he says.

Something smacks against my foot, jolting my ankle joint. I raise myself up on my elbows. I'm still plagued by pins and needles and I can feel damage scratching at my insides. The room swims around me and a thumping pain presses against my skull. Saul grabs my arm, drags me to my feet and pushes me so I'm leaning against the altar, staring right at the girl. Stella has sat the girl up.

"Heal me," she says, fear lacing her voice. Burns mar her face, creating a patchwork of glistening red and black sores. She's trembling as she holds her hands up for me to see. They're just as bad. "Heal me. This started inside. This body is dying. I'm dying."

I don't care about Stella, but I can't let the girl die. Stella's soul is burning through the girl's body, just as Adele said it would. How long was I unconscious for? Minutes? Hours? I glance over my shoulder to the door. It's still light outside, or maybe it's light again. I don't know. I'm not even sure I can heal her. She has to have sustained as much damage as Kim did when she was shot and it took me days to recover from that. I was strong then, this time I'm still healing myself.

"Heal me," Stella shrieks.

She grabs my wrist. My magic jumps into her, coursing through the body she's squatting in, pulling every shred of damage into me. It burns me. Lesions break out on my skin. I'm blinded by blood dripping from my eyes. The only thing I can smell is the metallic tang of the blood flowing from my nose. My legs sag and I crash to the ground.

CHAPTER NINETEEN

My neck aches as I wake up. It takes me a moment to remember why I'm laying crunched up with springs digging into my hip. I slept on Phailin's sofa. I sit bolt upright. Although the orange curtains are closed, they're thin enough for me to see it's still dark outside. I glance at my watch. It's barely seven. Phailin's voice filters through the sitting room door.

"I don't know. Four or five hours? Maybe six. It depends on when the trains are."

My brow crumples. Where is she planning on going?

"I'll be there."

I stand and make my way to the door, freezing with my hand on the handle. I can't storm out of the small sitting room and confront her, not after last night. For the first time, I felt like there was a chance we might get along.

I stagger back as the door opens inward, almost bashing me in the face. I turn and comb my messy hair with my fingertips, trying to pretend I wasn't listening in. Phailin's gaze flicks up and down me. Her lips draw into a tight line.

"Someone I used to know is willing to meet me."

I gape at her as my heart hammers against my chest. I have to swallow multiple times before I'm able to speak. "Do they know how to open a gateway?"

"Yes. Whether they'll tell me or not is another matter. I have to go. It's a long trip and you need to get ready for school."

My jaw becomes slack. "School? I'm not going to school. I'm coming with you."

She shakes her head firmly. "No." She begins pulling her dark hair back into a ponytail. "Look, this could be a dead end—or worse, a trap. You need to stay here and act like everything's normal."

"But it's not."

She uses her teeth to tug a hairband off her wrist and starts drawing her hair through it. "Maybe not, but whatever the outcome of my meeting, you will have to carry on with your life. You can't keep skipping school."

"You sound like Mum."

She arches an eyebrow. "And right now you sound like a brat."

I fold my arms and turn away. She's right. A little of the anger slips away from me as Phailin rubs my upper arms.

"I will let you know what happens and when I'm coming back. I'll probably be gone overnight, so don't worry or panic if I don't call tonight. All right?"

I nod, even though it isn't okay. I've already pushed Matthew and Sophie away. I can't do the same to Phailin. I can't let her cut me out of helping her find AJ. If her contact does remind her how to open a gateway, she will have all the power.

"I just want to help."

"I know you do."

I turn round. "I know you don't believe it, but I do love AJ."

She pulls me into an embrace. "It doesn't matter what I believe." She rubs my arms again as she pushes me away.

"What does school think is wrong with AJ?"

She shrugs. "Nothing."

"He's on the edge of getting kicked out."

Phailin's icy stare silences me. I catch the tip of my tongue between my teeth.

"I'm sorry," I say. "I wasn't thinking. I know you'll both leave as soon as we get AJ back."

I follow her as she stalks into the hallway and grabs her coat and handbag. "I'm sorry, too, Kim. I'm sorry you'll have to say goodbye to someone you care about. I'm glad you're willing to help me despite that."

I press my lips together, unable to think of anything to say. My heart aches, but deep down I knew I'd be saving AJ to give him up.

*

I raise my eyebrows as Sophie hovers by my desk in form. I motion for her to sit down, but she shakes her head. Her lips are pressed into a thin line. She's still angry with me.

"Did you stay at your dad's house last night?" she says. "You got off a different bus."

My jaw slackens. I'm surprised she noticed. "Mum's in the hospital." I'm not going to explain I went to Dad's to get changed after leaving Phailin's flat.

"Because of what happened yesterday?"

I nod.

"I'm so sorry. Is she going to be okay?"

I shrug. "I think she will be."

I play with my bag strap, running it back and forth through my fingertips. I can't stop thinking about Phailin. She'll still be on a train. I hope her old friend can show her how to open a gateway.

Sophie slips into her normal chair. "You could have called me." Her voice is soft, with no trace of anger. "Or sent a text to let me know what was going on. I would have listened."

I turn my face away and fix my gaze on the playing fields outside the window. The short grass is covered in a thick layer of frost, which sparkles beneath the low glare of the sun.

"Do the doctors know what's wrong with your mum?"

I suck in my quivering lower lip. If I talk about it, I'm going to cry. Besides, I can't trust myself not to blurt out the truth anymore. I want my best friend back, but I can't shatter her illusions about the world in the way Matthew destroyed mine. I know what it's done to me. I won't do it to her. I don't care what Matthew thinks. I am keeping silent to protect her. Aren't I?

"Kim, I hate fighting with you."

I twitch my mouth into a smile. "Does that mean we can hug and make up?"

"Yes."

Relief bubbles up into a massive sigh.

"If you're going to tell me what's going on."

I sink down in my chair, and the bubbles threaten to trickle out of my eyes as tears. The shrill school bell rings. Sophie puts her hand over mine and squeezes slightly.

"I'll go to the memorial garden at lunch time," she says. "If you're ready to talk, meet me there. Okay?"

I don't answer. Sophie sighs and hitches her bag onto her shoulder as she stands.

"I don't know what's going on with you, Kim, but I do know you never used to lie to me or keep things from me. Why can't you see I want to help you?"

"It's not that simple," I mutter.

"Yes, it is."

She lingers for a couple of seconds before turning and joining the stream of students heading out of the door. I don't move. I press my hands over my face and take a couple of shuddering breaths. I can't turn up at Chemistry in tears. School is the last place I want to be. I should have made Phailin take me with her. Or I should be looking for Gage. I have to find him before Matthew does. Most of all I need someone to talk to. Someone who knows about magic, not-angels, and AJ.

"Kim, are you all right?"

I force myself to lower my hands so I can look up at my form tutor. "Yes, just tired."

He sits on the edge of the desk and rests his hands over his thigh. "You're not staying up late playing video games, are you?"

I smile thinly. "I think you're mistaking me with my brother. I didn't sleep well last night, that's all."

I don't want to mention Mum. Dad told me he'd call the school at some point today to fill them in. No doubt once word gets round the teaching staff they'll look at me with concern and check I'm okay, even though it's obvious I'm not.

"Well, if you're sure you're all right, you'd better get to your first lesson."

I gather up my bag and wander past him, out of the classroom.

The corridors are still busy with students dragging their feet, not wanting to get to lessons. Normally I'd be one of the keener kids, moving along at a swift pace—especially to get to chemistry—but it's not the same without AJ here.

I could talk to my chemistry teacher, Miss Jenkins. She knows about magic. She almost died because her family—Sophie's family—couldn't keep up their end of the bargain they'd made with Taylor. Or Taylor's father. Or maybe even his grandfather. I dismiss the idea. She doesn't know I helped save her life. I'd be better off talking to Sophie's father, except he's the last person I want to be around. I've pretty much avoided going round to Sophie's house since he shot me. Even if I could pretend everything was all right around him, I'm not sure he could do the same around me. It was all I could do to convince him not to turn himself into the police.

There's only one person I can talk to: Phailin. But she's heading farther away from me by the second.

*

Sophie is waiting in the memorial garden when I arrive. She's sitting on Charley's bench, eating a sandwich, huddled in her coat, with a cheerful red scarf around her neck, matching gloves and a hat. Her caramel hair peeps out from beneath it. I can't make myself go any closer to her. Her back is half-turned to me. I doubt she even knows I'm here.

I want to confide in her, but all the excuses I've used to justify lying to her still stand. If I tell her about magic, it will destroy her world. If I tell her about magic, I'll put her in danger. If I tell her about magic, she might find out about her father's broken bargain with a Baneem. I don't want to hurt her like that, but I'm sick and tired of being alone and having no one to talk to. I want to be able to tell someone how much I miss

AJ, say words I could never say to Phailin without wanting to curl up and die of embarrassment.

I take a step back, ready to leave the garden, but Sophie turns and catches sight of me in the same instant. She smiles and waves. Even from this distance, I can see the spark of hope in her green eyes, hope that I'll confide in her and our friendship will be healed. My chest flutters as I stride quickly toward her.

"You came." She smiles brightly at me as she pushes her half-eaten sandwich back into its brown paper bag. She pats the seat beside her. "Let's talk."

I shake my head.

Her eyebrows twitch together in confusion. "Kim?"

"You're right, something is going on with me, but I can't tell you what." I swallow hard. "So I guess that means we can't be friends anymore." The words burn my throat.

Sophie's eyes sparkle. She blinks several times, but a couple of defiant tears slip down her cheeks. "What?"

"We can't be friends anymore."

She shakes her head. "You don't mean that." She stands and takes hold of my hands, clutching them so hard she pushes my bones and tendons together. I don't try hard enough to pull away, but I don't meet her desperate gaze either. "Kim, we've been best friends for five years."

I don't need to be reminded. I sniff back my own tears and raise my face skyward. The winter breeze chaps my cheeks and lips and stings my damp eyes.

"Things change."

"No, they don't. Not so much, so quickly. Tell me what's going on." Her grip tightens and she tilts her head to the side. "Where's AJ?"

"He's sick," I say through gritted teeth.

"Stop lying to me."

I rip my hands from hers. "Fine. He's gone. He left." More lies. Not that it matters anymore. I turn my back on her.

"Why didn't you tell me?" She touches my shoulder and tries to pull me round, but I shrug her away. "But that's not why you're throwing away our friendship, is it?"

I hunch my shoulders.

"That's crazy, Kim. You've lost AJ, and I'm really sorry about that. You know how much I liked him. But why would you take it out on me?"

I spin on my heel. "You're right. I'm crazy." I shout the words in her face. "Why has it taken you this long to see it? I'm the girl who lost her mind. It's what everyone else thinks."

"I never thought that." Her voice is quiet, wobbling on the brink of tears. "I always stood by you. Why are you doing this, Kim?"

I clench my teeth and my hands. I will not let my resolve waiver, no matter how much it hurts me. No matter how much I have to hurt Sophie.

"The only reason I still hang around with you is because you were pathetic enough to stay friends with me, which makes you a bigger loser than I'll ever be."

She gapes at me, shaking her head in disbelief. "Kim…"

"Seriously, you don't need me as a friend, Sophie. Why don't you just go and buy yourself some new ones with your daddy's money?"

She sinks onto the bench, hand pressed against her chest. "Go away."

"Has it sunk in yet? We're not friends anymore. You threw an ultimatum at me and this is what you get."

She snaps her head round to face me. "Go away." Anger flares her nostrils and ignites sparks in her eyes.

I take a step back. She begins to cry, her sobs escaping her violently. I turn and walk swiftly to the gated entrance to the garden. When I reach it, I glance back. She's buried her face in her hands. Tears trickle down my cheeks. I never wanted to hurt her. I never wanted to be so cruel. Why didn't she listen when I told her we couldn't be friends?

I cover my mouth with my hand to smother my own sobs. None of this is Sophie's fault. It's all mine. Matthew was right—I'm pushing everyone away. I leave the garden and Sophie behind. For the first time, I understand the gaping loneliness that Matthew and AJ must both feel. It leaves me feeling hollow and sick, like someone has carved my insides out with a melon scoop. I hate it. I hate myself.

*

A family meal is the last thing I need, but it's hard to refuse when Dad is being so insistent. Besides, there's nothing I can do until Phailin calls or until Gage shows his face again. Assuming Matthew hasn't already caught him and hauled him back to purgatory.

I sit with Dad and Chris in our local Pizza Hut, glancing at my watch every few seconds and my phone almost as frequently. I wish Phailin would call. She must have met her contact by now. There must be news.

"Do you need to be somewhere?" Dad asks.

I shake my head and scoop up a slice of pizza. I sink my teeth into the gooey mixture of cheese, pepperoni, and ham so I don't have to enter into a conversation about why I'm so preoccupied and anxious.

Chris picks at his food. Normally he'd scoff a pizza so fast you'd think he'd inhaled it.

"So," Dad says. "What do you two want first: the good news or the great news?"

I finish chewing my mouthful of pizza and swallow it a little too quickly in my hurry to answer his question. It feels like a chunk gets lodged in my throat, so I sip at my lemonade until the feeling passes. I'm surprised Chris doesn't beat me to answering, but he barely even looks up.

"The great news," I say. We need something to cheer our family up.

Dad grins as he reaches across and ruffles Chris's hair. Chris ducks away, curling his upper lip.

"I heard from the police today," Dad says in a low voice. "The record store isn't going to press any charges."

My chest momentarily feels weightless, as though I'm in a roller coaster that's just careened down the first big dip.

"That's fantastic news," I say. "It looks like my brilliant letter-writing skills paid off."

Chris isn't smiling.

"What's up?"

He shrugs. "I still did it though."

My expression droops and my jaw drops. I slide across the bench seat so I'm right next to him and hug him. He fights against me, pushing his palm against my chest, but I hold him so tightly he can't break free. I want to take his guilt and confusion away, but I don't know how. I can't turn the clock back or make him forget the entire episode. I can't explain to him it wasn't his fault, that Gage made him take those DVDs. So I just hold him, because Mum's not here to do it for me.

He manages to slip out of my grasp and edges away, his mouth drooping into a sour U.

"We're in public," he says. But even though his voice and his expression both tell me he hates me for making such a fuss in the middle of a restaurant, his eyes are grateful.

"It was a one-off," Dad says. "A momentary lapse of judgment. You've both been through a lot over the last couple of years. The record store understood that." He pats Chris on the shoulder. "You're not going to do it again, are you?"

Chris slumps down on the bench and hunches his shoulders. "No."

"Draw a line under it then," Dad says. "You don't need to dwell on it. It's in the past."

Chris nods, but still doesn't smile. It's going to take more than words to make him feel better about it. I clench my fist under the table. I won't let Gage get away with hurting my little brother.

"What's the good news?" I say.

"I spoke to Mum today. She's feeling a lot better. The doctors have put her on new medication. She sounded really positive."

I wish I'd been able to speak to her, and from the glum look on Chris's face, I'm sure he feels the same way.

"They're going to keep her in for a few days, and then she's going to stay at Aunt Sarah's until she's feeling herself again." Dad pauses and glances at each of us, his mouth forming a crooked line. "Is that okay with you two? Obviously you'll stay with me."

"Sure," Chris says.

I hesitate. "I'm glad Mum's feeling better," I say, carefully formulating the words in my mind before I speak them out loud. "I love spending time with you, Dad, but I think I'd rather stay at home." I hold my breath, waiting for his response.

His eyes widen a fraction, and then he blows a breath over his lower lip. "Why?"

I'm unprepared for that question. I was expecting him to say I wasn't old enough to be alone, even though I'm seventeen.

"Is it to spend more time with AJ?"

Chris rolls his eyes. "Gross." He covers his ears with his hands and mutters the words to a song beneath his breath.

I can't help but smile at him, but it quickly fades away. "AJ's gone."

I might as well give him the same story I gave Sophie. Even if Phailin and I do save him, he's not going to be a part of my life anymore.

"Gone?"

Obviously, I'll need to say more to sate his curiosity. "His mum got a job somewhere else. London, I think. They left on Sunday."

He whistles. "I'm sorry. Why didn't you say anything?"

I twist my half-eaten slice of pizza around the plate. "There was too much going on." I glance at Chris, sorry to involve him in my lie. "Anyway, I thought I'd stay at home because the peace and quiet would be good for studying, that's all."

Dad nods, before lifting his shoulders to his ears in a slow shrug. "I get it," he says. "I'm glad you're taking your exams so seriously."

"Thanks, Dad." That was much easier than I thought it was going to be. I lean across and pry Chris's hands away from his ears. "You can listen now. No more boy talk."

He sticks his tongue out at me and then takes a massive bite of pizza. At least he's getting his appetite back. I settle back in the booth and continue eating as Dad engages us both in small talk. For a little while at least, I want to enjoy the sense of normality that comes with being with my family.

My phone vibrates in my pocket. I pull it out and quickly scan the text message Phailin has sent from AJ's phone: I have what we need. Meet me at the flat after school tomorrow. We'll find him, I promise.

I smother a smile by taking a gulp of Coke. Between Chris getting let off, Mum improving, and Phailin's news, things are finally going right. Maybe once all this is over, I'll be able to find a way to make things right with Sophie and Matthew as well.

CHAPTER TWENTY

I'm still cut up inside from healing the girl when they come for me again, even though they locked me in a different room— one not lined with obsidian.

"Tell Saul I'm not fully healed," I say.

Flame Guy looks me up and down, his expression hesitant. His crony shakes his head and laughs.

"You look fine to me. Get up."

I don't. "The damage is on the inside."

He shrugs. "Not our problem, kid. Saul says you're needed, so here we are. Get up."

"Maybe we should tell Saul," Flame Guy says. "He looks pale. I don't think he's lying."

"So? We both know Saul's not gonna care." He kicks my knee, like it's going to compel me to get up. "I'm still waiting. Why are you keeping me waiting?"

I pinch my mouth into a snarl. This guy's attitude toward me is ice cold. A memory of reading super-hero comic books during endless train journeys flashes into my mind. This guy's no Bobby Drake, but Ice Man is a good enough nickname for him.

"Get up," he hisses.

I make a pretence of trying to stand but allow my legs to slip out from beneath me. I stare at them both, hoping one of them sees sense. Even if they do, it'll only delay the inevitable. Adele will still switch Stella's soul with that girl's. Saul will still expect me to keep them both alive and I'll still try for the girl's sake. What's her name? I stare at my hands. My fingers are twitching in a demented dance from the pins and needles plaguing them. I wish it was more obvious I'm not strong enough to do as much healing as…yesterday? The day before? I hate not knowing how much time has passed.

Ice Man grabs my elbow and pulls me up, half-tossing me into Flame Guy's grip. I hang between them for a second before making a feeble attempt to slip out of their arms. It doesn't work. Nothing will.

I let myself drift as they drag me to the altar room. I could refuse to heal either of them, but I'm sure Saul will kill the girl to prove to me resistance is futile. A grimace spreads across my face. Another pop culture reference. From superheroes to Star Trek. I'm clawing the barrel of desperation to try to make myself feel better, to somehow diminish the hopelessness of my situation. I don't want to help Saul, but I might as well be a puppet in his hands.

"Are you feeling better now?" Ice Man asks as he pushes the door to the altar room open.

My insides turn to acid as I see Mum. Two men, similar to my own captors in height and bulk, hold her at the far side of the room. She stands tall, chin tilted into the air, but the right hand side of her face is swollen and her lip is bloody. A dark purple bruise surrounds her eye like a grizzly tattoo.

Saul grabs the collar of my filthy tunic, wrenches me away from my captors, and pushes me into the room. I crash into the altar, which is now the only thing between me and Mum.

"I haven't recovered." The words blurt out of my mouth in a desperate plea.

"You will heal her," Saul says, "or she will die. I'm sure you'll find the strength from somewhere."

Mum refuses to catch my stare. She lifts her head higher and turns it away from me, so all I can see is the battered half of her face. Saul wraps his arm around my shoulder and jostles me in what should be a friendly fatherly gesture. In reality, it makes my body shudder and my gut convulse.

"Isn't this a lovely family reunion?" he says. "Don't you have anything to say to each other?"

Mum stares at him. A gurgling sound rumbles in her throat, and then she spits at him. The glob of spit lands on the floor.

"So much hostility, Phailin. Didn't you miss me?"

"Go to hell," she says.

Saul shifts his grip so his hand is clutching the back of my neck. "All right, if you don't want to chat, let's get straight down to business, shall we?" He turns to one of the brutes behind us. "Fetch Adele and Stella. Tell them we're ready." He cocks his head and fixes his stare on Mum again. "There's no sense in delaying any further, is there?"

"Don't do this," I say. My voice comes out as a frightened squeak. "Please don't. I'm not healed…"

He pulls me round and pushes me so my lower back is pressed against the edge of the altar. "I don't care. I knew you'd find an excuse, Aran. You'd find some way to try to defy me. It's why I had to up the stakes. The girl was just an experiment, you always knew that. Did you really think we'd use such a pathetic vessel for such an important task? I need someone who can get close to one of the Changed and there's only one I know of that comes when a human clicks her pretty little fingers."

I press my lips together, but they tremble under the pressure of a held-back scream.

"What are you going to do to him?" I can't bring myself to say Matthew's name.

"Kill him."

A sob chokes my throat. "No."

"No?" Saul lifts his eyebrows. "No? You'd choose the life of one of the Changed over your mother's?" He leans forward so he can whisper in my ear, only it comes out loud enough for everyone in the room to hear. "Now do you understand why it has to be her? If I'd chosen just anyone, I know you would have refused to help. You would have found a way to reconcile their death with your conscience. But you're not going to let your mother die, are you?"

"Don't be an idiot, Aran," Mum says. "He won't let me live."

Saul shakes a finger at her and then digs it into my chest. "I loved your mother," he says, "even after she betrayed me by stealing you from me. She did a lot for me and I won't forget that. You have my word. As long as you can keep her alive, I will not harm her."

"He's lying."

Part of me knows Mum is right, but another, stronger part wants to believe Saul's words if for no other reason than that it gives me a shred of hope to cling to. Emotions churn inside me, making it hard to think clearly. There's only one thing I know for sure. If I don't find a way to heal her body while she's possessed by a Baneem, she will die and it will be my fault. But if I do, I'm condemning Matthew to death.

Matthew is Shamari. He's strong enough to defend himself against a Baneem, but Mum will die. Except…he can't hurt a human. The perfection of Saul's plan taunts me, as does the cold realisation that I lose either way. Mum will die if I don't help Saul. If I do, Matthew might die because of me.

The fight floods out of me and I sag against the altar. I twist round as my legs collapse and I sink to the floor. I catch the edge of the altar in my hands and dip my head to them. I whisper so quietly no one can hear me: "I'm sorry, Matthew. I'm so, so sorry." I raise my face and stare at Mum. "I can't let you die."

She shakes her head and closes her eyes. "Naïve child."

Her rebuttal stabs at my heart. I clench my fists. I don't need her to understand or give me permission or thank me. I just need her to live.

Two shrill voices pull my attention away from Mum: Adele and Stella, back in her own body. What about the girl? I hold the question inside me, afraid of the answer. They step into the room and take in the scene. I must look pathetic, propped up by the altar while my own mother refuses to even look at me.

Stella looks past me to Mum and raises a fine eyebrow. "Huh. I'm suddenly more confident in this crazy plan of yours. Let's get this over and done with."

Whatever Saul has done to the girl, Stella obviously isn't in the loop. Does he trust her, or is she as expendable as Mum?

Saul drags me away from the altar into Ice Man's waiting grip. I don't resist, unlike Mum, who kicks and struggles like a wildcat as she's forced onto the altar.

"Don't do it, Aran." Her voice hisses out of her like she's spitting venom in the hope of stopping me.

I can't let her die.

Stella takes her place at the top of the altar, just like last time. Unlike last time, I force myself to keep my eyes open and watch.

Adele spreads her fingertips wide and holds her hands palms down an inch above Mum's writhing body. Her eyes flicker shut. The revolting odour of Adele's magic floods the room, but I'm numb to it. I'm numb to everything. Mum dry-wretches and struggles even more fiercely. Her body goes rigid and her eyes bulge. Her back arcs off the stone beneath her and the muscles in her arms and neck stand proud, as though they're going to tear out of her skin. She screams, the sound ripping through my consciousness. Adele raises her left hand. In answer, a white haze separates from Mum's body and floats up. Mum's soul.

Adele stretches her right hand out to Stella, who braces herself against the altar. Stella's body trembles and her head tips back, exposing the white flesh of her throat. Her scream is worse than Mum's, probably because it isn't long since this last happened to her. Her body must still be raw because I passed out before I could heal her. Her scream bounces off the stone walls of the small room and reverberates through my mind. When Adele tugs Stella's soul free, it comes away as a brilliant mist, far brighter than Mum's. I narrow my eyes and avert my face to shield myself from the brilliance.

Adele crosses her hands at the wrists. The two souls obey her command and switch places. She slams her right hand against Mum's breast and her left against Stella's. The two soul mists remain visible for a few seconds longer as they meld with their new homes and then vanish.

Stella's eyes roll back and her body drops to the floor. Mum gasps in air and sits up.

"Well, that was painful." It's Mum's voice, but not her words. She looks at me, her eyebrows raised expectantly. "You'd better buy me enough time, kid."

Ice Man releases me and shoves me forward. I come to a halt a couple of paces from Mum's body and for some reason, I hesitate. I want to save her life, but I can't shake the memory of the venom in her voice and eyes from my mind. She doesn't want me to save her. I don't want Matthew to die.

Saul curls his hand around my shoulder. "I promised I'd let her live if you helped me," he says. "I loved her, remember?"

What am I supposed to do? Let Mum die? I can't. I won't. I close the gap between us, rest my hands on her arm, and will my magic to take the invisible injuries away. Bursts of pain erupt around my body, quickly followed by a resurgence of pins and needles and a dark fuzziness in my mind. My body starts to tremble as it feels like someone is driving a thousand knitting needles through my flesh. Warm blood trickles down my nose and over my lip. The fuzziness makes my legs give way, but I drag myself toward Stella's body anyway. I put my hand on her arm and drag the damage onto myself, even though I barely have the energy or strength to do so. I won't give Saul any reason to hurt Mum. I will save her.

CHAPTER TWENTY-ONE

I can see something's wrong as soon as I step out of the stairwell. The light that normally illuminates the seventh floor of the block of flats has been shattered. Shards of white plastic are scattered on the ground. I step over them. The front window of Phailin's flat has been smashed in, allowing the wind to whip inside and twist the curtains. I breathe shallowly as I approach the front door. Someone has made an effort to pull it shut, but it flaps back and forth because there isn't a lock to restrain it anymore. The flat is dark.

I tug my phone out. I haven't had a message from Phailin since last night, but I wasn't really expecting one. I speed-dial AJ's number and press the phone to my ear, waiting for Phailin to pick up. As a polite, recorded voice informs me the call can't be taken, my heart rate increases. I try to swallow my fears away. She's probably still on the train, unable to hear AJ's phone ringing because of the rush of metal streaming over metal. Or maybe she doesn't recognise the ringtone. She'll see I've called any minute. I'll hear from her any second.

The rate of my breathing increases into sharp rasps, making me light-headed. I force myself to calm down, to time my breaths in and out to a count of ten. Hyperventilating isn't going to do anyone any good. Phailin is on the train. Everything is fine.

I should call the police. Perhaps the neighbours have already. I glance at the flats on either side, but they are both dark and silent. Their inhabitants are probably still at work. I get as far as dialling 9-9 before I cancel the call. Phailin will be angry with me if I bring in the police. I glance over my shoulder at the darkening sky. Beneath me, the city lights are starting to switch on. From here, I can see the alleyway that Phailin would have to walk through to reach the flat. There's no sign of her. Even though it's cold, my skin is starting to feel hot and clammy inside my coat. What if Phailin is inside? What if she's hurt?

I take a deep breath as I push the door open with my fingertips and step into the hallway, flicking the light on as I go. The sitting room door is open, inviting me to investigate. The computer monitor lies on its smashed screen, the sofa and chair have both been upended, and the fold-down table has been wrenched from the wall, leaving ugly gaping holes in the plaster.

"Phailin?"

I move from the sitting room to the kitchen. Every cupboard door and drawer hangs open, and all the contents have been tossed out. Broken plates, pans, dishes, and cutlery lie on the tiny floor space.

AJ's room has also been trashed. The single bed has been flipped onto its side. The chest of drawers lies on its front with its drawers emptied onto the floor. Tears sting my eyes as I look at the meagre contents of his life tossed carelessly around the room. A few pairs of jeans. A dozen T-shirts. Some part of me tells me to blush at the sight of his strewn boxer shorts, but all I can do is let out a sob. Textbooks and a few battered novels have been scattered everywhere. Most lie with their spines broken and their pages folded or torn.

The dark edge of a frame peaks out from beneath a drawer. I bend down to free it, careful to avoid the fractured glass front. Two photos sit side by side. One of Phailin, looking younger and less sad than the woman I know. The other is of me, smiling and shading my eyes. The invisible sun has picked out the red hues in my hair. My mouth quivers as I carefully pluck the glass out of the frame and lay it on the back of the chest of drawers. Now safe, I hug the frame to my chest and bow my head.

I've never been in Phailin's room before. It's only margin-ally bigger than AJ's and has received the same brutal treatment. Her possessions are just as sparse as his. A combination of smart and casual clothes have been scattered. Her quilt has been ripped down the middle, spraying tiny white feathers all around the room.

It makes no sense. Why would anyone toss the flat and not take anything? The computer would have been worth something. Unless it wasn't thieves. I press my hand against my chest and take deep breaths. I can't crumple. It won't help. I try to call her again, tears stinging my eyes with every unanswered ring.

I leave the flat and curl my hands around the balcony wall. I lean over a little and whisper Matthew's name and then shake my head. Whispering won't do any good. I draw icy air into my lungs and shout his name into the semi-darkness as loud as I can. I wait, counting the seconds away until I reach three hundred. Nothing. I'm not sure what I expected. I once stood on hallowed ground and screamed his name over and over, expecting him to hear me, but he couldn't. Even if he could, Matthew's not my guardian angel and he's mad at me. I shake my head and turn back toward the flat.

My heart practically leaps into my throat. Phailin is a few feet away from me, halfway between the stairwell and the door to the flat. Her hair is a little dishevelled, but otherwise she looks fine.

"Are you okay?" I say.

Her forehead creases at the top of her nose as she tips her head to the side. "Kim."

I swear her voice rises slightly into a question, but I dismiss it as shock.

"It looks like someone broke into your flat. I'm so sorry."

"Yes."

She crunches over the shards of the plastic light casing and wanders into the flat. I'm not sure what to do except follow her.

"You should call the police."

"No." Her tone is more wistful than angry or dismissive. "No need."

I frown. "Do you know who did this? Was it the Baneem?"

She spins round to face me. "Why would they do that?"

I shrug. I don't know. They wanted AJ and now they have him.

She moves into the sitting room and stands in the center. She doesn't move anything or check to see if anything is missing. She just stands there.

"Are you okay?" I'm not sure if I should go to her and hug her. "This must be a shock."

I want to ask her about the gateway, but I know I have to give her time to process what's happened. I'm not sure how I'd be reacting if it were my house that had been broken into. Mum would be in hysterics, but Phailin is stoically calm. She grimaces and rubs at her forearm through her military-style jacket.

"Where's your Shamari friend?"

I blink at her question. "What? Why?"

She turns to me, a false smile playing across her lips. "If you're right and it is the Baneem, maybe he could help."

"Maybe. But it doesn't look like magic was used."

She purses her lips. "No. But could you call him just in case?"

I narrow my eyes and take a half-step back toward the door. "I can't call Matthew. It doesn't work like that." I wish it did. Did AJ tell her about the feathers Matthew gave me?

She scratches at her hand, which looks red and raw.

"Are you hurt?"

"No. I need to speak to your Shamari friend. I need you to make it happen."

I take another step back. Something isn't right, but I'm not sure what. Why hasn't she mentioned the gateway herself? She knows Matthew can't come to Uralahnd with us. She knows he would try to stop me from going. I clap my hand to my mouth to stifle a gasp.

"You're not going to let me go with you, are you?"

She tilts her head to the side.

"That's why you want to speak to Matthew. You're going

to ask him to keep me here." I swipe my hand to the side. "Well, you can forget it. I'm going with you."

Phailin crosses the short gap between us and grips my shoulders. Her fingertips sink into the soft flesh just above my armpits. I yelp and squirm.

"Call your Shamari friend now."

"Why are you doing this?" I can see her hand properly now. It's raw from a fresh scald. "We talked about this. You said you'd let me help you."

"Plans change. Call him."

I twist out of her grip. "I already told you, I can't." I rub my sore shoulders while I fight the urge to run away from her. She's acting crazy, but I can't let her push me away. I have to go with her to Uralahnd.

"Kim?"

I twist round at the sound of Matthew's voice. He gazes at the devastation, eyebrows lifted.

My chest feels light. "You heard me and you came?" I'm smiling like a fool, wide-lipped and open-mouthed, but then I remember he won't let me go with Phailin to Uralahnd and my smile vanishes. I won't let either of them stop me.

His shoulders stiffen. "What happened here?"

I open my mouth to speak, but don't get a chance.

"Shamari." Phailin's voice is a relieved squeak. She grins at Matthew. "I need to speak to you. I have news about the Baneem."

"News? What news?" I say.

If she learnt something from her contact, why didn't she tell me? Clearly I was wrong when I thought we'd connected on Monday night.

She glares at me. "I'll speak to the Shamari. Not you."

I know she's not a fan of Matthew, but it's odd that she's not even prepared to say his name. She must blame him for not protecting AJ.

"If it's to do with AJ, it's my business," I say.

"It's not." She motions toward the sitting room and heads in herself.

I catch hold of Matthew's arm. "Something's not right. She's acting strange."

"Shamari," Phailin says sharply. "Do you want to hear this or not?"

Matthew hesitates. "You can talk to us both."

She throws her arms up and lets out a frustrated growl. "I really don't have time for this, but fine, have it your way."

She strides toward us both and doesn't stop. I shriek as her palm slaps against my forehead. The sharp scent of vinegar floods my nostrils. The room spins around me. Pain pulses in my skull. My knees feel weak and I sink to the floor.

I shove Charley's door open and see her lying on the bed with her blond hair fanned out over the pillow. Her arms are spread wide, palms up. Crimson blood drips from deep slashes on her wrists. Her blue eyes are open, staring at the ceiling. But they don't see. They're dull, empty.

Dead.

I scream. This isn't real.

My stomach lurches, and bile rises up my throat. I swallow and clap my hand to my mouth, sagging against the doorframe. I can't tear my gaze from the single lock of hair resting over Charley's porcelain cheek.

I dig my fingertips into the very real carpet beneath me. I know the hideous event I'm reliving isn't real. Charley died over a year ago, but I'm drowning in the starkness of a memory that has been locked away for so long. It's clearer now than the snatches I recalled when I found Kevin with his wrists slashed. I want to run, but I'm curled up on the floor, shivering and crying.

I force myself to open my eyes. Matthew is on his knees beside me. Phailin's hand is pressed against his head. It looks like he's staring through her, as dark tendrils snake over his body. He's not fighting back. Why isn't he fighting back? Is he caught in a memory like I was? Pain stabs at my chest. Even if he wasn't, he can't hurt Phailin because she's human. Isn't she?

I push up onto my forearms and then my knees. With a scream, I launch myself at her, pushing her away from Matthew and onto the burgundy carpet. She yells and reaches for my head. I slap at her arms, forbidding her from planting her palm on my forehead again.

"What did you do?"

Phailin snarls. "What he deserved."

She grabs my shoulders and throws me to the floor. She's far stronger than I expected. She crawls past me toward Matthew, who remains motionless. I grab a handful of Phailin's hair and pull back. She thrusts her elbow into my stomach. I don't let go. She raises onto her knees and tilts her body backward, pushing me against the wall. She slams back again and again. Pain gathers around my ribcage and shoulders, but I don't let go. A red burn materialises on her cheek, seemingly appearing from the inside out.

She inhales, the sound coming out as a pained and frightened hiss. "Damn. No more time."

She grabs my hand and wrenches it away from her head. Dozens of strands of coarse dark hair tear away from her scalp, leaving her bleeding. Then she turns and backhands me across the face. Gasping, I slide to the floor.

She glares at me and then at Matthew, who hasn't moved. He's still staring rigidly ahead, although now the tendrils have reached his eyes, drowning them in darkness.

"He's dead anyway. It's just a matter of time," Phailin says. "I didn't fail."

I grab at her as she runs toward the door, but she pulls free. I scramble to my feet, ready to chase her, but by the time I reach the door, she's gone. I can hear her feet echoing down the stairs. I itch to run after her because she might be the key to saving AJ. Only Matthew needs me. I can't leave him. I release the strands of her hair and slide down the wall beside Matthew, resting my hand on his arm. He's cold to the touch.

"Matthew?"

He convulses and chokes, as though waking from a nightmare. He probably is. I know how guilt-ridden his past has made him.

"Are you okay?"

He raises his hands and stares at them.

"What did she do to you? To me?"

"Magic." His voice is an unnatural monotone, a creepy version of his annoyingly calm voice.

I grip his arm tighter, as though the connection will snap him out of whatever's wrong with him. "But how? Phailin's human. I don't understand."

His brow creases ever so slightly. "I need to go home to heal."

My hand slides from his arm as he stands. I use the wall to get up so we're almost on an even level again.

"Home? You mean heaven?

A brief glimmer of a smile crosses his lips. "Something like that."

The last time he said those words, he vanished out of my life for almost a year. This time, I'm afraid if he goes I'll never see him again. He closes his eyes. For a couple of seconds his body shimmers, as though he's going to banish his physical form. Then his frown deepens.

"I can't."

"What do you mean you can't?"

He stares at me. I can't help but shudder at how alien his eyes look, consumed by darkness. "My soul is polluted by a lot of magic. It's stopping me from returning to my true form, which means I can't go home."

"Won't you heal in time anyway?"

He shakes his head. "The only place I can heal is home."

"A bit like vampires have to sleep in their coffins to regenerate?" He opens his mouth to reply, but I cut him off with a scowl. "And don't tell me vampires don't exist or that I watch too much TV." I plant my hands on my hips. "If you can't heal, what's going to happen to you?"

He shrugs. "I don't know. I've never been attacked with this much magic before."

"How do you feel?"

"Feel?" He stares at his hands again. "Weak."

I pace up and down the small hallway, between Matthew and the door, taking deep breaths while I try to think things through. "Okay. Is there any reason to think the magic won't wear off?"

"It doesn't tend to."

I pause mid-step, remembering Phailin's parting words: "He's dead anyway. It's just a matter of time."

"Will it get worse?"

"Maybe."

"And if it does?"

"I'll die."

I go back to pacing. "It can't be that bad." I growl and spin round to face him. "How can you be so calm?"

"I'm not." His expression shifts so his eyebrows are slanting up and his eyes are wide. "Does it help if I show my fear?"

I rock my weight back onto my heels. His comment is a stark reminder that his physical form isn't real. That everything about it—his appearance, his body language and facial expressions, even the timbre of his voice—is purposeful. He only shows emotion when he wants to.

I smother my face in my hands. "Why would Phailin hurt you? She told me she'd found out how to open a gateway. She said everything would be okay. Why would she do this?"

"I've got a better question: how?"

"Does it matter? You might be dying, Matthew. Phailin betrayed us."

"Did she?"

I glare at him. "Now is not the time for the holier-than-thou forgiveness act."

He smiles. "That's not what I'm doing, Kim. Humans cannot cast magic like that."

"Tia did. She killed Charley and Amy with magic, remember?"

"No. She used a ritual to embed magic in music as she was recording it. Humans cannot cast magic in the moment. Only a Baneem can."

"But Phailin isn't Baneem. Is she?"

"No."

"I don't understand why Phailin would hurt you."

"To save AJ?"

I want to shake my head, but something Phailin said when AJ first disappeared reverberates around my head. She told me Saul could make people do whatever he wanted them to do. I thought she'd done something terrible in the past, but what if she'd already made a deal with him when I was talking to her? What if she already had a way to get AJ back? Maybe that's where she really went and the rubbish she spouted about the gateway was just a cover story.

It makes sense, but it doesn't feel right. The way she acted didn't feel like Phailin at all.

Matthew's body quivers as the black tendrils spread a little farther across his form. His smile deepens, a silent indicator that he wants me to believe everything is okay. But it isn't.

"Matthew...your smile."

It isn't making my insides melt or my legs weak at the knees. I stare at his eyes, but I don't want to tumble into them. He banishes his smile, replacing it with an utterly emotionless expression. He inspects his hands again. I squint at him, so he's slightly out of focus. His physical manifestation is fraying at the edges. It's subtle, but I can see wisps of him coiling away and vanishing, as though he's no longer strong enough to hold his form together.

"My soul is weakening. It's starting to unravel."

I wish he'd inject emotion into his voice. Not hearing his fear isn't helping my own.

"What does that mean?" My gut aches with a truth my head wants to carry on denying.

"I am going to die."

I shake my head hard. "No. It can't be true. The magic will stop spreading. It'll subside, and then you can go home and heal."

He puts his hands on my shoulders, squeezing them gently. "I'm sorry."

I gaze at him with wide eyes. "You've got nothing to be sorry for. Especially after the way I treated you. I'm sorry about everything. I lied to you, used you, manipulated you and you still came back to help when I called." I bow my head. "You shouldn't have come. If you hadn't come back, you wouldn't be—"

"Dying?" His voice is solemn, which is the most emotion he's shown through it since Phailin attacked him. "This isn't your fault, Kim."

I turn, wrenching away from his grip, and kick the wall. "Yes, it is. All of it's my fault." I take a deep breath. "But feeling sorry for myself isn't going to help anything. We need to find a way to fix what Phailin has done to you before..." Matthew's lips part, but I cut him off. "Don't even try to tell me it's not possible."

He smiles. "I don't know if it is possible, but I'm fairly sure you can do almost anything you put your mind to." His eyebrows curve up to meet in the center. "But I'm not human, Kim. You can't just put a plaster or a bandage on and hope my soul knits itself back together." He reaches out and rests his fingertips against my arm. "I can feel the magic corroding my soul. I can feel myself becoming less and I have no idea how to fix it. Magic is my weakness, remember?"

"Your kryptonite," I say through a strangled sob.

His eyes narrow in confusion.

"Sorry," I say with a shrug. "I watch too much TV, remember?" I take hold of his hand. "Can you contact another Shamari?"

He bows his head in concentration for a few seconds and then shakes his head. "I can't return to my real form, go home, or communicate with the other Shamari. The damage to my soul has cut me off completely."

"Can I? I could go into the next territory and find one."

"I don't think you realise how big our territories are. Or how few of us there are."

"How big?" My stomach churns in anticipation of his answer.

"My territory is the UK and Ireland," he says. "France is a long way from here when you can't dematerialise."

I squeeze his hand, grateful for his attempt at humour. I know it's for my benefit. A misguided attempt to keep me motivated or something. I frown.

"Wait…how can your territory be that big? You said AJ had to stay in the city to stay safe."

He shakes his head. "No, I said he had to stay in my territory. Neither you nor Phailin asked how big it was. You both assumed it was a small area."

"And you didn't correct us." I bite the inside of my cheek. Now isn't the time to get angry with him. He's right—I made an assumption.

"Kim, what about AJ?"

"I can't think about him right now. I have to help you."

"Kim…"

"No." I jerk my hand away from his, as though his words have burned my fingers. "You're dying, but AJ is in Uralahnd and I don't have a clue how to get there. I was relying on Phailin and now…now…"

Matthew tries to touch my shoulder, but I bat his hand away.

"I might be able to help you, but AJ… I don't know what I can do for him. He's been gone for almost a week and I'm not closer to finding a way to get to him." I fold one arm over my stomach. Saying the words makes me feel sick. I breathe through my nose to calm myself. "I need to concentrate on helping you because the more I think about AJ, the more it hurts inside." I press the fingertips of my other hand against my chest, over my heart. "I can't lose you both."

Matthew nods once. "All right."

A little flutter of surprise erupts in my throat, making me let out a squeak. I don't understand why Matthew gives in so easily sometimes. Right now, I'm grateful he has.

"Won't the true Shamari know you're in trouble if you don't check in with them through telepathy?"

"Not for a long time. We don't have to communicate every day or even every week." His shoulders droop. "Time isn't really important to a creature who was never born and will never die. The true Shamari don't grow up or grow old. They just...are."

I sigh. There really won't be a cavalry of not-angels flying to the rescue. "We can't stay here," I say, glancing at the door, which is half-hanging off its hinges. "The neighbours will be coming home soon. They'll call the police."

I head into the sitting room and close the curtains so the devastation will be less obvious from outside the flat.

"Where can we go?"

"To my house? No one else is there."

I wait until he's followed me outside before I attempt to close the door. I have to settle for propping it against the doorframe. If the people on either side of the flat are self-absorbed, there's a slim chance they might not notice someone kicked it in.

I head down the stairs quickly, missing every second step. We've gone down three levels when a pair of teenage boys saunter toward us. They stop and snicker to one another. The taller of the two points at Matthew, openly laughing.

"You're a bit late for Halloween," he says. "Cool contact lenses though."

My jaw drops. It was stupid of me not to realise Matthew wouldn't be invisible anymore when I realised his other self-preservation techniques weren't working. There's no way I can get a dying not-angel covered in magical tendrils of darkness home without being seen. Not on my own.

Still laughing, the teenagers carry on up the stairs past us.

I take my phone out and pull up my contacts list. My thumb hovers over Sophie's number. I've got no reason to think she'll even take my call. I really hurt her yesterday, but I need her help. I take a deep breath and speed-dial her number.

"Kim." Her voice is flat.

"I'm sorry. I'll explain everything, I promise." I take a deep breath. "But I need you to meet me at AJ's flat. With your dad."

CHAPTER TWENTY-TWO

I'm drifting in and out, unable to stay fully awake but refusing to let myself fall into the pit of unconsciousness, so I'm ready the moment Stella brings Mum's body back to me. I hold her image in my mind, a focus that allows me to cling onto the edge of consciousness while my magic slowly heals and strengthens my body.

Saul and Adele are still in the room, but they've sent the four thugs away. They talk, their voices drifting closer and then moving further away, an ebb and flow of snatches of conversation that mean little to me. But sometimes their words make sense and strike cold fear into my heart.

"Are you sure he'll have the strength to heal them both?" Adele says, crouching before me.

I'm on the floor, in the corner of the room. Someone put me here, but I'm not sure who. My left shoulder and head are pushed into the corner. I manage to shift my head a little so I'm looking at Adele. Or maybe through her. My eyes flicker open and shut, open and shut, turning her image into a hazy mirage that seems more like a fairy tale wicked witch than flesh and blood.

"He will."

"This time." Adele stands and folds her arms. "To save his mother. But next time? When we need so much more from him?"

"There are other ways."

Adele moves away and her words fade into nothingness.

I won't help them again. I only did this to save Mum.

Only they have her now. Saul promised not to kill her, but he didn't promise to let her go. With her in his clutches, he'll use me like a puppet. Pulling my strings to make me perform to his every whim. Mum and I have to escape.

Stella's body lies on the floor close by, still. The only proof I have that Mum's soul is alive within her is the steady rise and fall of her chest. A body can't live without a soul, can it? At least, not for more than a few seconds. That's how long Adele held my soul out of my body. It felt like longer. It felt like I was dying.

I squeeze my eyes shut. When is Stella going to come back? I'm not even sure how much time has passed. A few minutes. An hour. More. It's impossible to tell.

"I hate not knowing." Adele's agitated voice floats back to me.

"Relax. We'll know if our plan has worked soon enough."

"If Stella makes it back."

"Finally."

I open my eyes and see Mum, flanked by Flame Guy and Ice Man. A burst of strength floods my body, empowering me to stand and lurch toward her.

"Get me out," Stella says. "It's burning in here."

Mum's skin is blemished by dark burns, but it's Stella's twisted presence inside her that robs her of her beauty.

"Did it work?" Saul asks as Stella lays her stolen body on the altar.

"Sort of."

"Sort of?"

"Can we discuss this once I'm out of this carcass?"

Adele steps up to the altar and raises her hands, but Saul puts his arm between her and Mum's body.

"Did it work?"

"The Shamari couldn't see my soul. I almost killed him outright, but that human bitch got in my way. It doesn't matter. I poured so much magic into his soul that it's only a matter of time. He will die." Stella pants the words out almost too fast for me to catch. "Get me out of this damn body."

Saul nods and steps back.

"Wait," I croak. "You have to let me heal Mum first."

We all know her body won't be able to cope with the trauma of having Stella's soul ripped out and her own forced back in if I don't. I lurch forward. Saul flicks his hand toward me. Before I'm able to reach Mum, Flame Guy has me pinned in his strong grip. I struggle against him, but I'm not strong enough to break free.

I stare at Saul, widening my eyes until they ache. "Let me heal her."

"Get me out," Stella yells, slamming her fists against the altar like a child throwing a tantrum.

I strain against Flame Guy's grip. "Please?"

I swear he loosens his grip ever so slightly, enough to let me edge an inch closer to Mum.

"Swap their souls first," Saul says to Adele. He looks at me, his mouth curling into a lopsided smirk. "Then you can heal them both."

"She'll die." I pull harder against Flame Guy and again, I'm able to move a fraction closer to Mum. But it isn't enough. "You promised."

I scream as the putrid stench of Adele's magic floods my nostrils. She coaxes both souls out of the bodies and flicks them over with expert precision. Stella slowly picks herself up off the floor while Mum's body convulses.

I almost fall onto my face as Flame Guy lets me go. Somehow, I manage to keep myself upright long enough to stumble to the altar. I crash into it, putting my hand over Mum's. As my magic connects to her, I can feel the mangled mess of her body. I start to pull it all onto myself. Immediately I know it's too much, too late, but I don't stop. I gasp at the burning pain that consumes my body, far worse than the normal plague of pins and needles. My nerves scream, my hand fights to jerk away as self-preservation kicks in, but my will is stronger. I will not let Mum die.

Her eyes open. They are like two brown beacons of hope shining from her scorched face. She's shivering, her teeth chattering together so loud they eclipse the sound of my own laboured breathing.

"Don't," she whispers.

I shake my head and ignore her, inciting my magic to carry on saving her. Warm tears ooze out of my eyes. Except they aren't made of salt water that can slip easily down my cheeks, they're blood.

"Don't."

Somehow, Mum drags her hand free of mine. I slump to my knees. My head slams against the unforgiving stone altar, but somehow I manage to keep myself awake. I make a grab at her hand just as she slides her fingertips into the pocket of her jeans.

Behind me, Saul laughs. His chuckle echoes around and beyond me, a phantom just out of my reach. I find the strength to grit my teeth and twist my burning face into a snarl. I want to kill him.

She twists her hand round and presses something smooth and flat into mine. I curl my fingers around it, without ending our fragile connection. The damage pouring from Mum into me is endless. My magic fights to spread the damage across my body, but there's no part of me that isn't raw. Blood bubbles into my throat, making me cough and gag until I've expelled it all. Darkness beckons to me, inciting me, but I stare at Mum. I need her to live. I've never had to face anything alone. I'm nothing without her. We're both running out of time.

"I won't let you die." My words are weak and distorted. I'm not even sure I said them out loud.

I'm slipping closer to a darkness that's more frightening than any I've ever faced before. It's not a healing stupor opening its arms to welcome me, but death.

A strong arm drags me from Mum and throws me to the floor. Before I can fight to stand, Saul plants his foot on my chest, holding me flat against the floor. I can barely raise my arms to try to push him away. He laughs off my pathetic attempt at resistance.

"I'm not going to let you kill yourself," he says. "I still need you."

Globs of darkness weigh down my lashes, creating a grisly set of bars across my vision. But I see Mum. She rolls over, so her cheek is pressed to the altar. She stares at me and flops her arm over the side. I reach out to her, but Saul has pushed me too far away from her. Our fingertips remain a few millimetres apart. Too far for me to continue to heal her.

"Live," she whispers.

Her eyes drift shut. Her arm trails limply against the side of the altar. Her chest falls still. The tremor in her body subsides.

Saul lifts his foot from my chest. I curl into a tight ball on my side, holding a scream inside my throat. I will not fall unconscious. I will not allow the darkness to relieve my grief and pain, not even for a second.

A white haze rises out of Mum's body, a balm to my grieving eyes. Am I imagining seeing her soul rise ever upward? Adele is watching it, too, her expression sombre. So is Flame Guy. Saul's gaze remains firmly fixed on me. His face is a terrifying void of emotion as the soul of a woman he claimed to have once loved floats toward the ceiling and vanishes.

CHAPTER TWENTY-THREE

I hate waiting for Sophie and her dad to arrive. I fill the time by trying to put the flat back in some kind of order because it's better than sitting in silence, twirling my thumbs. Matthew is sitting on the sofa, staring straight ahead. Although he isn't showing any outward signs of pain—or any emotion—the black tendrils have gradually gotten thicker. Some have merged together, creating a fluid grid of darkness.

When I squint, the edges of his form are hazier than before. I'm not sure how long he has left, if he'll gradually disappear a fragment at a time, or if there will come a point when the remnants of his soul simply implode into nothingness.

"Matthew, what did you see?"

He shifts his vacant stare to me. I'm crouching on the floor beside the computer table, carefully picking up shards of monitor glass.

"When she pressed her hand to my forehead, it was like I was finding Charley all over again."

Regret shrinks his mouth into a hard line. "I'm sorry."

It was a memory he'd locked away, deep in the recesses of my mind. Finding Kevin with his wrists slashed had brought back a flash of it, but now the whole thing is laid bare, like a wound made raw from scratching.

"How old were you when you died?"

"Nineteen."

I grimace. Too young to be hung and have your body burned

at the stake for witchcraft. "Two years older than I am now. Is that what you saw?"

"No."

I debate pushing further, but I know it would only cause him pain. I give up on the final tiny fragments of glass that are trapped in the carpet fibres and start picking up the chairs, folding them and leaning them neatly against the wall in the corner of the room.

"I saw my family burn." He clasps his hands together. "Those are the memories she made me relive. One after another. First my parents. Then my two sisters. Finally my younger brother."

My jaw becomes slack. "I…didn't know they'd died in the same way."

"It was my fault."

My phone rings, giving Matthew the opportunity to look away and clamp his lips together. I check who's calling in case it's Sophie. Seeing Dad's name and number flash out, I cancel the call.

"I don't believe it was your fault," I say to Matthew. I can't let him clam up on me now.

"I invited a Baneem into our home."

I sit beside him and put my hands over his. "Did you know what she was?"

He shakes his head.

"Then how can it be your fault?"

"In the same way you believe that what's happened to AJ and I is your fault. My actions caused their deaths. I didn't want it to happen. I certainly didn't mean for it to happen, but that was the outcome. I fell in love with a Baneem and she destroyed my family."

I gasp. "Why?"

"It's what she did. She'd done it to other families in other villages before mine. She tore communities apart and brought the fury of the witch finder general down upon them."

"What did she gain from it?"

He shrugs. "I don't know. She moved from lover to lover. As soon as each one decided to reject her, she destroyed them."

He tips his head back and stares at the ceiling. "I met her one market day. She was beautiful, funny, and intelligent. I thought she was gentry, but she denied it, even though she could read and write. I'd have done anything for her—except desert my family." His shoulders rise a fraction. "So she implicated them in witchcraft, one by one. By the time I realised what she was, I'd lost them all."

"But why did she have you killed?"

"Because I rejected her. Knowing what she'd done...I couldn't stand to look at her."

"Matthew." I want to hold him and take some of his pain away. I can't imagine what it must be like to have such intense guilt gnawing away at you for over four hundred years. "You're not going to die again," I say firmly. "I'll find a way to save you, I promise." I grind my teeth together. "I shouldn't have let Phailin go. I should have found a way to stop her. Maybe she could have undone the damage she caused."

"I doubt it."

"But she did this to you."

"If it was Phailin. It's not possible for humans—"

"To cast magic like that. I know. You told me." I pinch the bridge of my nose. "I'm sorry. I'm not angry at you."

"I know."

A knock at the door provides a welcome interruption.

"What happened here?" Sophie says, glancing around as she steps into the sitting room doorway. She stops, mouth agape, staring between me and Matthew. Her dad is only a beat behind her, only his eyes narrow in fury the second he sees Matthew.

Sophie folds her arms. "Who's he and what's wrong with him?"

"I'm sorry I had to call you." I lower my face, unable to look Sophie in the eyes. "But I...we need your help."

Technically I only need her dad's help—or, rather, the use of his car—but I need Sophie. I need the support of my best friend.

"With what? Makeup removal? Or clearing up after your friend trashed AJ's flat?"

I tap my foot. Why is she making this so difficult? My chest tightens. She's being this way because of how horrible I was to her. I hope I didn't go too far to save our friendship. I press my hands against my face, breathing into them for a second, before I look up and meet her angry stare.

"Matthew is an angel." I nod toward him. "And he's dying."

Sophie's eyebrows lift, making her eyes widen so much she could be a Disney cartoon. She laughs, clutching her belly with her hands. Then she stops abruptly and all the humour drains from her face.

"Seriously? You treat me like garbage and then call me here to lie to me?" She turns to her father. "Let's go. We've wasted our time."

Mr. Jenkins doesn't move. Sophie scowls at us both, turns and stalks out of the flat.

I run after her, ignoring her father as he tries to grab hold of my arm. "Stay with Matthew," I say on my way out of the door.

I catch up with her in the stairwell. "Sophie."

She stops and looks up at me. She's half a level below me, so a dozen concrete stairs separate us.

"Is this your idea of a joke? You treat me like crap and then expect me to believe in angels? What else is real, Kim? Ghosts? The boogeyman?"

I dip my chin to my chest. "It's not a joke, Sophie. You wanted to know what secrets I've been hiding from you."

"Yes, I did, but I didn't expect you to tell me a fanciful pack of lies."

"I'm not," I say, struggling to keep my voice calm. "Magic is real, too."

She laughs again, but the sound is consumed by bitterness rather than humour. "Get lost." She turns to go down the next flight of stairs.

"AJ has been kidnapped."

She freezes, one foot on the step below her. She opens her mouth, but snaps it shut again as a couple wander past on the level below. I can just see them glancing up at Sophie. She gives them a friendly smile, prompting them to turn away and carry on toward their flat.

"I'm not lying," I say once we're alone again. "It happened last Thursday."

"We went bowling on Thursday."

"After that."

"Are the police involved?"

I shake my head. "They can't help."

She taps her fingertips against the metal banister. "Because of magic and angels?"

I sink down into a crouch, hanging onto the banister to steady myself so I don't topple down the stairs. "I know this is hard to take in—"

She cuts me off with a sharp shake of her head. "You've got a funny way of apologising. I don't want to hear anymore lies, Kim. I gave you chance after chance to tell me what was really going on, but all you did was pile lie on top of lie. And then the things you said yesterday..." She steps back up onto the half-landing and squeezes her eyes shut. "Why are you doing this? How can you expect me to forgive you when you're still lying to me? What you're saying isn't even halfway to believable."

"I'm not lying." I swallow to rid myself of the sour taste in my mouth. There's nothing I can say to make Sophie believe me.

"Would you come inside so I can show you something?"

I glance behind me. I hadn't heard Matthew approaching. Even dying, he's soundless.

Sophie folds her arms. "Show me what?"

"Something that will make you believe," he says.

She throws her arms up and lets out an exaggerated sigh. "Fine. Whatever."

I'm relieved when she trudges up the stairs and follows Matthew back into the flat.

As soon as we're in the sitting room, he bows his head. His wings sprout from his back. Sophie gasps and stares at him with wide eyes and gaping mouth while her father sits in the armchair, teeth clenched together. Matthew's wings are no longer mottled, but black. The magnificent feathers begin to fall one by one, exploding into minute bursts of light as they hit the ground.

"Matthew…" Shaking, I reach out to him. "Your wings…"

His brow quivers. "It looks like the damage is worse than I thought."

I watch hopelessly as Matthew's feathers continue to drop and dissipate. They're not just feathers, they're fragments of his soul. "Can you retract your wings?"

He squeezes his eyes shut in concentration for a few seconds. Slowly, they vanish, but not before another dozen feathers have fallen and been consumed.

"I hope that was convincing enough," he says.

"You really are an angel," Sophie says.

"Yes."

"And you're dying?"

"Yes."

She turns to me. "And AJ? He's really been kidnapped? Why?"

I hold my breath. Now isn't the time to withhold anything from her. "Because he's not entirely human."

It's hard not to glance at Mr. Jenkins, whose eyebrows are hooding his eyes. Sophie blinks at me, her slack-jawed expression surprised but not disbelieving.

"He has magic," I say hurriedly. "He can heal. His father is a horrible man and took him. We can't go to the police because they wouldn't believe any of this. And now his flat has been trashed, his mum's missing, too, and…"

She pulls me into an embrace, rubbing my back to calm my tears. "I'm sorry." She drops her head against my shoulder. "I'm so, so sorry."

I hug her. "No. I'm sorry for everything. For the lies, for pushing you away."

We hold each other, both crying so hard it's impossible to tell whose body is shuddering the most.

After a few moments, Sophie lifts her head. "What do you need me to do?"

I turn to her father. "We need to get Matthew back to my house."

He pats his hands against his knees with an annoyed grunt. "My car is in the car park."

Sophie purses her lips. "Dad, why don't you look surprised by any of this?"

He clears his throat.

"Kim's not the only person who's been keeping things from me, is she?"

"I needed help a couple of months ago," I say quickly. "Being a judge, your dad is pretty powerful."

She rolls her eyes. "I know that." Her tone is grumpy. "But seriously? Angels and magic exist and you both kept it from me? Why?"

I lower my head. "To protect you. Finding out about this stuff blew my world apart. I didn't want to do the same to you."

"And when Kim asked you for help, you bought all this straight away?" Sophie says.

Mr. Jenkins shrugs. "Having an angel manifest in front of you, wings and all, will make you a believer pretty quickly."

Sophie rolls her eyes. "No kidding."

"We should go," Mr. Jenkins says stiffly. "Before someone calls the police." He stands and helps Matthew to his feet. "Keep your head low until we reach the car."

Matthew does as he's told. I follow behind, my footsteps growing slower and heavier as we leave the block of flats and walk the short distance to the car park. Mr. Jenkins's massive black Land Rover squats neatly in a space. Sweat breaks out across my skin. I can't forget how Mr. Jenkins forced AJ and I into that Land Rover at gunpoint and delivered us to Taylor. The last time I was in that car, we brought AJ, unconscious, back to Phailin.

"Are you okay?" Sophie asks.

"Just worried about Matthew and AJ."

"What do you need to do to save Matthew?"

I shrug. "He's a walking, talking soul. The magic is attacking him and corroding it. Matthew described it as unravelling."

I squint and stare at Matthew as he stoops to get into the back of the car. The edges of his physical manifestation have become more fluid. Wisps of his soul dissipate into the dark air. Every muscle in my body becomes tense with fear.

"If we don't do something, he's going to drift away."

Sophie's green eyes are thoughtful. "So you have to find a way to contain it?"

I stare at her blankly.

"Can't you put his soul in a real body? Wouldn't that stop it from drifting away?"

I gasp and clap my hands together in front of my mouth before pulling her into a hug. "Sophie, you're a genius."

She strikes her left arm over her chest and flourishes her right arm out to her side, bowing over her knees.

"I do try," she says, standing. Her nose wrinkles as she smiles. "Front or back?"

I hesitate. She opens both doors, allowing me to see inside. I can't help but remember sitting in the backseat, cradling AJ in my arms, not knowing if he was going to live or die. Now Matthew is sitting rigidly in that same seat, dying. I don't want to get into this car ever again, but I can't make a scene without Sophie questioning why. I've already made things difficult for her father, I can't make it worse. I don't want Sophie to ever find out he abducted or shot me. Taylor drove him to that. Sophie's father is a good man.

"Back." I slip onto the seat and shut the door behind me.

*

I leave Sophie and Mr. Jenkins in the kitchen to talk while I join Matthew in the sitting room. My mouth is dry as I sit on the edge of the sofa beside him. I'm not sure what to say or do. I'm used to seeing Matthew strong and confident, not afraid. Not that he's openly showing his fear, but the fact that he isn't projecting any emotions onto his face tells me everything I need to know. The black tendrils make him appear inhuman, like a creature that wouldn't be out of place in my worst nightmares. I tap my fingertips together.

"Sophie suggested we could put your soul in a body to stop it dissipating." I glance at him from the corners of my eyes, trying to gauge his reaction. His expression doesn't change. "It's kind of grim, but there might be a John Doe in the morgue or something."

"I don't know what a John Doe is but—"

"Someone who can't be identified."

"It won't work."

I frown. "Can't your soul animate a body and make it live again?"

"No."

"What about someone in a coma? Someone brain-dead?" I say hurriedly. "Someone who will never wake up."

"It won't work," he says firmly. "Even if it were moral, which it isn't, my soul is too powerful. It would burn straight through a human body. Even now."

I stare past him at the chintz sofa fabric. "Literally burn it?" I say, aware of how distant my voice sounds. "From the inside out?"

"Yes."

I run my fingertips over the back of my hand, causing the fine hairs to rise and prickle, as a memory tugs at my mind. There was a scald on Phailin's arm. I raise my fingertips to my cheek, remembering the red burn that blossomed on her face, and then cover my mouth with my hand. The burns. I bend over slightly, breathing hard through my sudden urge to throw up.

"Kim?"

"Phailin's skin was burning from the inside." Should I be relieved or terrified by the conclusions my mind is leaping to? "Matthew, is it possible for a Baneem to possess a human body?"

"No. The same thing would happen. The body would be destroyed. Not as quickly as if a Shamari did it, but within hours."

"She said she was out of time…" I shake my head and wrap my arms around my stomach, trying to squeeze out the cold sense of dread settling there. "Phailin was possessed, wasn't she?"

He lifts his shoulders in a half-shrug. "It's an explanation that makes sense."

"I can't think of any other way that a human could suddenly start throwing magic around like a Baneem, can you?"

"No."

"Does that mean she's dead?" She can't be. It would destroy AJ.

Matthew purses his lips. "Not if she was healed in time."

"AJ."

Matthew turns his head so he can look at me. I make the mistake of staring back. Even though his aura is too weak to pull me in, the dark void of his eyes makes my body turn to ice.

"Wouldn't you do anything to save your family?" he says.

My mouth quivers. "Phailin was right. AJ's dad can make people do whatever he wants."

"You can make anyone do anything with the right leverage," Matthew says, lowering his voice. "Remember what Sophie's father did?"

"I'll never be able to forget what he did and I'm pretty sure I won't be able to forgive him." I curl a lock of hair around my fingertip. "But I do understand why he thought he had to do what Taylor told him to. He was trying to save his family. Sophie can't ever know what happened. I don't want him to lose his daughter because of Taylor." I drop my head into my hands, clutching my hair in my fingertips. "I don't want to lose AJ because of Saul, either. And I don't want him to lose his mum."

More than ever, I need to find AJ and probably Phailin, too.

"If our theory is right, you mustn't blame AJ or his mother for what has happened to me."

I try to laugh, but the sound that comes out of my mouth is too laden down by anger and fear. I cup his cheek in my hand. Even though the oily texture of the darkness covering his form revolts me, I don't pull away.

"Your supernatural ability to forgive others is annoying at times," I say, forcing fake humour into my voice. "God knows I don't deserve your forgiveness, but you've given it to me anyway." I run my thumb across his cheek. "What I don't understand is why you can't forgive yourself."

Matthew shrugs and gently pushes my hand away from his face. "I don't need to forgive myself. I need my family to forgive me, but they're dead."

I brush my hair back and puff my cheeks out. There's nothing I can say and no solution I can offer him. Not that it will matter if he dies. My heart grows heavy in my chest as I temporarily push AJ to the back of my thoughts.

"I think Sophie is right. You need a body to stop your soul from dissipating," I say firmly. "But it has to be one that won't burn up. Any ideas?"

"No. I'm sorry."

"Rest. Let me worry about how to save you. Just hold yourself together, okay? Promise me you won't give up."

He smiles weakly. "I promise."

I know he'll do his best. If there's one thing I can rely on, it's that Matthew doesn't break promises. I stand and breathe in deeply.

"I'd better go and talk to Sophie. I have to tell her everything."

"Almost everything," Matthew says.

"Yes." I slip my hands into my pockets. "Almost everything."

*

"I brought you a drink." Sophie sets the tall glass of lemonade down on the desk beside my hand.

I pause from staring at my monitor long enough to nod and smile my gratitude. She sits on my bed, pulling her knees to the side so she can rest the soles of her feet against one another.

"Dad's gone home. He's going to tell Mum I'm staying with you tonight."

Her statement prompts me to grab my phone. I tap out a quick text to Dad as Sophie carries on talking: *I'm okay. Studying hard. Sophie is sleeping over tonight xx*

I glance over my shoulder. "Your dad was happy with that?"

"Nope. But he didn't put up much of an argument either. He knows I know he's hiding something about how he really found out about magic. I promised not to push if he lets me help you." She narrows her eyes a fraction. "For the record, I know you know what the deal is with Dad, too."

My head is spinning with who's supposed to know what.

"But it's not up to you to tell me," Sophie says. "Dad can tell me his secrets himself." She picks at the toes of her thick black tights. "All he would say is that Mum knows nothing about magic, so I guess I'm in the keeping-secrets business now, too." She purses her lips and stares glumly at the bed.

"I'm sorry," I say.

She shrugs. "You'll make it up to me somehow." She nods at my computer monitor. "Any luck working out how to give your angel friend a body he won't turn into ashes?"

I take a sip of the lemonade and then gently tap the edge of the glass against my chin, just below my lower lip. "Maybe. Unsurprisingly, the first thing that came up was Frankenstein."

"The novel?" Sophie shudders elaborately, snaking her shoulders and back as she lets out a disgusted grunt. "A) It's pretty sick to make a body out of bits of different people; b) surely you'd run into the same crispy charcoal problem; and c) how would you animate it anyway? Unless you've got a secret lab of nastiness hidden somewhere."

I can't help but laugh at her words, which I know was her intention. "It took about that long for me to dismiss the idea."

She leans back onto her hands. "But you said 'maybe,' so what have you found?"

"Have you ever heard of a golem?"

She rolls her eyes up. "Sneaky annoying critter who ends up dropping into a volcano with a magic ring? I don't see how that would be helpful."

I giggle against the rim of the glass, causing ripples to chase each other across the surface of the lemonade.

"Aren't golems a mythological thing?" she says, leaning forward onto her knees. Her expression is a lot more serious now.

I nod. "Creatures made out of mud and animated using symbols representing the word of God."

She whistles. "Get you, little research monkey. Will it work?"

I shrug. "I don't think it's even possible."

"You've got a dying angel downstairs and a boyfriend who can heal, but you don't think making a golem is possible?"

Put that way, it doesn't seem so farfetched. "There's no proof one has ever been created," I say. "And even if they could be, they're supposed to be dumb."

"Because they're not real," Sophie says. "They're an animated lump of mud."

I nod.

"So no vocal cords. No tongue. Why would they be able to speak? But using one as the housing for the soul of an angel would be different, right?"

I love her optimism. This was why I needed Sophie back in my life. For the first time since I told her how crazy my life has become, I'm truly glad I involved her.

"Assume for a second it's possible to create and Matthew's soul will be able to animate the hunk of mud. There are two questions you need to ask yourself."

I spin round in my chair, lacing and unlacing my fingers while I wait for her to carry on.

"Will mud be any different to a human body? And can Matthew live like that? Maybe that's a question for him. The golem won't be pretty, especially if it's made by you, Miss Unartistic, and he'll be effectively trapped inside it. It'll be like a prison."

"But he'll be alive."

She shrugs. "And that will probably be enough, but you need to let him decide."

I bite my thumb at the edge of my nail. "I know and I will. After I figure out if it's even possible. There's a professor, Dan West, up at the university who's supposed to be a specialist in Jewish folklore. I was going to go up there tomorrow to speak to him."

"Skipping school. Again?"

My shoulders slump.

"I'll come with you."

"I need you to cover for me at school, Sophie. It'll look too suspicious if we're both off."

She scowls at me. "What about Matthew? Are you going to leave him alone?"

"I can't take him with me."

"I'm not sure you can leave him either. You said there's still one of these evil magic people around."

"Baneem," I say. "And yes, there is. Gage." I say his name like she should remember him, but she doesn't. The only people who do are those who were affected by his magic. Me, Kevin and Tia. "But he's not involved in this and it's me he wants to hurt."

"Are you sure about that?"

I wish I was surer than I am. "Matthew will be okay. I'll only be gone a couple of hours."

I'd also never forgive myself if Sophie stayed with him and the Baneem did attack. I can't let my best friend become another one of their victims.

"Go to school," I say firmly. "Cover for me. As soon as I have any information, I'll text you."

She bobs her head from side to side. "Fine."

A slow smile spreads across my lips.

"What?" she asks, fidgeting on the bed. "You look like the cat that got the cream. Pardon the cliché."

"You're right about a golem looking awful if I made it." My smile spreads into a grin. "But you're really good at art. You could make it."

She stands and smacks me on the top of the head. "Hello? You do know that drawing is different to sculpture, right? Just because I can do one doesn't mean I can do the other."

"You've got a better chance of creating something beautiful than I have. Besides, didn't you do a sculpture project in art last week?"

"I'm doing it." She folds her arms across her chest, jutting her lower lip out in a sulky pout. "It takes more than a couple of lessons to plan and create a piece of artwork. You're asking me to create a human-sized sculpture with no preparation and in a short space of time. I don't think I can, Kim."

I widen my eyes and give her a toothy grin before whispering "please" through my teeth in the most childish manner I can.

Her expression softens, and then she laughs so hard she almost doubles up. After gulping in a few breaths, she stands upright and flicks a tear from the corner of her eye.

"Fine. If you can work out how to make this golem real, I'll make it for you." She sticks her hand out. "But I'll need to spend some time with Matthew making sketches and things. If I'm going to do it, I'm going to try to do it right."

I accept her hand and squeeze it tightly as we shake on it. "Deal."

CHAPTER TWENTY-FOUR

The cell door clangs shut and the surrounding bars protest with a high-pitched whine.

"Kid."

I ignore Flame Guy and slide down the wall, too exhausted and battered to stand. I've barely been given time to heal and unconsciousness still beckons, but I fight it off. The buzzing effect of the obsidian vibrates through my jaw into my body.

"AJ."

I flop my head in his general direction. He's framed by the fierce sunlight spilling in through the open doorway, casting most of his features in shadow. His heavy fists are curled around the black bars.

"For what it's worth, I'm sorry about what happened to your mother."

I stare at him blankly, unable to summon hatred toward him. He's just Saul's goon. He's not the one who's responsible for Mum's death. If anything, he gave me a chance to save her by letting me go. I hope Saul doesn't punish him for it.

"Did you see her soul?"

I blink. Drying globs of blood drop from my eyelashes onto my cheeks.

"This is a place of magic. You can see things here that are invisible on Earth, like a soul leaving the body. You saw it, didn't you?"

"Go away."

The corners of his mouth droop down. "I thought you should know you weren't imagining it. She's at peace now. Try to take some comfort in that."

Comfort? The only comfort I need right now is to feel my hands around Saul's neck.

I turn my face away from Flame Guy. "Go away." It's an effort to summon venom into my voice, but somehow I manage it.

He sighs and then stomps toward the door, slamming it shut. I'm alone in the darkness. I don't want to be alone.

I flatten my palms over my face, dropping whatever it was Mum gave me to the ground, and press my fingertips hard against my forehead. I'm the reason Mum's dead. I'm the reason Matthew's dying. And Kim… She must have figured out my involvement in Saul's twisted plan. She must hate me right now. I would. I do.

I try to direct my hatred toward Saul, but it hits a mirror and bounces right back. It doesn't matter that I'm in pain now, my body broken inside and bloody, because I deserve it and I'm going to stay conscious, whatever it takes, so I can feel every shred of the pain clawing away at my insides. Whatever Saul has planned for me next, I deserve it.

I press my lips together to stop myself from crying and snivelling like a pathetic kid. Part of me snaps that I'm acting like a child. Feeling sorry for myself won't do me any good. Is hating myself the same as feeling sorry for myself?

An emotion presses against my skin from outside my body, an overwhelming sense of compassion and love that makes me quiver and wrenches my gut because it's so at odds with the dark feelings within me. Slowly, I allow my hands to drop away from my face and open my eyes. At the right edge of my vision, a white haze flickers. My chest constricts. The haze hovers less than a foot away from where I'm slouched on the ground, radiating love.

"Mum?" I can barely squeeze the word out of my throat, which is clamping up.

The haze drifts a few inches closer. Concern creeps over me like a mother's hands searching her child for injuries. Outwardly, I must look like a hideous, bloody mess. But there are no injuries on my skin. The unhealed scars I got from trying to save Mum lie inside, crisscrossing my body like a net.

Her soul edges closer still and when she pours regret over me, I'm unable to hold back the tears. As my shoulders shudder and I sob, she settles around me. Her touch is cold and oddly comforting, but it isn't the same as being held in her arms.

"I'm sorry." I'm not sure she can hear me and "sorry" really doesn't make up for what I've done, but I don't know what else to say. "I'm sorry. I just… I thought… I believed… Oh God. I'm sorry." I grip the edge of the bed and grit my teeth. It doesn't stop me crying. "I really screwed up."

The emotion she's radiating changes to one I can't describe, but it feels like she's trying to tell me it's okay.

"It's not okay. How can it be okay?" I stand through her and wheel away, ignoring the driving dizziness that plagues me as I clutch my greasy hair in my hands. "It won't ever be okay. You're dead."

I drop to my knees and wrap my arms across my stomach, grabbing my sides. I'm crying so hard I'm pretty sure I'm going to throw up, but I can't stop myself. Mum's soul moves closer again. I narrow my eyes and stare at the pale haze through blurred tears. The edges of her soul are evaporating off, like ice vapour.

Before I can say anything, my stomach convulses and pushes what little is in there up, burning my throat and my mouth as I wretch violently and spew up a combination of acid and blood. The attack leaves my stomach muscles aching. I scoot back and prop myself against the bars of the cell.

"You're fading."

She approaches me again, enveloping me in sorrow and regret.

"You have to go."

It must be the obsidian that's corroding her soul—it must be. My magic is held within my soul and somehow the obsidian nullifies it.

"You have to go."

But she doesn't go anywhere. She hovers around me, giving me the closest thing to a hug she can. In just a few seconds and without any words at all, she's able to convey love and forgiveness and…hope?

"Please go."

I'm not sure what happens to souls after death. I don't know if there's an afterlife. I guess there must be something. How else could she still be here, with me, if death destroyed the soul? How could Matthew and the other Changed exist if death destroyed the soul?

There's less of her now and the intensity of her emotions is fading. Why won't she go? I choke out a sob. Because of me. She won't go because of how pathetic I'm being. Can she feel my emotions in the same way I can feel hers? Is she connecting directly to my soul? Can she feel the strength of my hate? Does she know I want to die?

Her sorrow grows stronger and stronger until it's the only emotion I can feel from her. She knows. It shifts to something firm and strong, which tries to instill a desire to fight within me.

I shake my head. "I can't. I tried to fight. It didn't work."

I feel her soul become stern, edged with held-back anger. I don't want her to be angry with me, but I'm not sure I know how to fight anymore. I'm not sure I have the strength to try only to fail again. How can she believe in me so much when I screwed up so badly? How can she still love me when I'm the reason she's dead? I ruined her life the day I was born. She should hate me.

She lets a little of her anger slip. My chin quivers as it jolts into me, as effective as if she'd shouted in my face, to grow up and get a grip. She's right. I can't give up and die here. I don't know how Saul is going to make me continue to help him, but I know he'll find a way. If I give in and let him, what difference will Mum's death have made? Saul let her die to break me, but I need to use my grief as fuel.

The stern anger Mum is directing at me fades to reassurance. I wipe my hands over my eyes, smearing blood across my cheeks. I have to at least try. I owe her that much. It isn't enough to say the words. I have to make myself believe in them, too, or she won't leave and the obsidian will corrode her soul until nothing's left. I can't let that happen. I can't lose her twice.

Her soul dips toward the floor a foot away from me. In the light from her soul, I'm able to see a folded piece of paper. It's what she gave me with her dying strength. I lean toward it, pluck it from the ground, and unfold it with shaking hands, eyes growing wide as I reveal a gateway diagram.

I straighten my back and tilt my head against the bars. "I'll fight. I promise I'll fight."

I hope it's a promise I can keep. She's given me a way out. Or it would be if I wasn't stuck inside a cell that forbids the use of magic. I trace my fingertips against the edge of her soul. I wish she could really hold me. I wish I could hear her voice one last time. "But you have to go before this cell destroys you. I can't watch you die again. Please."

Her soul draws away and for a moment, I think she's going to leave. Instead she surges forward again, wrapping around me tightly so all I can feel is the chill of her soul and the intensity of her love for me.

"Please go." My voice is reduced to a forced whisper.

Even though I said them a few minutes earlier, they're still the hardest words I've ever had to say. I don't want her to leave me alone. I don't know how I'm going to cope without her or how I'm going to stay strong. I need her, but I have to let her go.

"Go."

She rushes up, vanishing through the ceiling and I know she's gone forever.

CHAPTER TWENTY-FIVE

Dan West isn't what I'd expect a university professor to look like. To be fair, I'm not sure what I expected, but it definitely wasn't a good-looking thirty-something with tousled blond hair and sideburns cutting down to his jaw line. I stand at the back of the lecture theatre, watching him deliver an animated talk to a group of eager, mostly female students. I hug Sophie's art folder to my chest, feeling overwhelmed and out of place.

The lecture seems to be about the progression of Hebrew writing, from ancient pictograms to the modern day. It means very little to me, and most of the technical terms Dan's using are above my head. I guess I'd understand more if I'd taken English language instead of literature.

He flicks to a new slide which shows a crooked pictogram, kind of like an L on its side.

"This is pey," he says. "It means 'mouth,' which is more commonly translated as 'speak.'"

I lift my head and stare at the slide.

A girl in the front row puts her hand up. "It doesn't look like a mouth."

Dan chuckles and clicks the slide on. "Is this better?"

My heart hammers in my chest as I stare at the pictograph: two long arcs, connecting at the corners, like a childish drawing of an eye without the iris and pupil. I've seen Matthew draw it and then speak into my head. I drew it twice on his feathers to contact him. I'd never thought of it as a mouth before. But now it's being pointed out to me, I see it clearly.

"The origins of the word can be found in the Semitic scripts from around 2000 B.C. As you can see, at that point it did look like a crude mouth," Dan says.

He carries on talking, but I tune his voice out and continue to gape at the symbol on the slide. The script of the Shamari. For the first time since I clicked onto the page about golems last night, I feel like my crazy plan might actually work. Golemancy must be rooted in the same history as the pictograms the Shamari use to trigger their abilities.

At the end of the lecture, a gaggle of girls hang around to ask questions and bat their eyelids at Dan. I feel like I'm on the set of an Indiana Jones movie and that at any moment a bumbling sidekick is going to run in and drag Dan off on some kind of adventure. My cheeks redden as I realise how ridiculous I'm being, but my crazy thoughts are a good distraction from worrying about Matthew. I hope I made the right decision to leave him alone.

"Hello."

I blink and shake my head a fraction at Dan's greeting. I hadn't even realised the girls had gone and he'd tidied up his papers. Now he's standing a couple of steps below me, smiling warmly.

"Hi," I say, immediately sounding like a stupid teenager.

"You're not one of my students. Can I help?"

"I'm in sixth form and I'm doing an art project. I was wondering if I could ask you some questions about golems." My lies rush out as I wave the art folder at him.

He raises his eyebrows. "I'm not sure I see the connection between art and golems." His blue eyes twinkle as he tilts his head to the side. "Shouldn't you be in school right now?"

"I got released for the morning to come and talk to you." I still hate that lying has become so easy for me.

"It might have been sensible for you to ring ahead and make an appointment," he says. "That way you could have skipped being bored during my lecture."

I dip my chin. "Are you too busy?"

He laughs. "Luckily for you, I've got a spare ten minutes or so. Do you want to grab a coffee?"

I curve my mouth into a frown.

"I've got all the information I need up here," he says, tapping his temple. "Besides, the campus café has a better atmosphere than my stuffy office. Come on."

I follow him out of the lecture theatre building and along the covered walkway that stretches the length of the university campus. I can read between the lines. Dan West doesn't want to have to worry about being alone in his office with a seventeen-year-old girl. I don't blame him for wanting to avoid that situation.

The cafe, just off the main walkway, is pretty much entirely beige. The linoleum is beige, the walls are beige, and the wobbly tables and padded chairs are beige. I can't help but curl my lip as we wander inside and order drinks.

"I'll get them," Dan says, as I order a hot chocolate.

I don't complain, even though heat flushes into my cheeks.

"So," he says once we're sitting down. "Tell me about your art project."

I run the handle of Sophie's art folder back and forth through my fist. "We have to do a project based on mythology," I say, rattling off the cover story Sophie and I worked out over breakfast this morning. "Only Greek and Roman stuff is off-limits because that's what we did our initial art studies on."

"Ah, so your teacher is encouraging you to be more creative and to look beyond the most popular and well-known mythologies?"

I nod.

"Why Hebrew mythology? I would have thought you would be more drawn to Celtic mythology. Or perhaps Norse." His gaze slips to my auburn hair as he's talking.

"I wanted to be different," I say.

He scratches his chin. "All right. But why do you need my help?"

"Because I want to be accurate in my representation of a golem," I say firmly. "I've done some research, so I know they're made out of mud—"

"Clay," he says. "River clay to be precise."

I press my palms to my cheeks in an effort to stop them glowing. It doesn't work.

"Sorry. Carry on."

"I know they're made out of river clay and that you need to put a word on their forehead to activate them." I glance down at my hands. "But that's it."

We both smile at the waitress who brings our drinks over. Dan grabs a couple of sachets of sugar, holds them side by side, and tears the tops off. He taps the white crystals into his drink and then stirs it. His spoon clanks around the outside of the cup.

"The word is emet, which means 'truth,'" he says. "The idea is that emet brings the golem to life, but by changing emet to met, you can deactivate the golem."

I lift my eyebrows.

"Met means death. That's just one variation. Another is you need to create a shem, which is placed into the golem's mouth to give it life. Removing the shem takes that life away."

"Shem?"

"A small scroll with one of the true names of Yahweh inscribed on it in Hebrew."

He grabs a napkin and pulls a pen out of his shirt pocket and begins to write down a long series of glyphs. It takes me a moment to realise they're probably Hebrew letters or words. Once he's done, he twists the napkin round and shows it to me. The inscription is far longer than I would have imagined the word "God" to be.

"Which version works?" I bite my lower lip the second the words have slipped out.

Dan chuckles. "In the 1500s, a golem was allegedly made using the first method by Rabbi Eliyahu of Chelm. According to a source from almost a century later, when the emet was changed to met, the creature turned to dust." He takes a sip of his coffee. "In the sixteenth century, the Rabbi of Prague, Judah Loew ben Bezalel, apparently used the shem method to create a golem to defend the city."

"What happened to it? In the myth," I say, before quickly taking a quick sip of my drink.

"There are various tales," Dan says. "One account says the golem fell in love and became violent when it was rejected, so the shem had to be removed to stop it going on a murderous rampage."

"Sounds like Frankenstein's monster."

Dan grins. "In a way, the monster from Mary Shelley's tale is a golem. Throughout mythology and literature, man has always been portrayed as having a desire to be able to mimic god and create life. It hardly ever goes well. Take Frankenstein as a case in point: He tries to be like God and instead creates a being so hideous he can't bear to look at it. The monster itself is not a thing of evil until it is rejected by its maker and then by humanity as a whole. Then he seeks revenge on Frankenstein, systematically killing people he loves."

"A recurring torture, like Prometheus," I say.

"You take literature as well?"

I nod.

He lifts his cup and takes another sip, his eyes smiling at me over the white rim. "Maybe that's something you could incorporate into your art project."

"How strong is clay?"

Dan raises his eyebrows at my question. "You tell me. You're the art student. Don't you work in clay?"

I take a gulp of my drink, frustrated.

"It's both strong and brittle," he says. "Think about it. In its natural state, you can mould it. Then you fire it. Not only does it withstand the temperatures in a kiln, but it changes and becomes hard and is no longer malleable. Of course, if you dropped a fired piece of clay onto a hard surface, it would break. Strong and brittle, like man."

"Is that why it was used to create golems?"

He shrugs. "I've no idea. It sounds like a pretty good idea, though, doesn't it?" He cradles his cup in his hands and leans back in his chair, grinning to himself. "It's always important to look beyond the known beliefs and facts," he says. "A lot of the time, the reasons behind the symbology of certain materials wasn't recorded because it was known and passed down through oral tradition. Besides, does it matter for your art project? Surely art is about shining a new light on something we take for granted?"

I'd never really thought of art in that way before, probably because I'm lucky if I can draw a recognisable stick man. Sophie would probably like this guy and his ideas.

I pick up the napkin. "Can I take this?"

"Sure."

I'm not sure if it will help. Matthew would probably remind me that God and Yahweh are simply labels given to the Creator by humans.

"Could you draw the other symbols you were talking about, please?"

It won't hurt to go for broke and try both methods. If this doesn't work, Matthew will die. I hand him the napkin back, watching closely as he draws three sigils.

"This is emet," he says. "Truth." He puts his fingers over the first two sigils. "Now it's met. Death."

I can't help but shudder at the thought of being able to destroy Matthew so easily. I raise my eyebrows to stop my forehead crumpling into a frown. Is it that easy for the Creator to destroy the Shamari if they break His rules?

"Thank you," I say, as I carefully fold the napkin up and slip it into the art folder.

"No problem. It was lovely meeting you…?"

"Kim." I hold my hand out for him to shake.

"Nice to meet you, Kim," he says, accepting my hand.

I stand and hold the folder to my chest again, but I pause mid-turn. "Does the shem need to be written on special paper or with something specific like charcoal?"

"No," he says with an amused grin. "Is everyone in your art class this thorough?"

I shrug. "Probably not."

"Good luck," he says. "I hope you get a great grade."

I force a smile, wishing a good grade was all that's riding on my ability to use the information he's given me to create a golem instead of Matthew's life.

CHAPTER TWENTY-SIX

I lie on my side, staring at the dark floor because I don't have the will to stand. I need to heal, but the obsidian prison won't allow it. I'm not sure why I'm still alive. I hold my hand in front of my face and force myself to focus on it. I'm not burning up. If the obsidian nullifies magic, I should be burning up.

I was stupid not to realise it before. Adele lied. The obsidian isn't stopping me from using my magic, but it is subduing it to the point where it's too weak to do anything other than keep me alive. I clutch my knees tightly. I'm not sure how that helps. It won't give me a solution to how to get out of here. Everything I've tried to do since the moment Saul stepped into my life has failed.

I tried to fight him in the alley, but I was too weak.

I tried to use my magic as a beacon to alert Matthew to my location, but I was too late.

I tried to escape Saul and his thugs, but I was too slow.

I tried to save Mum.

I grit my teeth against the tears that overwhelm me. I promised her I wouldn't give up, but it's hard when everything feels so hopeless. I need her here, helping me figure out what to do. I can't do this alone.

I lift my head and use the back of my hands to wipe the tears from my eyes. I am alone. No one is going to help me. Mum isn't coming back.

"I'm sorry." My voice rasps in my throat and sounds louder than it really is. I clutch my hair in my hands, covering my face with my forearms. "I'm sorry."

I repeat it over and over until I'm barely whispering the words out. It really is my fault Mum's dead. Whatever Stella did to Matthew is my fault, too.

"I'm such an idiot. Idiot." It's a new word to repeat. A self-destructive mantra that paralyses my weak desire to fight.

"I think the word I'd choose is 'pathetic,'" Adele says.

I lower my arms from my face slowly, blinking against the sunlight pouring through the doorway. She and Saul are standing outside my cell, staring at me. Flame Guy and Ice Man are here, too, standing with their backs against the wall. I didn't hear any of them enter the room, let alone walk right up to the cell.

"Go to hell." There's no force behind my words. There isn't even any anger. They're hollow and empty, which is exactly how I feel.

Adele presses her hand against her breast. "I'm hurt. I thought we were getting along quite well. I guess I was wrong."

I twist my body, so I can bury my face against the bench.

"You've changed your clothes," she notes. "I'm curious as to why."

I clamp my lips together. There's not much difference between one set of blood and sweat-stained clothes and another. Except my clothes remind me of home and Mum. They remind me who I am. Besides, my jeans have pockets, which are perfect for hiding a neatly folded sheet of paper.

"I think he's ready," Adele says.

I don't know what they have planned for me, but I know I'm not ready.

Saul scratches his chin and peers at me. "Maybe."

What is he looking for? Think, AJ. He half-starved me. Left me alone. Abused me. Used me. Murdered my mother. Threw me back in here without letting me heal. The only amount of kindness I've been shown was by Flame Guy. He's done it all to destroy me. To rob me of my will to fight. And he almost managed it.

I push up on the bench, using my wobbling arms to help me stand again. I cover the short distance to the bars in a handful of strides and curl my hands around them, clenching so hard I reveal the whites of my knuckles.

"I will never stop fighting you." Anger hisses into my quiet voice. I back it up by looking him directly in the eyes, not blinking as I silently dare him to look away first.

He reaches his hand through the bars to pat me on the shoulder, but I drop my body out of the way and stagger back.

"Yes, you will, Aran." He taps a fingertip against his pursed lips. "I'd hoped being responsible for your mother's death would be enough, but I obviously underestimated you." He smiles, but his eyes remain hard and cold. "Your girlfriend…" He clicks his fingers. "I forget her name."

"Kim," Adele says, smirking.

"Did she mention someone called Gage to you?"

I hold my breath, but don't allow the angry mask to slip from my face.

"I'll take that as a yes. I sent Gage to play with Kim in order to keep her pet Changed around. Another thing you were wrong about, Aran. I do have people on my side. Lots of them."

Anger wraps around my gut, snaking up my throat, contorting my mouth into a grimace.

"But we don't need her anymore, so we can let him loose on her," Saul says. "I'm sure he'll enjoy it. He really hates her."

He steps back as I throw myself against the bars, standing just out of reach as I thrust my arm through and flail for him.

"Not because of me." They're words I desperately want to believe but can't. "Because of you. You're a sick, twisted bastard."

Saul laughs and smooths his hair back nonchalantly. "Actually you're the bastard if you want to get technical. And it will be your fault, Aran. If you'd played nice like you were supposed to, I would have called Gage off."

I shake my head. He's proved himself to be nothing but a sadistic liar. He would let Gage hurt Kim for the fun of it.

"Ready or not, I don't want to delay any longer." He signals to his thugs. "Take him to heal and then bring him to me."

I back away as the cell door is unlocked and Ice Man and Flame Guy enter. There's nowhere for me to run, but I still struggle as they each wrench one of my arms behind my back and frog-march me out of the cell.

As soon as we're clear of the door and the oppression of the obsidian, my magic kicks in. The effect sends my body into painful spasms. My back twists, my toes curl, and my hamstrings tighten, forbidding me from walking, forcing them to carry me.

I'm taken to a windowless room, with walls painted in yellow ochre. A lantern hangs on the wall opposite the door, lending the room a shuddering orange light. Ice Man releases me the second we're over the threshold. I'm saved from slamming onto the floor by Flame Guy, who steadies me and leads me to the back of the room, where he lays me down beside the wall. I curl into a ball as pins and needles drive into my skin. Through half-closed eyes, I watch Ice Man take up residence to the left of the doorway. Somehow, I summon the strength to grab Flame Guy's arm before he manages to stand up straight. There's no strength in my grip, but he hesitates anyway.

"Please," I rasp. "Let me be alone?"

His jaw tightens, relaxes, and then tightens again. "Sorry, kid, I don't think that's a good idea."

"AJ."

He scratches at his chin.

"Where am I going to go? There's no windows. You and Ice Man will be outside the door."

His eyebrows lift. "Ice Man?" There's an amused chuckle in his voice.

"Please?"

"I don't know…"

I try to tighten my grip on his arm, but pain forbids my tendons from working properly. I squeeze my eyes shut and clamp my teeth against a pained groan that leaves me gasping.

"You know what the healing stupor does to me. Please?"

He stands, gently easing his arm away from me. I watch him with wide, imploring eyes as he walks backward for a couple of paces, turns, and slaps Ice Man lightly across the chest.

"Let's stand outside."

Ice Man shoots him a narrow-eyed glare. "Why?"

"Look at him." Flame Guy gestures toward me. "He's going to pass out in a couple of minutes. We should at least let him have a bit of dignity and leave him alone while he heals."

Ice Man chuckles under his breath. "Dignity? He's wearing clothes that stink of piss and shit. I think we're past that."

I thought I was past caring what anyone thought of me, but my cheeks blaze with heat at his comments.

"Come on," Flame Guy says. "Give the kid a break."

"You're going soft," Ice Man grumbles, but he shrugs and wanders outside anyway.

Flame Guy pauses before shutting the door. He makes eye contact and gives me a small nod of his head and an even smaller smile. I manage to tease the corners of my mouth up in a tiny gesture of thanks. He shuts the door, leaving me alone. Giving me a chance to escape.

I pull the paper with the gateway drawing out of my pocket and unfold it. My hands are shaking so badly that the image jumps wildly in front of my eyes. I try breathing slowly through the pain and the crippling effects of my magic, but it doesn't make any difference. I smooth the paper out on the floor and sit up, gnawing my thumb as I stare at it.

There's nothing in the room except for the lantern. They certainly haven't left me with a handy supply of charcoal with which to draw a gateway.

Why charcoal? Mum never told me its significance. I'm not sure she knew. Matthew must, yet he didn't let Kim in on the secret when he gave her his feathers. It must be something dating back thousands of years to a culture I know nothing about. I should have paid more attention in the handful of religious education lessons I went to—maybe I'd have found some clue in the bible or in Jewish mythology or something.

I grit my teeth to calm myself. Going round in circles about what I don't know isn't helping. I don't know how long I'm going to be left alone, but I do know this is my only shot at getting out of here. Assuming I can create a gateway. The Baneem can't, but humans can. I can see the drawing and recognise it for what it is. When I look away, I hold the memory of it in my mind. It's a good enough start to let me hope I'm human enough to open a gateway and get out of here. But I need a substitute for charcoal. Right now anything I could draw with would work, but there's no handy pens or pencils in here either. There's nothing but me. I breathe in sharply.

Me.

I raise the backs of my hands in front of my face so I can see the blue cut of my veins beneath my skin.

Blood.

I tug the belt out of my jeans, push the sleeve of my T-Shirt as high as it will go, and wrap the leather strip around my upper arm, just above the elbow. I thread the end through the buckle without securing it, and using my teeth, I pull it tight enough to feel pressure but not so tightly I cut off the supply of blood to my arm. I've left enough slack on the buckle to be able to press the prong against my wrist. I hesitate, wondering if I've got what it takes to hurt myself. Even if I do, am I strong enough to stay conscious while I'm bleeding? I don't have time to be squeamish or to second-guess my plan. This is my only chance.

I take a deep breath and gouge the metal belt prong into my skin.

I have to grit my teeth to stop myself from screaming. I can't make a sound, or Flame Guy and Ice Man will come back into the room. A thin thread of red appears in the wake of the prong, and the skin on either side of the jagged cut blazes a deep shade of pink. At first there's only a trickle of blood, but it starts to drip faster. I work quickly, forming a circle on the wall just large enough for my shoulders. I gasp as the edges of the wound start to knit themselves together. No. I can't let the wound heal. I bite my lower lip and jab the belt prong into my vein. I have to swallow back sobs as I work it from side to side, making the hole larger and the flow of blood faster. I leave the belt prong in place. I know from when Saul stabbed me and left the knife in my gut that my magic won't be able to heal it.

I keep glancing down at the paper as I divide the circle into eight equal parts and begin to draw a glyph in each section. I have no idea what they represent and I don't care, as long as it works.

By the time I'm ready to draw the last glyph in the center, I'm lightheaded. Coloured spots are dancing before my eyes, like the after-image caused by glancing at the sun. I can barely feel my body, it's so consumed by the intensity of my magic. I tug the belt prong free of my wrist, trusting to my magic to heal the wound before I bleed out. Swaying, I draw the thirteenth glyph in the very center of the gateway and slam my palm onto it.

The blood outline glows brightly. Power floods out of it, knocking me backward. Light dances across the walls as the flame of the lantern flutters and sputters. I stuff the drawing into my pocket, crawl toward the gateway, and thrust my arms through it, then my head and shoulders. Slowly, I pull my broken body through the small hole. Light blinds me, and I can't breathe. It feels like I'm teetering over nothingness. I pull myself further and then fall, my legs, ankles, and feet sliding through the gateway with ease.

I slam against a hard, cold surface. With my last remnants of strength, I turn round in time to see the gateway shrink and snap shut.

My thoughts turn to Kim. She needs my help. I have to warn her about Gage. But I can't hold off the healing stupor any longer. I curl up, praying I'm somewhere safe, as my eyelids flicker shut and I welcome sleep.

CHAPTER TWENTY-SEVEN

I smother a yawn behind my hand as Sophie, Matthew, and I walk toward the river. I've never seen the city so dead before. A pale crescent moon hangs in the sky, not bright enough to offer me any comfort. We're guided by the overlapping pools cast by the amber streetlights. We don't talk. Sophie is carrying a rucksack. Matthew looks relaxed, but it's too easy to see the way the edges of his physical form are fraying and drifting away. I clutch a piece of charcoal in one hand and the shem in the other. I copied the Hebrew script Dan had written on the napkin onto a piece of Sophie's watercolour parchment. I still don't know if my plan will work.

I yawn again. I tried to sleep for a few hours before we left the house. All I ended up doing was tossing and turning, afraid my alarm wouldn't go off and I'd sleep through the low tide. Every time I did manage to drift into sleep, I saw AJ, trapped in darkness.

We turn onto the cycle path, which overlooks the riverbank. The streetlights are spaced a little further apart and aren't as bright as along the road, leaving intermittent splashes of darkness along the path. The artificial illumination doesn't spill down the whole bank. Sophie pulls her rucksack off her shoulder, opens it, reaches inside, and pulls out a large torch. She flicks it on and shines it down the bank. The stark white light glistens on the calm surface of the water and the thick wet mud we'll have to slide down. Just at the base of the bank, I can see a streak of orangey-red clay.

"I brought you some clothes, Matthew," Sophie says. "They're my dad's, so they're not the height of fashion or anything, but they should fit you." She runs her gaze up and down him. "They'll probably be a bit baggy."

Matthew gives her a vague smile, but his attention is really focused on the clay. I step onto the bank and lean down so I can grab the long rushes in my hands to help me down. Matthew curls his hand around my shoulder. There's barely any pressure behind his grip and tendrils of his soul drift away as a result of the contact. I gulp and gaze up at him. He pulls his hand away and stares at it, mouth downturned and eyebrows slanting up toward the center of his forehead.

"This will work," I say.

I don't wait for him to object or argue. I stow the charcoal and shem safely in my coat pockets and start making my way down. I manage to maintain a steady pace, taking it one step at a time, but the edges of my feet ache from gripping the bank through my trainers. I step from a grassy section onto dark mud and my foot slips. I twist and grab, but end up sliding down the bank on my bum. The cold, wet mud seeps through my jeans, making my skin feel slimy. I wipe my filthy hands on my thighs, but dark streaks are left behind. Sophie follows me, her descent almost as ungraceful as mine. Matthew is next. He walks down as though he's on the flat, never once having to reach out for support.

Sophie chucks the rucksack back up to the grassy section and then stares down at the clay.

"Let's do this," she says, turning to Matthew. "Lie down."

He raises his eyebrows.

"Somehow, we have to get you inside the golem, yes?"

He nods.

"So I figured building the golem around you would be the easiest solution to that problem."

Matthew's mouth twitches at the corner. "All right." He doesn't move to lie down.

"What's wrong?" I say, even though I can guess.

"I'm adjusting to the idea of being trapped."

I shake my head. "Don't think of it like that. The golem will save your life." I hope.

"I know, but…" He shakes his head and takes a step forward.

"But?"

He bows his head and closes his eyes. "I'm wondering what I'll be."

"An angel with a real body?" Sophie says.

"Shamari," Matthew and I say in unison. I laugh. He doesn't.

"My aura has already faded. I can't flow between my forms anymore." He lifts his hand and traces a pattern in the air. Nothing happens. I can't even tell what ancient glyph he was trying to draw. "I can't tap into my abilities either. Everything that makes me what I am is gone."

"You'll get it back," I say.

He twists round so he's barely a palm's width away from me, staring down into my eyes. Even without his aura, his expression is terrifying and makes my legs quiver.

"How?" His voice is full of bitterness tinged with fear.

"We'll find a way to heal your soul." I raise my chin into the air, returning his stare with steely defiance. "But only if you fight. You can't let yourself die because you're too much of a coward to live."

The tension in his shoulders drifts away. "I'm tired, Kim."

I brush the tears away that are prickling my eyes. "Don't you dare give up. I need you. I don't care how selfish it sounds. I need you."

"Guys." Sophie is crouching at the water's edge. "This is all very touching, but the tide won't stay out for long. There's only a couple of feet of clay visible now. Plus, it's freezing. When the water does start coming back in, we'll be kneeling in it before we know it. Correction: I'll be kneeling in it and you'll be nice and cosy on the bank." She gives me a grin. "Are we doing this or not?"

"Yes, we are." I smile at Matthew. "You heard her—we don't have time to debate this. You've had all day to deal with your doubts."

"I know. And believe me, it's all I've thought about." He gazes across the water. "You know it might not work anyway?"

"It will."

He tilts his head back, so his face is angled toward the heavens. The breeze disturbing my hair and chilling my skin doesn't touch him at all, but the moonlight illuminates his form. He's a beautiful, brilliant soul we're about to encase in clay. Possibly forever.

"I don't know if we'll be able to find a way to heal you," I say. "But at least we'll have the time to try."

"After you've saved AJ."

"Yes." I'm not sure what he expects me to say. Right now, he's my priority because he's dying in front of my eyes.

A peaceful smile crosses his lips. "Good."

"Does that mean you won't stop me going to Uralahnd if I manage to find a way?"

His mouth jerks into a grimace.

"Did you find Gage?"

"No."

My stomach momentarily feels lighter. "Then I'll find him and make him help me get the instructions for a gateway."

"Kim…"

I throw a play punch at his shoulder. "Your big brother routine is getting really boring."

He smiles. "Sorry. You're the first friend I've had since I died. The first time," he adds with a wistful roll of his eyes. "So yes, I want to protect you. And yes, I care about you." He stares at his feet. "I need to tell you why I didn't take AJ to purgatory when I found out he was half-Baneem."

I chew the inside of my cheek as apprehension tickles my gut.

"He made you happy and he was willing to sacrifice everything to save you."

I try to blink back a sudden surge of tears. "You're an ass."

"Why?"

"Because you're making me cry like a baby." I pull my sleeves over my hands and rub at my eyes and cheeks, but the tears keep flowing.

Matthew's smile deepens.

"Now are you going to lie down and let Sophie get to work or not? Because all this soppy crap is wasting time."

He nods and lays down beside where Sophie is standing. The clay squelches as Sophie kneels and scoops some up into her hands. I watch as she works the clay over Matthew's manifestation. The torch, which rests on the ground beside her, casts a halo of light around the golem as it takes shape beneath her hands. She moulds the features around Matthew, using her fingers to scoop away the excess clay, but the thickness of it lacks definition. It has more shape than the grotesque images of golems I found on the Internet, but it's still an ugly lump of clay.

I turn away, unable to watch her any longer. Matthew is going to be trapped in a creature that people will be afraid of. He won't be able to use his aura to make himself invisible. I press my hands to my eyes. I convinced him to do this. What have I done?

I take a breath. It's not forever. It's a temporary fix. The Shamari will be able to help him. I lower my hands from my eyes and freeze.

Gage is standing on the bank above us with his arms folded loosely, smirking. He raises his chin toward me, acknowledging my wide-eyed stare.

"Very intriguing," he says. "You know it's pointless, don't you?"

I resist the urge to glance back at Matthew and Sophie. I can't let Gage rattle me. I have to believe our plan is going to work, even though my heart is quivering and it's hard to keep my breathing slow and steady.

He tilts his head to the side, curiosity sparkling in his eyes. "What is it you're trying to do? Encase his soul in mud?" He laughs so hard tears seep out of the corners of his eyes. He wipes his thumb and fingers across them and shakes his head. "Seriously, Kim? You're pathetic."

I clench my fists. I'm not pathetic. I'm not the weak little girl he used magic to seduce and tried to kill a year ago. Not that he'd know it. He's too busy buffing his ego to see the young woman I've become. I press my lips together to suppress a smile. His arrogance is my only advantage.

"Whatever happens, don't stop," I say over my shoulder to Sophie.

Growling, I run up the bank toward Gage. I don't make it. My foot slips on the damp grass. I slam onto my chest, gasping as the air is knocked from my lungs along with my pride.

"Kim!" Sophie's warning comes too late.

Gage's hand closes around my hair before I'm able to draw in a breath and scramble to my feet. I grab it, but tearing pain screeches through my scalp. He pulls, drags me up the bank, and throws me to the ground. Tiny stones graze my palms and knees as I break my fall. Muttering a curse, I brush tears from my eyes.

"What were you going to do?" He stands over me with his hands in his pockets. "Attack me?"

Narrowing my eyes, I lift my head. "I beat you once before."

"Because of your pet Shamari. But he's not coming to your rescue this time, is he?"

I stand and brush the grit from my jeans. Obviously I remember things slightly differently. Yes, Gage almost killed me. Yes, Matthew had to release me from Gage's manipulative magic. But I was the one who knocked Gage out when he turned his magic on Matthew. Sadly, there isn't a handy desk chair lying around out here.

I focus on Gage's smirk as he lazily watches me stand. I grind my teeth, round my shoulders, and ram him. He lets out an odd sound as we both barrel to the ground, something caught between a laugh and a surprised grunt. I sit on his chest and plant my hands on his shoulders, pressing them to the ground. His chest vibrates beneath my palms in a deep laugh.

"Who opens the gateway for you?" I say.

"I knew you were into me." His eyes sparkle as he shapes his mouth into a grotesque kiss.

I curl my upper lip. My expression of disgust changes into a squeal as he grabs my arms. I fight his strength, but he uses his weight to roll us over, throwing me onto my back. My body thuds against the riverbank, making me wince. I struggle as Gage pins me to the ground, his body pressed against mine. Bile burns up my throat, bubbling into my mouth. I swallow it back. My chest heaves, and a guttural gurgling noise escapes my mouth as I gag. Gage leans in for a kiss. I flail my hands, slapping his face over and over, until he jerks back with a snarl.

"It's a bit late to play hard to get, isn't it? Last time we were this close you were begging for it." He makes himself heavier, so I can feel his body against every part of mine. It would serve him right if I threw up on him, but I can't make myself, so I spit in his face instead.

"Only because of your magic."

I tug my eyebrows down. Why isn't he using his magic now? If he wanted to, he could make me do anything. He could use it to manipulate Sophie or to finish Matthew off.

As if reading my thoughts, he strokes his thumb across my cheek. "I don't need magic to kill you."

Trembling from his touch, it's all I can do to keep my head still and not try to drive it into the ground to get away from his touch.

"Is that why you're here? To kill me?" I force myself to stare into his brown eyes, pretending to be braver than I feel. They reflect the mud perfectly. "Have you stopped playing your stupid little games?"

"Stupid?" He slams his fist across my face, smearing blood from my nose across my cheek. "You couldn't stop me screwing with your family, could you?"

I can't sniff away my tears without pain shooting up my face. "What did you actually achieve?" I spit the nasally words into his face. "Mum's coming home. Chris isn't in trouble. You failed."

He curls his hand into a fist and holds it primed, with his shoulder twisted back. "Don't you get it yet, Kim? Because I was here, messing with your family, your pet Changed stayed, too. I didn't fail. I set him up to die."

For a second, it feels like the ground has dropped away and I'm falling through a black hole of realisation.

"But he isn't dead, is he?" I say.

"Not yet." His mouth twists into a smirk. "But he will be, just like your sister."

Gage drives his fist into my face. My lip splits, spilling drops of blood into my mouth. Heat blossoms across my cheek. Pain drives into my cheekbone. I force myself to grin, even though it must be an ugly sight. I can't give up. I can't let Gage win. I have to fight through the pain, find a weakness, make him angry, throw him off-balance. I need a plan, but it's hard to think while he's crushing my chest.

I hurl another insult at him to buy myself time. "Tia murdered my sister. Not you. You might act big, but you're stupid and pathetic and weak."

He pulls his shoulder back to strike me again, but I bring my knee up into his groin. His face reddens and his mouth drops open in a wheeze. I push him off me and kick him again, harder than before. He curls up, hands clutching his crotch. Jumping to my feet, I strike him again, this time in the stomach, before dropping into a crouch beside him as he trembles and groans pathetically. If Saul sent him, then chances are he can lead me through Uralahnd to AJ.

"Tell me who opens the gateway for you."

His whips his hand out, grabs my ankle, and tugs. I fall back onto my bum and immediately try to push my weight forward onto my hands. Gage is faster. His fist crashes into my breastbone. I'm left on my back, gasping, unable to move as he straddles my chest, squeezing the air out of me.

"Why do you want to know?" He circles his hands around my neck but doesn't apply pressure.

Stay strong. Tears bubble behind my eyes. I can barely feel my face. I have to stay strong. "You know why."

"So you can rescue your boyfriend?"

He leans down. For a second, I think he's going to kiss my neck. Or my face. Or my bloody, swollen lips. I can't bear for him to touch me like that again. I kick with my legs and scratch at his face, but he laughs off my futile actions as he whispers into my ear.

"Doesn't that make you just like me?"

My body stiffens, and the fight freezes within me. I'm nothing like him.

"I use humans to get what I want. You want to use me to get what you want. Your pet Changed has probably got you thinking you're so much better than me, but you're not, Kim. You're the same. You need magic."

I try to shake my head, but he applies enough pressure on my neck to stop me.

"No," I say through gritted teeth. "You want to hurt people. I want to save someone. There's a difference."

He raises his eyebrows. "Really?"

I push my hands between his arms and try to prise them apart, away from my neck. He locks his elbows and squeezes harder, pushing his thumbs against my windpipe.

"Even if I did tell you, it wouldn't matter," he says. "They're probably stripping your boyfriend of his magic right now, so they can use it to power a hidden army that will decimate the Changed."

"You're lying." It's all I can do to gasp the words out.

"Why would I lie? It's not like you're holding a gun to my head, Kim. It's not like I'm begging for my life." His mouth curves into a grin. "You can't save him. Just like you can't save your pet."

I squeeze my eyes shut to block out his face. I will save them both. I have to save them both.

"Face it, Kim, there's nothing left for you to do but die."

His thumbs press harder against my windpipe. The ground beneath me feels like it's turning to sponge and absorbing my fading body. If I die, so will AJ. If I die, so will Matthew. If I die, so will Sophie. I have to live. I have to fight.

I completely relax my body, holding what little breath I have inside my lungs. As Gage's grip relaxes, I allow my head to loll to the side. He sits back, shifting his weight from my chest to my gut. It's hard not to groan, exhale, or show a flicker of pain on my face, but somehow I manage it. The ground and air are so cold they've leeched all the warmth from my skin. I could almost believe I was dead. I hope he does, too.

His weight lifts off me. Grass scrunches to my left and then whines. Has he spun around? I feel his footsteps through the ground. His shoes send little shockwaves through the earth each time they strike. He's moving away from me. Toward Sophie and Matthew.

I breathe out slowly and quietly gulp a breath in. My head pounds. My fingers and toes tingle. The fresh air makes me feel a little better and lends me energy and strength.

I open my eyes. Gage is standing at the top of the bank, looking down on Sophie and Matthew. He pushes his shoulders back and begins to sing. Even a small amount of magic will be enough to kill Matthew, thanks to the pollution already blackening his soul.

I won't let Gage hurt my friends. He's done too much to my family already.

I get to my feet and run, slamming my palms against his back. He wobbles and falls, flipping head over feet down the steep bank through the sticky mud and slimy clay. He slides to a halt with the rising, murky water lapping at his dark hair.

I half-run, half-slide down the bank and then tumble. I tuck myself into a ball and allow myself to roll. Mud and clay coat me from head to foot by the time I land beside Gage. I grab his shirt, bunching the fabric in my hands as I haul him onto his back.

"Tell me who opens the gateway for you," I say, bringing my nose close to his.

He doesn't answer. Or move. He stares up at the crisp night sky. He doesn't blink.

My chest tightens. The clay is drying into a mask that forbids the emotions clawing inside me from manifesting on my face. He can't be dead.

His head is at an odd angle on his neck. I search for a pulse, but there isn't one. I press my hands down on top of his chest and push, push, push, trying to force life back into his body. The muscles in my shoulders start to ache. I don't care. If he's dead, how will I open a gateway? How will I help AJ? This isn't what I wanted.

My hands, slick with clay, slip. I fall across his chest, sobbing so hard my stomach heaves. I push up and grab his shirt again. All the anger I felt toward him has drained away.

Gage is dead. AJ is out of my reach. I've failed.

CHAPTER TWENTY-EIGHT

"Kim."

Sophie's insistent voice nags at me until I'm forced to turn to face her. My tears have cut tracks through the dry clay, inviting cold air to chill the narrow slivers of exposed skin.

"I've finished," she says, sweeping her hand over the golem.

It's better than I could have expected but worse than I might have hoped. Recognisable as a human form, it lacks the subtlety and shape of a real person. The light of Matthew's soul is completely eclipsed by the clay, except at the mouth, which Sophie has left open and hollow.

"Whatever you have to do, do it," Sophie says. "We can't stay here much longer."

She's right. The water laps around her knees as she kneels beside Matthew and the golem. It slips back and forth, cutting small pockmarks in the base of the golem with each sighing breath. But I can't move. I'm frozen beside Gage.

"It was an accident."

I want to believe Sophie, but the truth is I meant to knock Gage down the bank. I meant to hit him as hard as I did. I just didn't expect him to die. I didn't want him to die.

"Matthew needs you."

She's right. If I let my guilt cripple me, Matthew will die. I rock back, pull one leg out from beneath me, and stand with jerky movements. My arms hang slack by my sides. Sophie and Matthew are only a handful of steps away, but each one is a chore as I tug my feet out of the mud with a pop.

I drop down beside them, my knees slapping against the clay. Thick splodges splash up onto my clothes. It makes no difference, they're already covered and heavy. I probably look as unnatural as the golem does. I make an attempt to wipe my hands on my jeans. It doesn't help. I reach into my pocket and tug out the shem, smearing streaks of damp red clay over the paper. I hope it doesn't matter.

"Hold on," I say to Matthew.

His mouth twitches into a barely visible, weak smile. I hold my breath as I slip the shem into the golem's mouth, resting it in the empty space between the opening and Matthew.

Nothing happens. The golem remains still and lifeless. Matthew's fading manifestation is still visible within the golem but separate from it. It didn't work. Why didn't it work? According to the myth, all I had to do was put the shem in the golem's mouth. If not-angels, magic and gateways to another world can exist, surely bringing a golem to life is possible?

I fish the paper napkin that Dan had written on out of my coat pocket, unfolding it with shaking fingers. I try to write on the golem's head with the charcoal, but the clay just coats the black stick, making it useless. I shove it back in my pocket, and using my fingertip, I copy the Hebrew word emet onto the golem's forehead. It's not neat. The Hebrew letters that form the word are jagged and cut deep into the clay. I don't care. It has to work. I watch closely, expecting Matthew's soul to glow and fuse with the golem. I expect the clay figure to sit up and smile at me.

Nothing happens.

I allow the filthy napkin to slip out of my hand. The wind catches it, carrying it away like a fluttering dove. Except it doesn't carry hope with it—only defeat.

"It's all right," Matthew says. "You tried." The clay funnels his voice, making it sound hollow.

I shake my head, pressing my quivering lips together. Sophie puts her hand on my shoulder, but I shrug away her comfort.

"It's not okay." My voice quivers in my throat. Sobs choke me and make my chest heave. "The Baneem took my sister from me. They've taken AJ from me. They tried to hurt my family. I. Will. Not. Let. Them. Kill. You."

I rest my fists against my skull, pressing hard to drive away the headache that makes my head heavy and my thoughts dull.

"Why didn't it work?"

"Golem's are myths," Matthew says.

I glare at him. "You're a walking, talking myth. You exist. This should have worked. We needed it to work because we don't have time to figure something else out."

Even if it does work, the magic would still be poisoning his soul, but at least it wouldn't be able to fray any further. I can't let him die.

I tug the shem out of the golem's mouth and unwind it. As I do, I smudge clay over the Hebrew letters. I don't know exactly what it says, only that it's one of the names of God.

"Maybe I copied it wrong." Except I can't check because the napkin is gone.

"What if it had worked?" Sophie says.

Blinking, I jerk my head back.

She gestures toward the golem. "There's nothing linking Matthew and the golem together, so if it had worked, we'd have a mindless, walking lump of clay hulking around."

"He's inside it."

"But he's not connected to it."

I tilt my head to the side. She's right. It was never going to work.

I wrap my arms around my waist and lean forward over my knees, so my face hangs above the clay golem.

"Gage was right. I'm pathetic."

"No, you're not," Sophie says. "We just have to figure this out. Your idea is sound. Matthew needs a vessel that can contain his soul…" She hesitates.

I can guess what she was going to say: what's left of it. A second shudder ripples across my shoulders.

She clears her throat. "We have a vessel. Now we need to work out how to fuse Matthew into it."

I shake my head. "What good will it do if we can't animate the golem?"

She arches an eyebrow. "What makes you think we need to?"

I stare at her.

"Maybe Matthew's soul will give it life." She dips her gaze and tucks her hair behind her shoulder, coating the caramel strands in red clay. "Forget it. It was a stupid thought."

"No. No it wasn't." I lean across and hug her so tightly I think I'm going to squeeze the air out of her lungs. "You're amazing, you know that?"

Red flashes across her cheeks and she shakes her head. "I'm really not. I'm not even sure what I said." She shivers and tucks her chin into her coat. "If you've got an idea, hurry up and do it. It's freezing out here and the river is rising."

The water is sloshing around my bent legs. I can feel the tug of the tide pulling at my coat. For the first time, I realise I'm not very cold because the clay coating my body is providing a warming layer. Sophie isn't so fortunate. Her skin is pale and her lips are turning blue. We're running out of time, but I do have an idea.

I grin. "We don't need to animate the golem because Matthew's soul will."

She bobs her head from side to side. "It sounds better when you put it like that."

"It wasn't God's name that we needed on the shem, it was Matthew's."

Sophie stares at me blankly. Matthew's lips purse thoughtfully. I wish I could see the rest of his face or his eyes, but they're obscured by the golem.

"Think about it. By using one of God's names, we were asking Him to empower the golem. What we really need is your soul to inhabit and animate the golem. So we need your name."

I turn the shem over, tug the charcoal out of my pocket, and—using the clean end and Sophie's back to lean on—write Matthew's name on the paper. I don't know how to write it in Hebrew. I pray it doesn't matter. I go to roll it up and then hesitate.

"Matthew, what's your full name?"

His lips twitch into a thin line, like it's a big enough secret to die for. Or perhaps he can't remember. Four hundred years is a long time.

"Tell me."

He must be trying to remember. God, he has to be able to remember.

"Matthew Bryce." His voice breaks with long repressed pain.

"B-R-Y-C-E." I say each letter aloud as I write it down, pausing long enough for him to object if I'm spelling it wrong. I roll the shem up, hiding his name one letter at a time.

"Please work," I say, as I place the shem back, pressing it against Matthew's lips.

Brilliant light radiates out from it, so bright I have to shield my eyes with my hand and turn my face away. The rays burst through the golem, obscuring it completely. Intense heat spreads outward, prickling my skin. Sophie grabs me and drags me back to my feet, pulling me away from the water. We collapse on the muddy part of the bank. I look back in time to see all the light get sucked back into the golem's mouth with a loud whoosh. Coloured lights flicker in my vision as the aftershock of the light is burned on my retinas, leaving me squinting.

The golem begins to change. The clay moulds itself, refining the curves and lines that Sophie carved until they are human and beautiful. As the light fades, the red hue of the clay slips away like a lizard sloughing off its skin. What is left behind is pale ivory skin, covered in droplets of river water which glisten in the torchlight.

"Wow," Sophie says. "He's...umm..." She clears her throat and covers her mouth with her hand, smearing clay across her jaw and lips. "Clothes."

She scrabbles across to the rucksack and then slips down the bank to Matthew. I can't tear my eyes away from his face. It's like I'm seeing him for the first time. He looks the same, but there's a vulnerable quality to him now. His eyes, open and staring, are still so dark they suck light into them. I force my gaze to his naked chest, half-expecting to see him breathe. But I don't. He's not alive now any more than he was seconds before. He's still not human.

He sits up as Sophie piles the clothes she brought onto his lap. Her cheeks blaze red, and her gaze darts around uncomfortably. He blinks, opens and closes his mouth, lifts one hand and then the other, and flexes his fingertips. Every movement is slow and laboured.

"How do you feel?" Sophie asks.

He tilts his head up and looks at her for the first time. "Heavy." Even his voice is slower and deeper.

She reaches out and, biting her lower lip, touches his face with the tips of her fingers. She presses a little harder, but her fingertip doesn't make any impression in his skin.

"You feel like stone," she says. "But you look human."

He blinks again and stares at his hand, wiggling each finger in turn. "My soul must have shaped the golem when we fused together." He turns his face toward me, an action which takes a handful of seconds to complete. "Thank you."

I smile through my tears and nod. I can't speak. I'll cry harder if I do.

"Can you stand?" Sophie asks. "We really can't stay here."

He nods and flattens his hands against the ground and pushes himself upright. Sophie squeals and grabs the clothes before they tumble into the river. The redness spreads from her cheeks, up her nose, and across her forehead. Matthew wavers on his feet. Sophie stands beside him, wrapping an arm around his back and propping him up with her shoulder. He drapes his arm around her neck and offers her a grateful smile. She doesn't see it, she's too busy looking everywhere but at him.

"A little help," she says.

I get to my feet and slide down to them. Between us, we manage to help Matthew up the steep and slippery bank.

"Get dressed," Sophie says. "Before someone sees you and arrests us." She turns her back on him and tries to brush the redness away from her cheeks.

Finally, my tears give way to laughter. My knees weaken, almost pitching me to the floor, but somehow I find the strength to remain standing. I can't collapse. I can't rest. AJ still needs me. Gage might be gone, but there are other Baneem out there who travel between Earth and Uralahnd.

"It's safe to look now," I say quietly.

I smile to myself as the deep blush returns to Sophie's cheeks, shining like a beacon through the clay streaks. Matthew has managed the oversized trousers, but is struggling with the buttons. I'm not sure if it's because he's never had to push tiny pieces of round plastic through small slits or because he's finding his new fingers clumsy.

Sophie wanders over to him. "Let me help."

Matthew doesn't resist as she gently brushes his hands aside and quickly does up the buttons. The deep blue shirt looks good on Matthew, even though it's several sizes too large and gapes at the collar. He is attractive. I turn away. Just admitting that to myself makes my heart ache more fiercely for AJ. I have to find him. I will find him.

I wander to the edge of the bank and look down. In the time it's taken Matthew to dress, the water has risen to swallow the clay bed again. We left the torch behind on the mud bank. Its beam illuminates Gage's body as the water laps at it and tugs it away from the bank. The current embraces him and slowly drags him away toward the sea. I wish the memories he left behind were so easy to wash away.

CHAPTER TWENTY-NINE

The muffled buzz of Sophie using my hairdryer drifts through the wall as I wipe the steam away from the bathroom mirror and stare at my reflection. The long, hot shower has left my cheeks flushed and eased away the deep worry lines marring my forehead. I know they'll return, but for now the water has washed the mud and clay from my skin, leaving it feeling soft and revitalised.

Gage has left his mark. Blue splashes across my cheek, and a dark red slash cuts down my lower lip, punctuated on either side by swelling. It's hard to put my lips together and even harder to smile. I should be smiling. We saved Matthew. Gage is gone. But all I want to do is curl up in a corner and cry.

I touch my fingers to my throat. There's a pair of symmetrical dark bruises over my windpipe where Gage pressed his thumbs. Further round my neck are pink, finger-sized pressure points. It's not the first time he's left strangle marks I've had to hide, but it is the last.

I drape the towel over the rail, pull on my pyjamas, and pad through to my room. Sophie is sitting on the bed, pulling a brush through her hair. My hairdryer lies beside her.

"Feeling better?" she says, glancing up.

I shrug. How can I feel better knowing I'm responsible for someone's death? Even if it was Gage. Even if it was to protect my friends.

Sophie pats the bed beside her. "You should try and get some sleep."

I don't accept her invitation to sit down. I know the second I let myself get comfortable I'll fall asleep. I thought I could rest, but during the walk home, all I could think about was AJ and how badly I've failed him.

Yawning, Sophie stretches her arms above her head and flexes her back. "We all need some sleep." Her mouth quirks into a wiggly frown. "Can Matthew sleep now?"

I raise my eyebrows. "I have no idea."

"He's downstairs," she says. "Maybe we should go check on him before we sleep?" She reaches for my bedside clock and checks the time. "Five. I don't think either of us are going to make it to school today. Luckily it's just pre-Christmas drivel. Nothing we can't miss."

Christmas. It's a week away. Just over a week ago, my biggest worry was whether or not Phailin would accept my invitation to spend Christmas Day with us. Now everything's changed.

I follow her downstairs. We find Matthew in the kitchen, standing barefoot in the midst of broken shards of glass. When he sees us, his face slowly changes from a blank expression. He tugs the corners of his mouth down and then forces his eyebrows down into a crease. I'm not sure what his forced expression is supposed to convey.

"I'm sorry," he says.

"What happened?"

He reaches for a glass from the cupboard, picking it up carefully between his thumb and fingers, but as he lifts it out, it shatters with a loud pop. Sophie and I jump back. Shards of glass patter onto the tiled floor. Matthew's expression drifts back into a blank state, and he shakes his head, leans back against the work top, and grips it in his hands. The work top cracks and splinters beneath his touch, revealing the cheap chip board beneath the surface. He lets go and hangs his head.

"Don't know your own strength?" Sophie says, edging closer.

"Obviously not," he says. "I'm sorry."

I retrieve a dust pan and brush and start cleaning up while Sophie picks her way over the glass to take his hand and lead him to the breakfast bar.

"You'll get used to your new body," she says.

She hops up onto a stool, smiling. He lifts his head, and, although his expression is blank, his eyes are sorrowful.

"Sophie's right," I say. "You'll get used to it. No one else is going to be here for a few days, so you have time."

I grab an old newspaper from the recycling bin and tip the glass shards onto it before wrapping the sharp package up carefully.

Sophie covers her mouth with her hands as she yawns loudly. "Sorry." Her cheeks flush. "I really need to sleep. So do you, Kim." She tilts her head to the side as she looks at Matthew. "Can you sleep?"

His shoulders rise and fall in a mechanical shrug. "I don't see why I would need to." He holds his hands palms up and then turns them over. "I'm not flesh and blood."

"Maybe you should lie down and try?" Sophie says through a fake smile. "He can use Chris's room, right?"

"Sure."

Matthew's eyes open and close in what I think is supposed to be a blink, but it's too slow and controlled to be a reflexive reaction. I shudder. His new body is unnerving in a way his physical manifestation never was. That was believable. I suppose because his expressions and reactions were a natural part of him, whereas now he's having to choose every little movement of his clay shell.

He waits for Sophie to slip off the stool and follows her toward the kitchen door.

She pauses on her way to the stairs. "Are you coming?"

I shake my head. She narrows one eye and raises the opposite eyebrow. I've never seen her look quite so stern.

"I'll go up soon. I promise."

She lets out a heavy sigh and tuts at me, but she doesn't push the issue any further. I'm glad.

I go into the sitting room alone. I'm not sure what to do. Sophie's right—I should sleep. My mind is too thick and heavy to come up with any kind of plan for finding a Baneem. Will Matthew still know when a Baneem is using magic close by?

Matthew. The look in his dark eyes haunts me. He's trapped in a clay prison because of me.

I sink down onto the sofa. I don't know what to do. I don't know how to find AJ. I don't know how to help Matthew mend his soul. I don't know how to take my brother's guilt away or make Mum feel like she's in control again.

I twist my legs up onto the sofa and lie down, using my bent arm as a pillow. I don't try to stop my eyes from drifting shut. Maybe once I've rested things will be clearer. My body feels heavy and I stop resisting the exhaustion that's been banging to get in. I let myself succumb to sleep, holding AJ's lopsided smile in my mind.

*

A distant hammering disturbs me, slowly pulling me out of the dizzying darkness of a dreamless sleep. I rub my eyes. I don't feel rested at all. My limbs are still heavy and it's as though someone has stuffed my head full of cotton wool. I check my watch. It's just gone seven. I sit, flexing my neck to each side to try to ease the painful kink that's left from laying in an awkward position. The banging continues, too loud to be a product of my imagination. I stand and let my feet carry me on auto-pilot to the front door, yawning and rubbing my neck as I go. I smooth my pyjamas down before I open the door, expecting to see a postman, grumpy from having been kept waiting so long.

My body tingles with a spike of adrenalin. Blood rushes to my head, leaving my face flushed. I sway forward, too dizzy to stay upright, and AJ catches me, sets me back on my feet, and propels me inside in the same action. He glances over his shoulder at the empty street before kicking the door shut. It bangs and rattles in the frame.

He keeps one arm around my shoulders and cups my chin in his free hand, tilting my face up. Concern is etched on his face. Deep worry lines crease his forehead and crinkle around his eyes. His lips are parted slightly as he silently runs his dead gaze over my face and neck. The creases fade to nothingness as he clenches his teeth. His body stiffens. His muscles flex.

"What happened to you? Was it Gage?"

"Yes, but it doesn't matter." I put my hand on his chest, feeling the fast thud of his heart against my palm. "Gage is dead. He can't hurt anyone anymore."

I expect the tension to drain out of him, but instead my words make his muscles twitch. His arm drops away from my waist.

"Saul will send more. We have to go." He turns away from me and presses his eye against the spy hole.

I assume he sees nothing because he sags against the door.

"It's okay," I say. "You're safe now."

He shakes his head and his mouth downturns in a glum frown. My chest aches. It hurts to see him looking so broken. I press my hands against his face, and the soft stubble on his jaw tickles my palms. I run my thumbs over his grimy cheeks, noticing tear tracks that have cut through the layer of dirt encrusted on his skin. I want to kiss him, but his lack of contact holds me back.

"I tried to get to you," I say, blinking back tears. "I'm so sorry I couldn't."

He shakes his head. "You don't need to be sorry."

But I am. It's only been a week, but he's lost weight. His skin is taut and dry and his hair is lank and greasy. He's wearing the same clothes I last saw him in. The clothes he went bowling in and rolled around in leaves in. Except they're heavily stained with blood and other things I don't want to think about. They stink so badly it's an effort to stop my nose wrinkling. Blood stains his right wrist and lower arm, but I can't see any trace of a wound. I don't want to imagine what Saul did to him. I'm pretty sure nothing I could conjure up would be as bad as reality.

"We have to go," he repeats. "We're not safe. Saul wants me, but he'll..." He trails off, clenching his teeth together and squeezing his eyes shut. "I'm so sorry. This is my nightmare and you're hurt because of it."

Opening his eyes, he runs his thumb across my lower lip, his touch so light it's nothing more than a whisper. He pauses at the ugly split. The comforting scent of his magic pours around me, enveloping me and holding me closer than he is. The rich mossy smell overpowers the stench from his clothes. Warmth flushes through my mouth as the anger drains out of the swelling and the cut knits itself back together. I catch his hand in mine.

"You don't need to heal me."

I let him jerk his hand away. He touches my cheek in the same soft, tentative manner, removing the dull ache I've been feeling since Gage punched me. Next his fingertips drop to my throat. I tip my head back a little, exposing the bruises. I want his touch to be more real and solid. I want to trade his fingertips for his lips. But once the warmth of his magic has passed, he drops his hand to his side and lowers his face into shadow.

"Thank you." I search his face to guess at what he's thinking or feeling.

He swallows. "Matthew..."

"Matthew is all right." It might be an oversimplification of the truth, but right now it'll do.

AJ blinks and turns his face toward the wall. I can hear his breath hitching in his throat as his chest shudders.

"It's okay—"

"No. It's not." He snaps his response, his face hard, his eyes cold.

I touch my fingertips to my quivering lips. I thought I'd said the right thing.

His brow softens as he slowly shakes his head. "I'm sorry."

I place my hand on his arm, silently accepting his apology. There's so much I want to ask him and tell him. I want to find a way to soothe his anger. But most of all, I just want to feel his arms around me and his lips against mine. I want to know he's okay, even though he blatantly isn't. Whatever happened is clinging to him, dragging him down and keeping him from reaching out to me.

So I reach out to him. I step closer, pressing up against his chest. He tenses and a small gasp of resistance escapes him. He raises his chin to avoid me as I bury my face against his collarbone. His T-shirt is stiff and itches my cheek. It's impossible to escape the smell of sweat, blood, and worse. I don't pull away. Beneath the stench of captivity, I can still smell AJ and that scent is earthy and warm and comforting.

"We have to go," he says, his voice strained.

"No," I whisper, wrapping my arms around his back. "I know you don't want to run anymore."

I press my palms against the dip between his shoulder blades, hoping the strength of my embrace will help him feel a little safer.

"It doesn't matter what I want," he says. "I can't let Saul get hold of me again. He'll use me to hurt more Shamari. I don't want to be responsible for any more deaths. I have to run and so do you. We both know it doesn't matter if I'm not here. He'll use you to get to me. Like—" His voice breaks into a strangled sob.

I don't push him to explain. All I need to do is calm him down.

"We'll find a way to stop Saul," I say. "You, me, and Matthew. You'll never have to run again. I promise."

I hold him tighter still, pulling his body against mine. It doesn't matter that he isn't holding me back because I can feel a little of the tension fleeing his body, one muscle at a time. He sags against me, his back curving, allowing him to curl into my embrace. I look up, watching his face as I run my hands over his shoulders, up his neck, and along his jaw so I can cradle his cheeks.

He blinks quickly and repeatedly. His gaze holds mine, but there's no life or light held within his chestnut eyes.

"Do you trust me to find a way?" I say. "Do you believe in me?"

His mouth quivers and a shuddering breath escapes his lips. He doesn't answer. I didn't really expect him to. I push myself onto my tiptoes and gently kiss his closed mouth. I don't need him to reciprocate. I just need him to know how much I care and how fiercely I'll fight for him because I don't know what else I can do to ease his pain and fear.

"I love you."

Just three small words, spoken in the quietest whisper, but they ignite a small smouldering spark deep within his eyes. I can only put one name to it: hope.

THE END

ABOUT THE AUTHOR

Clare Davidson is a character driven fantasy writer, teacher and mother, from the UK. Clare was born in Northampton and lived in Malaysia for four and a half years as a child, before returning to the UK to settle in Leeds with her family. Whilst attending Lancaster University, Clare met her future husband. They now share their lives with their young daughter, their cats and Rukia the Finnish Lapphund.

CONNECT WITH CLARE DAVIDSON

Website: http://www.claredavidson.com
Facebook: https://www.facebook.com/ClareMDavidson
Twitter: https://twitter.com/ClareMDavidson
Goodreads: http://www.goodreads.com/ClareDavidson
Mailing List: http://eepurl.com/zpjGf

REAPER'S RHYTHM

(HIDDEN: BOOK 1)

When everyone thinks your sister committed suicide, it's hard to prove she was murdered.

Kim is unable to accept Charley's sudden death. Crippled by an unnatural amnesia, her questions are met with wall after wall. As she doubts her sanity, she realises her investigation is putting those around her in danger.

The only person who seems to know anything is Matthew, an elusive stranger who would rather vanish than talk. Despite his friendly smile, Kim isn't sure she can trust him. But if she wants to protect her family from further danger, Kim must work with Matthew to discover how Charley died – before it's too late.

BROKEN BARGAIN
(HIDDEN: BOOK 2)

When you know magic is real, complacency is not an option.

It's a new school year and ten months since Kim's sister died. She wants to forget about magic, rebuild her life and start fresh. But it's not easy when she has to lie to everyone: her family, best friend, Sophie, and secretive new guy, AJ.

But when Sophie's grandmother falls ill, Kim can't help but notice the parallels to Charley's death. Convinced she's the only one who can help, Kim sets out to discover what's really wrong with Sophie's grandmother.

TRINITY

Kiana longs to walk through a forest and feel grass between her toes. But she is the living embodiment of a goddess and has enemies who wish to murder her. Her death will curse the whole of Gettryne. Locked away for protection, she dreams of freedom.

Her wish comes true in the worst possible way, when her home and defenders are destroyed.

Along with an inexperienced guard and a hunted outcast, Kiana flees the ravages of battle to search for a solution to the madness that has gripped Gettryne for a thousand years. Pursued by the vicious and unrelenting Wolves, their journey will take them far beyond their limits, to a secret that will shake the world.